KNIVES

RUTHLESS KINGS MC™
BOOK TEN

K.L. SAVAGE

ISBN: 978-1-952500-31-2

PHOTOGRAPHY BY WANDER AGUIAR PHOTOGRAPHY
COVER MODEL: GABE LADUKE
COVER DESIGN: LORI JACKSON DESIGN
EDITING: INFINITE WELL
FORMATTING: CHAMPAGNE BOOK DESIGN

FIRST EDITION PRINT 2020

2

TABLE OF CONTENTS

To all the outsiders, the runts, the lonely souls, our Ruthless Readers,
We know what it's like to be the ones looking in. We know what it's like to feel isolated, hopeless, and so alone you don't know where to go or how to get out of the bubble you've found yourself in.
There is always love. There are always people willing to welcome you with open arms. We are those people. You have us.
Pop. That. Bubble.
It feels good to be set free.

PROLOGUE

Fifteen Years old

Silence is the clearest speaker of all. Its words ring loud and true.

I read that somewhere a few years ago etched in a bookshelf in a library. I ignored it at the time because I didn't understand what the statement meant. Silence doesn't speak. Silence doesn't make noise.

But silence spoke volumes when I started high school last year, and that's when the understanding clicked in my mind.

It's what happens in the quiet that means the most.

Teenagers are brutal. Physically, mentally, and emotionally. They are bullies, plain and simple. And even worse are the ones who stick around to watch me get my ass beat. Every damn day. No one says a word. They laugh, they point, they watch.

It's because I'm a nobody.

I'm scrawny, I'm short for my age, I have long hair that's dirty because I have no money to get it cut. I'm only allowed to shower once a week to save on the water bill because everyone else in the house has to bathe too.

I'm a natural target.

I'm the kid everyone avoids. I'm the kid no one trusts. It's easy to be an outsider when I've never fit into any group, made friends with any kids, or have had a home to call my own. I don't have parents, and the kids love to remind me every day that I don't have a mom and dad.

As if I could ever forget that I've been on my own for a long time.

My caseworker found me living on the streets a few years back after running away and sent me back to another foster home. It's my tenth one since I was eight. It used to bother me, not having that sense of family, but I've learned not even family is all that cracked up to be. My foster home has ten kids. Our clothes are always dirty. We go days without eating a proper meal. We get slapped around some, so it has skewed my idea of what family is. The foster parents are only in this for the paycheck.

I've learned to trust no one because everyone disappoints.

Well, I take that back. There is one person. My foster brother, Mason. He is a year older than me and takes the 'big brother' role seriously. He's a protector. He's always standing up for me when the kids at school call me a loser, a freak, a creep, a bastard. Other kids don't make fun of Mason. They wouldn't dare. Mason is already over six feet tall, and muscular, while I'm pathetic and weak.

It's not like the kids at school are wrong about me. I'm all of those things because I don't know how to be anything else, but it's time for me to learn. Mason won't be around forever to save my ass, so it's up to me to make the change, to be my own protector. When Mason turns eighteen, he is going to be out on his ass because the system doesn't keep adults, and where will that leave me?

Alone.

Vulnerable.

And with no one in my corner.

It's why I need to find a way to protect myself. A weapon of some sort. Something that's quick, agile, and fierce. I want my weapon to say, 'don't fuck with me'.

Maybe then the bullies will see how serious I am.

I'm tired of always looking over my shoulder. It's exhausting, and I want to be done being afraid.

Like right now.

"Hey, loser!"

I keep my head down and shrug the raggedy blue backpack up my shoulder. It's torn, stained, and the straps are barely hanging on to the last bit of thread. I stuff my hands in the hoodie pockets and walk faster. The sooner I get off this back road and onto the main road, the better.

"Hey, freak, I'm talking to you."

"Yeah, we're talking to you. It's rude to ignore us."

"I bet he's scared."

The three of them taunt me, but I know better than to pay them any attention. I'm damned if I do, and I'm damned if I don't.

My breaths come out quicker. Sweat starts to bead across my neck. I knew I should have taken the other way, but it adds on another twenty minutes. The back road is abandoned, and everyone dumps what they don't want back here along the sides of the fence that block the road off from someone's property. Tall weeds stand tall among a few silver trash tins, rusted bikes, and old sewing machines strewn all over the ground. This road is a homeless person's dream, but horrible things happen here because of the weapons laying around.

This road always has a massive amount of random trash all over it. It's why everyone in town calls it Miscellaneous

Way, because anything and everything can be found. Even bodies.

And I don't want to be one of them.

If I only had a weapon that could go the distance, that could protect me from a few yards away; then I'd have a chance at escaping these guys.

"Thomas," Murray singsongs my name, then hits one of the trashcans with the bat he always has in his hand.

The loud clatter startles me. I trip over my own feet, which only draws a big, ugly laugh from the three bullies. I hate this life. Everyone says it gets better, but when? I'm face down in the dirt, rocks are digging into my hands, and I can hear their footsteps getting closer. Nothing about this is *better*.

I'm a dead man.

I look around for something to protect myself with, but all I see are some rusted knives on the ground next to a busted-up kitchen sink. It's probably not rust; it's probably blood that's been there for far too long. But they are the only thing within reach.

I dig my elbows in the ground and scurry toward the knives hiding in the grass and reach for the closest one. It's a useless steak knife.

You've got to be kidding me. Why couldn't it be a butcher knife? Something big and scary?

I get to my feet and throw the one in my hand, launching it with a panicked grunt, but the blade comes detached from the black handle, and the threat falls short.

"Oh my god, you're so stupid. Did you honestly think that would work?" Louis says. He's shorter than the others, only around my height. I'm sure if he was all alone, he'd turn into a scared dog like me.

Falling to the ground, I gather the last four knives in my hand, ready to use them if I have to. A spider crawls around the blade, then scrambles to my hand. Its legs are light on my skin, a tickle. In a way, I feel like it's good luck. Unlike most people, I'm not afraid of spiders.

Insects, reptiles, and animals only attack when they feel threatened. Humans attack whoever the hell they want to, when they want to. Or just because they feel like it. It's why I think out of everything this world has to offer, humans are the most dangerous.

The spider falls off my arm and disappears into the grass, leaving me alone against my enemies.

"What are you going to do with that, Thomas?" Murray asks in a mocking tone, digging the baseball bat into the ground as he takes a step. "Are you going to stab me?"

My hands shake as I slice the knife through the air. "I… I might if you come any c-closer," I stutter, then lick the sweat off my top lip. The backpack slides down my shoulder into the crease of my elbow, and I drop my hand to let it fall to the ground.

"You think you can kill someone?" Murray tosses his head back and laughs, placing a hand in the middle of his chest. He abruptly stops laughing and taps the aluminum bat against his left foot. "I could kill you," he sneers at me, then spits. "You are worthless. You take up too much space. You breathe my fucking air. You don't deserve to breathe my air!" He swings the bat, and I hear the swoosh of it as it barely misses my face.

Stumbling back, I trip over my backpack, and when Murray goes to hit me in the face, I roll away and stab his leg, then yank out so I can still have my weapon.

"Mother fucker!" he screams, adding most of his weight to his other leg. He points the bat at me, red-faced with anger. "You're a dead man, you hear me? Dead."

Louis tries to attack me next by taking the bat from Murray, but I move to the side and bring the knife down on his back, slicing directly into his shoulder blade. Louis pitches forward with a pained grunt, and his grip loosens, causing the bat to clink to the ground. The blood spreads

11

across his shirt and drips down until it's soaking into his jeans.

I'm waiting for guilt, for the voice in my head to tell me to run, but only adrenaline is speaking to me, and it's telling me not to stop until all of these assholes are bleeding. For good measure, I kick Louis in the stomach, and he cries out in agony.

"How does that fucking feel? Huh? How does it feel?" I scream, then pick up the bat and slam it against the stab wound on his back.

"Stop! Stop, no more. Please," he sobs.

"Stop?" I ask, barking out a chilling laugh. My eyes fall on Murray, who is currently backing away from me. "You want me to stop? That's rich coming from the lot of you! You didn't stop beating me last month when I asked you to. I pissed blood for a week!" I yell, tears blurring my eyes as I slowly make my way toward Murray and Pete. Pete is the quiet one, the one that follows but never says or does anything because deep down, he knows he is just as weak as I am. "I'm going to—"

A hand pulls me back and yanks the bat from my hand along with the knives.

I whip around to punch whoever it is in the face. I'm done. I'm fucking done with the constant bullying, the pain, the crying. I'm sick of it. I lift my arm and clench a fist, preparing to fight again, when a hand grips around my knuckles.

"It's me, Thomas. It's Mason. You're okay. You aren't alone."

"They were attacking me. I didn't know what else to do. I...I..."

"You did the right thing." He grips my shoulders and tugs me behind his oversized body and hands me back the knives.

Why can't I be more like him? Why do I have to be stuck in this body?

"Problem, Murray?" Mason asks him, swaying the bat left to right.

Louis groans from my left and somehow manages to get to his feet. He stumbles back over to his friends and sags against Pete. I stare down at the knives in my hands, speckled with blood, and I still don't feel guilt.

I feel like the job isn't finished.

"Yeah, your fucking boyfriend here is a psycho!" Murray pulls up his pant leg and shows Mason the wound on his leg. "Look what he did to me."

I hate it when they call us boyfriends. All because we aren't blood related, and Mason is always coming to my rescue.

"And what were you going to do to him?" Mason slams the bat against the trashcan next to him, denting it.

"Nothing he didn't deserve," Murray hisses.

And that's when Mason surprises me. His hand disappears behind his back, and lifts his red shirt, grabbing the handle of a gun. I gasp and take a few steps back. This isn't like Mason. Where the hell did he get that?

"You have two seconds to get the fuck away from my brother before I put a bullet in your head. You've been warned a hundred times from me. I'm done giving out chances." Mason cocks the silver gun, the cylinder spins to lodge the bullet in place, and the three boys that have been picking on me instantly freeze.

"Woah, Mason. Just hold on a second," Murray says, trying to calm Mason down.

I tug on Mason's sleeve, but he doesn't look my way. He's bound and determined to stare at them on the other end of the barrel. "Mason, what are you doing? Let's go home."

"We won't pick on him anymore, I swear. Let us go," Murray holds his arms wide and steps back. "We'll go. No more trouble."

"I think I need to go to the doctor," Louis moans.

"Shut up, Louis," Murray snaps, staring at the gun as the sun shines against the sweat dripping down his temple.

"Mason, let's go home. Please," I beg him. I don't want any more trouble. Mason has come to my rescue one last time. He's risking himself for me, and I don't want to be responsible for ruining his life too.

"I'm going to call the cops if you don't put the gun down," Louis warns us, fumbling for his pocket.

Mason's jaw ticks, and his chest rises and falls in a burst of anger. He's really holding himself back. His body is shaking, and his face is red.

"Mason, put the gun down," I beg him. "They aren't worth it."

"Yes, they are," he says, taking his eyes off the trio for a moment. He stares at me. Mason seems a lot older than seventeen years old right now. "You don't deserve the treatment they give you. It's up to me. I'm your brother. Me. I protect you."

Okay, so he's a year and three months older than me. Same difference.

"And I protect you too," I say, wrapping my hand around the barrel of the gun to get Mason to drop it.

"They aren't going to stop until you're dead, Thomas." Mason jumps when he hears sirens in the background, and with every second that passes, they get closer.

Mason lifts his gun again, pinching his lips with determination as he aims at Pete. Time slows as I turn my head and grab onto his arm to stop him. "Let go, Thomas! Let me do this," Mason grunts, fighting me.

"No. We can't—" My ears ring, and the heat from the bullet leaving its home is hot on my palm, burning me. I hiss and yank my hand away.

"Murray!" Pete yells, and that's when my stomach churns as I peer over my shoulder, seeing Murray with a gunshot wound in the middle of his chest.

"Oh my god," I mumble.

Mason doesn't hesitate. He lifts the gun again and aims it at Pete, letting another bullet fly. My mouth falls open, and I'm on the verge of puking. Pete's neck snaps back when the bullet lodges between his eyes. Mason swings his arm and lands on an injured Louis, but he is on the ground, gasping for air and blood bubbling out of his mouth.

I must have nicked his lung somehow when I stabbed him.

The sirens are anxiously close now.

"Mason, we need to go. We need to get out of here." Oh my god, what did he do? How can we get out of this?

"We have to tie up all the loose ends, Thomas." Mason squats next to Louis. A fifteen-year-old kid who sat in the back in Biology class today is going to die.

I didn't want this. Did I? I only wanted to go home, to get away, I wanted them to let me be, but they couldn't. They had to keep pushing. I stood up for myself and maybe I got carried away. I was protecting myself.

I never thought Mason would find me and commit murder.

Mason slides the gun between Louis's lips and pushing it down his throat until Louis gags. When he coughs, he spits up blood. Tears trickle down his cheeks, and he slides his eyes to me, silently begging me to help him.

"You aren't ever going to hurt anyone again," Mason says to Louis.

Louis grips Mason's bicep with a bloody hand, squeezing it, but doesn't have the energy to push him off.

I can't have Mason kill someone else for me. I'm not worth it. I run to him, and right as I'm about to launch myself at my foster brother, my feet digging in the sand to push me off the ground, he pulls the trigger.

The breath is knocked out of me when blood splashes against my face, warm and wet. I close my eyes, not wanting to see the raw scene in front of me. I can't figure out how to breathe. I'm panicking. The sirens are getting closer, the world is caving in, and the only person I could count on just ruined his life for me.

How am I going to live life without Mason? He's the only reason I'm alive.

"Thomas, open your eyes and look at me. Look at me!" He shakes my shoulders until my eyes snap open. "Breathe."

I manage to pry my wet lids back and peer into the eyes of the only person that's ever given a shit about me. I'm trembling.

"The cops are going to come, and they are going to arrest me."

I shake my head back and forth, dislodging the pools of water filling my vision. The droplets drip down my cheeks, and when I look away from Mason, I see three dead bodies. Blood is everywhere.

So much blood.

"Thomas, I need you to run."

I'm so confused as to how we got here. My stomach is rolling. I think I'm in shock, or maybe I'm dreaming. "We need to get out of here Mason. Let's go."

"There isn't time. You need to hide. They are going to be here any minute. I want you to go to that biker bar we pass all the time, okay? Tell them I sent you. Tell them you don't have anywhere to go."

"What?" This makes no sense. Why the hell would he know any bikers? "Bikers? Mason, you aren't making any sense. Come on, we can cut through here—" I point over the fence where the mountains are "—We can keep running until we are far away from here, and we can start our lives."

"No. Someone has to take responsibility for what happened here, and it's going to be me. I shot them. I do the time. You always take responsibility. For everything you do, you hear me, Thomas?"

"Mason, please. You're all I have. This was all my fault. Let me take the blame. This is my fault. If I had taken the

16

other route, you wouldn't have looked for me and grabbed that gun from... where did you get it?"

"That doesn't matter."

The sirens are only a block or so away. I turn around to look down the road to make sure we are still alone. "Please, we don't have much time. Mason, let's go. Let's go now." I tug on his hand and try to pull him to the fence, but he stays in one spot, unmoving, the blood spreading across the ground and touching his sneakers.

"Let's go. Why aren't you coming!" I yell. "Damn it, Mason. You're the only person in the world who has my back. I need you. If you do this, I'll never see you again. Please."

"I will always have your back. Always." His head jerks when the sound of squealing tires comes ripping across the road. He pushes me toward the abandoned building. "Go. Go, Thomas. Now!"

I stumble when I see the rolls of dusty clouds from the police cars speeding down the road getting closer and closer. The sirens are ear-splittingly loud. The hints of red and blue lights are already filling the distance. I don't want to leave him. I open the wooden door to the rundown shed. It's dark, musky, and cobwebs are all over me. The only light that spills through is from the window that's clouded with dust and grime. The bottom right square is broken, but I can see Mason from this spot.

The wet, humid air sticks to my skin, and when I grab onto the ledge of the window, beads of sweat mixed with blood drip down my lips. I almost lick them.

Almost.

Until I remember it isn't my blood I'm about to lick. I wipe my mouth on my shirt sleeve and hope Mason makes it out of this situation okay.

"Put your hands behind your head!"

I inhale a sharp breath, staring at a cop who has his weapon drawn, pointing it directly at Mason.

17

"He's armed!" the cop announces, and three other officers flank each other, pointing their guns at Mason.

Four cops.

Four guns.

One Mason.

No hope.

"Please," I beg, someone, anyone, to not take Mason away from me.

"Put down the weapon," the cop barks at Mason.

"Okay," Mason says, giving me a quick parting glance. He has no fear, at least none that is showing, which only makes me admire him more. But I know the look he gives me, and it isn't one filled with hope.

It's one that says goodbye.

He leans down to place the gun on the ground, but the barrel is pointed at the police officers, and the first gunshot sounds.

Then the next.

And the next.

I place a hand over my mouth to stifle my sobs when I see Mason's body jerk until he is boneless on top of Murray, Louis, and Peter.

I flip to my back and slide against the wall, unable to look out the window a second longer and cry silently. My best friend is dead. For some fucked up reason, he decided I was worth it.

Worth what? I have no idea.

"Fuck, Ripley. He was putting the gun down," one officer says.

"Like it matters." One snorts. "Look at the kids he killed."

"We didn't know the story. He was just a kid himself. You never pull that shit again; do you understand?"

"Yeah, Nolan. I got it."

"Call it in. Let's get this crime scene taped off and these bodies bagged."

I cup my hands over my ears and begin to rock back and forth. I don't know how long I sit there, but the zippers of the body bags are so loud they break me open. The sirens come and go.

And soon, the only thing left is silence.

The wind blows through the broken piece of the glass, blowing against the sweat on my neck. All I can see every time I blink are the bullets piercing through Mason's body. I stand on unstable legs and open the wooden door that leads outside. It's colder outside. The night sky reminds me of the night I lost my entire family.

My real family.

My sister. My mom. My dad.

It's only fitting I lose Mason on a night that feels so similar. Cold, beautiful, star-filled, and the crickets... yeah, the crickets were just as loud as the night of the accident. Life goes on even when you don't want it to.

Taking a lungful of air, I make my way to the left, and the door behind me slams shut. My nerves are shot, and I jump from the loud boom it brings over the empty pastures on either side of the road. My heart thumps in my chest as I stare at where Mason was shot hours ago.

Four people died today, right here, right in the middle of the road, but it's like it didn't even happen. The road is clear, disappearing into the edge of the sky. The silence, the world around me, the crickets... everything is as it was, but I'm changed forever.

There are only the puddles of blood drying in the sand of the road. It's the only proof to let me know it wasn't a dream.

It's evidence to reassure me that I'm alone.

I wipe my cheek on my shirt sleeve again, dragging the material across the dried blood and wet tears. I place my hands on my hips and start walking, because what else am I supposed to do? I see my backpack out of the corner of my eye behind a trashcan, and I debate if I want to take it.

19

If it's up to me, I'll never go back to school. I'll never get close to anyone again.

I remember the biker bar Mason brought up to me and told me to go to. It's a place we used to pass every day walking to and from school to go home. The place scared me, but he loved it. He loved the tough and rough look, the bikes, the women, the leather. Mason was always badass like that though, and if he wanted me to go there, then I'm going to go.

Picking up my backpack, I toss it in the trashcan and cover it with a lid. I give one last look to where I saw Mason's body fall.

What am I going to do without him? In the last two homes, he protected me from perverted dads, handsy moms, and disturbed kids. When he could, he protected me at school.

And he died doing the one thing he always did.

What can I do to return the favor?

Go to the bar.

Where the badass bikers are going to kill me, probably.

I tuck my hands into my pockets, my fingers brushing over a ball of lint, and hunch my shoulders as a rare howl bursts through the air. A coyote. They probably smell the blood in the road, hoping to feast.

When the highway comes to view, it's empty, nearly as abandoned as I am. I take a left, the soles of my shoes scuffing against the asphalt. I'm not afraid to admit I'm crying. I know I shouldn't. My foster dad says, 'Men don't cry. Men aren't allowed to cry.'

But I've lost the only person that's mattered to me in a long time.

I don't know how long I walk. I keep my head down, eyes glued to the road, watching the bumps of rocks in the pavement vanish from my footsteps.

A grumble of bikes comes from up ahead, and it has me jerking my head up, seeing a headlight float in the night as it turns left, the opposite direction of where I am coming from.

I stop at the edge of the fence where the road turns to gravel, and the old, beat-up bar looks like it's about to fall apart. It's made of wood planks, and there isn't a sign to tell me if the bar has a name. Loud music spills from the inside, and all the chrome of the bikes lined up out front shine against the red neon skull sign hanging on the inside of the window.

My feet drag against the gravel, the rocks crunching under my converses. I thought I'd be afraid, but after everything I've just been through, what I've seen, what's the worst these guys can do to me? Kill me?

I dare them.

I pause at the door, which is wide open, and decide to walk in. The air is warmer in here from all the bodies moving around. Smoke hangs heavily in the air, and the floor is sticky against my shoes. My adrenaline is crashing. My body is starting to shake, and my eyes are pooling again. I'm hoping I'm in a safe place because I think I'm about to lose it.

No one notices me yet in the dark room. I don't blame them. Men are watching women strip on the poles; some men are having sex, screwing right here in front of everyone. I look over my shoulder, wrapping my arms around myself when I slam into something solid.

"Who the fuck are you, slim?" a raspy dark voice asks me.

When I turn to him, his eyes widen in surprise. It must be the blood all over me.

"Slim, what the fuck happened to you?"

I'm too distracted. The lights, the music, the conversations, everything is so loud.

"Hey." The man lays his big paw on my shoulder, shaking me. "Slim, you okay? Hey," he snaps his fingers in

21

front of my face, and I know he can see how scared I am. I don't hide my emotions well. "Come here. Follow me." He lights a cigarette and throws an arm around my shoulders, forcing me to walk as he does.

There are a few other men by his side, huge guys. They remind me of Mason, in a way. Like grown-up badass versions of him.

But he'll never be able to become them now.

The music dies down as we walk to the back. The lights are brighter, and the music is a dull thump against the walls. The guy opens a door, revealing a huge table with a skull engraved in it. He pulls out a chair and drops his arm from my shoulder. "Sit," he says.

Like I'd ever disrespect a man eight-times my size.

I sit down quickly as he takes a seat in the chair at the front of the table while the other two men flank either side of him. They are wearing the same leather vests, but his says Prez, while the other two say VP and SGT at Arms, respectively.

Whatever that means.

"Want a drink?" he asks.

I nod eagerly. I'd love some water.

The VP opens a mini-fridge in the corner and pulls out a brown bottle, opens it with his forearm, and sets it in front of me.

"I'm… I'm… not old enough to drink," I say, my voice shaking.

The three of them laugh. "Kid, we know that. You look like you need it, though. Go ahead; it'll be our secret," says the VP.

I wrap the bottle in my hand and bring it to my lips. I've never had beer before. It's cold, and it tastes like shit, but it feels good. Half the bottle is gone by the time I place it on the table.

The man that calls himself the Prez leans forward, crossing his arms on the table. "Now that you look like you aren't about to pass out—"

"—He might throw up," the VP jokes.

It isn't funny. I might.

"Slim, do you know where you're at?"

"Biker bar," I mumble, wiping my lips of beer foam. "I…" I start to rock again, pressing the palms of my hands against my eyes. "He told me to come here. I don't know where else to go."

"This is Ruthless Kings territory you're in. What happened to you? I need you to tell me everything. Are you bringing bad shit to my club?"

I shake my head and yank the knives out of my pockets, slamming them on the table. "Mason. Mason saved me. These kids followed me, but he was my foster brother, and he saved me—"

"You're Mason's brother? You must be Thomas."

I lock eyes with the Prez, a hundred emotions suddenly swirling in me. How do these guys know about me and Mason?

"Yeah."

The Prez's eyes soften. "He's said a lot about you. Says you're smart. That true?"

I shrug my shoulders at the Prez. "I know how to survive. Barely. Mason…" My eyes start to water again. "He's dead. He died. He killed the guys following me, and the cops killed him. Before it happened, he made me hide and told me to come here. I don't know where else to go. Where do I go? I'm sorry. I don't want to cause trouble, but I don't have anyone else. Mason was all I had. I tried to protect myself with these knives, but Mason had a gun."

"Fuck. I was wondering where it went." The man who calls himself Prez slides his fingers through his beard and tugs on the silver strands on his chin. "I need you to tell me

23

everything, from start to finish, and don't leave shit out, okay?" Prez says.

"Mason died, you sure, Slim?" the VP asks. "He had real promise in becoming a prospect. Damn it. Damn it!" he shouts, kicking the mini-fridge so hard, the door breaks off the hinge.

"Let's all calm down," Prez states, and the two men surrounding him take a seat, the VP breathing heavily like a raged bull. "Start from the beginning, and the more you can tell me about those cops, the better, okay?"

"Yeah," I nod, swigging my beer. "Yeah, okay."

The man across the table reaches in the middle and grabs the only weapons I have. I try to steal them away from him, but he is quicker, lifting them up in the air so I can't get them. "I think I can teach you how to make a pretty cool weapon out of these knives."

His patch says SGT at Arms, and the guy's arms are the size of my head. "They are old, rusted to hell, but we can shape them up and make a badass ninja star. We'll break the blades, then weld them together in the middle. After all this is settled, of course. It will be easier for you to learn since you're so small."

I hate being small. I blush and glance away, twiddling my fingers together. A rag is placed down in front of me. "Clean yourself up, Slim. Get that blood off you. And there ain't nothin' wrong with being small. It's here that matters," the VP taps my chest, "and here." Then presses his finger against my temple.

"That's really fucking sweet, but I need information. You two keep getting off track. Slim, fucking speak before these assholes start going on about something else. I want retribution for what happened to Mason," Prez states.

I take another swig of beer to gather some sort of courage and meet the eyes of the Sergeant at Arms. He gives me an encouraging nod, and I take a deep breath before returning the Prez's gaze.

24

"I'm the kid that gets bullied, and there were these three kids that always liked to give me a hard time. I don't have family and neither did Mason. We lived in a shit foster home, but he took it upon himself to always save me. He was my brother. My best friend. I owe him everything."

"Mason was good like that," Prez nods, a genuinely sympathetic tone in his voice. "Go on."

I do. From start to finish until I'm sobbing like a damn baby, because I feel like it's all my fault. Mason would be alive if it weren't for me. I have to prove myself to him now, so he didn't die for nothing. I need to be more than I've ever been.

"We will have our lawyer draw up some adoption papers. We're going to send you to a new school. When you turn eighteen, it's up to you on what you want to do. Prospect or get the hell out of dodge, but I think you'll like it here. I got a kid about your age named Jesse. Relax, Slim. You're with us now, but that's the only beer you're getting from me until you're a man. Got it?"

I nod eagerly, wondering if I'm dreaming, but when I rub the damp towel over my face and see red, I know this is reality.

Mason sent me to a place where I'd be safe. Even in death, he is protecting me. I'm not going to let him down. This place, if they will allow it, will be my home, and I'll be everything Mason wanted to be.

It's the least I can do after everything he has done for me.

25

CHAPTER ONE

Present day

"Ninety-Eight. Ninety-nine. One-hundred." I lift my chin over the pull-up bar one last time and drop to my feet, then fall to the floor and get into a push-up position. I place one hand behind my back and grunt as I push down. I do three sets of ten, alternate my hands, then do three more sets of ten on the other side. A bead of sweat drops from my forehead, rolling down my nose, and splashes against the floor.

I don't work out because I want to. I work out because I have to. I refuse to be weak. I refuse to not be at my strongest. I refuse to be that small, scrawny kid that didn't know how to hold his own.

Dropping to my back, I call out for Yeti, our resident white pitbull, and I hear the clobber of his paws against the wooden floors. When he is at the door, I point to my feet, and his pink tongue is out of his mouth as his stocky frame comes and sits on my feet.

"Good boy," I praise him, placing my hands across my chest to begin my sit-ups. Every time I hit my elbows to my knees, Yeti gives me a big wet kiss on my cheek, which gives me that much more motivation, because who doesn't love kisses from dogs? My abs begin to ache and tighten. I do five sets of twenty sit ups, only taking a few seconds between sets to catch my breath. By the fifth set, my body is shaking, and when I fall to the floor to stop, Yeti barks at me, slobbering all over my legs.

"Yeti, I don't want to. God, I'm tired."

He barks at me again to finish the last twenty. He always knows when I want to quit, and he always gives me fucking lip when I want to stop.

"Okay, okay. I'll do it. Just give me a second to breathe."

He growls, showing his teeth, threatening me that I better get off my ass or he'll do something about it

"You're a ballbuster," I mutter, taking a deep breath and sit up, exhaling the breath. Yeti licks me before I fall back, only to come up again. My stomach cramps as I crank out the first half. I have ten more.

My muscles protest, and I start to slow. "I can't, Yeti." Every sit-up, every crunch of my abs, and every time my elbows hit my knees, I let out a painful groan.

Five more.

Inhale. Exhale. Inhale. Exhale.

Three.

Two.

I think I'm going to puke.

One.

"Damn it!" I collapse on the floor; arms spread out as I gasp for air and sweat my body weight. Yeti's weight leaves my feet, and he cuddles up next to me, shoving his nose under my dead arm. "You kick my ass, Yeti. Ever heard of giving a guy a break?"

27

He lifts his nose and snorts, spraying fucking dog snot all over me. "Thanks for that. I appreciate it." I groan as I sit up and sling my shirt off, then wipe the sweat off my face with it.

I walk towards the kitchen and lift my arms to grab the trim of the door and stretch, leaning my body out of the entryway. It's quiet here since Boomer and his members left. They only came for Christmas, and since that was a complete shitshow, just like everything else is around here, I'm sure he was excited to get home. Especially since he missed Christmas with his ol' lady Scarlett. She decided to stay back with Homer, the old man who is officially part of the MC, according to Boomer.

Now, there are just a bunch of us assholes and a few kids to fill the noise.

I'm not going to lie; I'm one of the few that likes the ruckus.

Chaos, strife, and pain are the only mistresses I need to keep me awake at night. And you know who checks all those boxes?

Mary St. James.

She's far from a damn saint and reaps nothing but pure havoc on me. I swear the only reason for her existence is to get under my skin and piss me off. Well, mission fucking accomplished. She's sassy. She's wild. She's fucking fierce.

And all that adds up to one hell of a dynamite package that I want to ignite if I could get over how fucking crazy she drives me. I swear to god, if there was a cliff every time she cocked an attitude with me, I'd fucking jump off it.

She's maddening, but I know underneath the red lipstick that is supposed to make a statement, and the black leather jacket that hugs her breasts when she zips it up, Mary is scared.

With what happened to her, she has every reason to be. She's one of the girls that we rescued in Atlantic City; the chapter Boomer is taking over. The so-called Ruthless Kings

28

that didn't deserve the name bought and sold women. Doc's ol' lady, Joanna, she was a part of it too, along with Boomer's ol' lady, Scarlett.

Hell, I would think having Joanna here would help Mary, but she's bound and determined to lose herself in the pit of the hell created by the Atlantic City members. She did her best to join the cut sluts on their mission to suck and fuck every member in the clubhouse, but no matter how hard she tried, none of us would touch her.

We might be bastards in some way, shape, and form, but we don't use women who are only looking to feel something other than fear. When a woman wants to be a cut slut, she does it because she wants to; she wants to be used in every hole, in every way. And if that's their choice, more power to 'em. All of us know Mary isn't like that. She's a good girl. When we found her, she had on pearls and a fucking cardigan.

And now she's dressed for a rock and roll concert.

Don't get me wrong; some of those leather pants she wears has me watching her walk away longer than I should. Her new look fits her behavior. I'd be sad to see it go, especially since getting to know her. I don't know much about her past; she doesn't talk about it, but pearls and cardigans? They don't match the hellraiser simmering beneath her skin.

Does it mean I want to touch her flames?

Abso-fucking-lutely.

Does mean I'm going to?

No.

She annoys me too damn much, and I know she can't stand me either. She got me coal for Christmas. Coal! As if I've been naughty this year! Please. I'm a fucking angel wrapped in a damn bow, and my halo shines brighter than the damn horns she has on her head, I can say that much. She got mad at me for getting her a fake leg because she still walks with a limp after getting impaled by a piece of wood. I thought it was funny.

And she hates me for it.

But it's the kiss I hate her for.

Maizey pointed out at Christmas that Mary and I were under a mistletoe when we were arguing, and I just got fucking tired of always fighting with her, so I pulled her in by her hair and kissed her to shut her up.

I didn't think I'd actually like it.

And goddamn it, I hate her for giving me the best damn kiss I've ever experienced in my entire life. That chaos, strife, and pain I live for, that's constantly roaring inside of me, came to an abrupt halt as our mouths became one. Time slowed. Sounds ceased. And when our tongues slid together, we forgot we were enemies, and we gave in to one another.

Her lips were velvet, and her breaths were sweet like candy. I was getting lost in those flames I should always stay away from.

Until she hit me in the gut with that peg-leg I bought her. Then, she stomped off in a hissy fit, leaving me fucking harder than nails and confused.

Confused because all I wanted to do was run after her, slam her against the wall, and own her mouth again.

It's been two weeks, and every single night I'm waking up from a wet dream, cock in hand, and come coating my stomach. I have never had that happen, even when I was sixteen and getting erections because the fucking breeze blew.

Mary has inserted her havoc in my veins, mixing herself in with the other three mistresses constantly whirling around inside me.

I'm wound up tight, and I'm ready to sling a few of my ninja stars, maybe draw some blood. But now that things are quiet at the club, I'll just go get another tattoo to help take the edge off. The more I have to be around that damn woman,

30

the tighter she winds me, and the more I want to remind her that when we kiss, the last thing we do is hate each other.

We *want* each other. I know she feels it too.

"You want to take a picture? It lasts longer," Badge grumbles with a slight curl of his lip as he pulls out a chair at the table. He doesn't take his eyes off me as he sips the plain black coffee from his mug. Badge is a prickly guy, and on a good day, he might not bite your damn head off.

"Let me grab my camera. There's nothing I want more than your ugly mug framed next to my nightstand. I'll kiss it every night before I go to bed."

"You're so fucking weird, Knives."

It's true. I never joke about anything. Why bother, when the truth can make people that much more uncomfortable?

That's the only rule I have always made sure applies to me, until recently.

The truth is a wicked bitch, and everywhere I turn, she's roaring her ugly head at me. For instance, I'm starting to wonder if I actually like Mary, and that truth makes me uncomfortable. I'm going to ignore it.

Nothing good can come out of her and I being together. Two people that don't like each other. That's like a hurricane and a tornado finding their way into each other's paths, ready to destroy.

But the whisper of truth is still there, telling me I want Mary more with every second that passes. I want to kiss her again to see if what I feel is the same or if it was a fluke, but there is no way she's going to let me near her again.

And she shouldn't.

I've done too many bad things, and even though she pretends to want the cruel side of temptation the MC offers, she isn't ready for it or me.

Like Tongue, I'm a bit fucked in the head, but not in a crazy sense like Tongue is. I'm not going to be bringing home a fucking swamp kitty and calling it 'Happy.'

31

I'm crazy in the sense that I don't feel grief for what I do. I cut, I draw blood, I inflict pain, and I never want the pain to stop.

I want to keep cutting, keep them pleading for help. I want to hear the victims begging me to stop. I love making them bleed so much they pass out, so I wait until they wake up, maybe give them a transfusion, and I do it all over again.

And I'll keep going until there is almost nothing left.

Give them hope that they will be able to live, and when I see their smile, their thankful, relieved smile with blissful tears raining down their cheeks, that's when I'll sling my ninja star across the room and lodge it directly in their foreheads.

And even after all of that, I'll still feel nothing.

Yet I think of Mary and I feel everything.

"Jesus fucking Christ, Knives. Stop looking at me." Badge slides the chair back and stomps away toward his office, where all the fancy gadgets are.

I wasn't looking at him. I zoned out.

See what she's doing to me? I need to get with Tongue. He and I like to sharpen our blades together, or sometimes he helps me make a new ninja star. I have one I haven't used since it's been made, and it's the one made of the knives I found the night Mason died. I should use it.

And I almost did on the cop who pulled the trigger first. I waited and waited, and then he became Chief of Police, but then he died of a fucking heart attack, and now the man that replaced him is my friend.

Well, ish.

We do each other favors, like when Sarah's SUV got blown up, and we wanted to make sure a report wasn't filed? I called him. Paid him. And we are in the clear.

It's good to have the law on your side, which is why I'll never understand why Reaper gave Badge the ultimatum.

The other cops involved in Mason's murder moved away right after, and I haven't been able to find them since. But I will.

And when I do, I'll use the knives from that night, and I'll bring myself some sort of peace.

Sarah comes into the kitchen, and the dark memories fade, replaced by a grin as I watch her tiptoe. She's holding her stomach, which is still flat, and slowly, gently, and quietly walks to the coffee pot. Sarah is pregnant. After what seems like forever, Prez and his ol' lady finally get their happy ending, but Sarah isn't fully excited just yet. She's afraid of every move she makes because she doesn't want to miscarry again.

She's isn't that far along. Eight weeks, maybe? Twelve weeks is usually the safe space for women not to worry about miscarriages, at least, that's what Doc told us.

"What are you doing?" I ask, crossing my arms over my chest.

Sarah yelps, holding her hand to her chest and taking deep breathes. Then, she lets out a gasp, sliding her hand to her stomach to make sure nothing happens. Her hand being there won't stop a miscarriage, and I think she knows that. It's only about comfort at this point. "Knives, you can't do that. You scared me," she says, taking a second to gather her breath. She tucks a strand of hair behind her ear and starts tiptoeing again to the coffee pot.

Even though Doc said she can have one cup of coffee a day, she doesn't want to risk it, so Reaper bought a decaf coffee machine for her instead. She stares up at the cabinet above her and opens it, but the mug is just out of reach.

And she won't reach for it. She's too nervous to stretch her body. I'm worried about her. I understand she's scared, but she needs to realize that normal, everyday things she always does aren't going to hurt the baby.

"Here, why don't you sit down, and I'll get it for you?" I walk out of the hallway between the kitchen and the gym, and Yeti follows behind me. When Sarah sits down, Yeti falls at her feet, then stares at all the entrances to the kitchen. He's protecting her.

"Thanks, Knives. I know, I'm crazy for acting this way, but I'm so nervous."

I grab the mug, set it on the counter, and pour the decaf coffee to the rim. God, I can't imagine the withdrawals she must be experiencing. I have to have caffeine every day. "Here you go." I place the mug in front of her, and she uses her hands to cup each side. I bet it's nice and warm. "It's okay to be afraid, but don't be so afraid that you stop living your life. Okay?"

"We've wanted this for so long, and if we lose another... Knives, I don't know what we would do."

She tries to hold it in, but soon enough, the tears spill right out of her.

I don't know what to say. I haven't experienced this situation before. I want to say, 'you'll try again.' It's the logical answer, but kind of heartless, because I'm not being sympathetic. I used to be. The teenage me would have cried right along with Sarah, but I haven't cried since that night.

Tears dropped are energy wasted.

"Why the hell is Sarah crying?" Reaper barges into the kitchen, and I lean back in the chair, crossing my hands over my chest to protect my heart.

If there is one thing I am afraid of, it's Reaper's ability to yank someone's heart out of their chest and not blink twice as he watches it beat to a slow, irreversible stop.

"I'm hormonal, Jesse! And I'm afraid of everything I do. Knives was trying to encourage me! Don't be mean to him."

My brows raise to my hairline as Sarah buries her face in her hands and sobs. Reaper wraps his arms around her, and then gives me the stink eye when he notices my shirt is off. "You could have covered your hairy chest," he says. "You're a goddamn werewolf."

I rub my hands down the fur, and Sarah turns around just in time to see me do it, which has me stopping, but her cheeks turn red. Something flashes in her eyes, and I stop rubbing down my chest, because she whispers something to Reaper and runs toward his office, leaving me wondering what the hell I did.

I know I'm hairy, but I'm not hairy enough to clear a room.

Reaper points a finger at me. "I'm saying this once. Walk around with a shirt on after this. Sarah is hormonal and the sex… is fucking amazing. She's always needing sex, and apparently, men shirtless really get her revved up, but I don't need my woman revved up over anyone but me, got it?"

"This has happened more than once?" I raise an eyebrow, trying not to laugh.

"Knives."

"Oh, okay. I wouldn't call it a pattern, Prez. Just a coincidence. Hormones are like that."

"And Slingshot, Patrick, Badge, and Tank. One second with their shirts off and she comes running to me—" his eyes widen when he realizes what he is saying. "You have my permission to always be shirtless until she has the baby." Reaper runs down the hall after his ol' lady, whipping his shirt off to get down to business before he enters his office.

"You're welcome!" I shout after him, which earns me the middle finger. This won't be the last time I'm half-naked in front of Sarah. I have to listen to my President, right? I snort, taking Sarah's coffee in my hand and taking a sip, only to spit it right back out when I taste the lack of caffeine.

How do people drink this?

My cell phone ringing from my bedroom has me getting up, pouring the coffee down the drain, and getting a new cup of coffee. I sit back down, letting the ringing come to an end. I don't feel like talking to anyone. They can leave a voicemail.

I'm thinking about how everyone around me is finding their ol' lady and being happy, but I don't know if I'm capable of feeling happiness like that. My soul was damaged a long time ago, and there is no way it can be repaired.

Then the kiss I shared with Mary plays in my mind, and I remember a sliver of healing that started to thread the gaping hole in my spirit together again.

No, who am I kidding?

I'm   beyond   repair.

CHAPTER TWO

Crap.

This is the second time in a week I've been pulled over. The first time, I got out of it because I flashed the cop a pretty smile, but it didn't work this time. Probably didn't help that I was apparently "rude", and "uncooperative", and "being booked for wanton disregard for safety".

So sue me, I'm not perfect.

The cell door slides shut, the metal clanking as it slams against the wall, locking into place. It smells like piss in here. I know I'm a bit reckless, but landing in jail for a speeding ticket, of all things, is a new low for me.

Even if it was kind of fun for a moment.

When I'm speeding down the road, the rush is almost too hard to explain. My foot against the pedal, pressing it against the floor as the needle on the speedometer climbs to the red lines. The engine roars, and when I hit 110 miles per hour, I feel like I'm flying, like I'm free.

Then a damn cop had to flip on his lights and ruin everything.

I grab the metal bars and push my face against them. "Hey, come on. Let me out of here. I don't belong here. My speedometer is broken, honest." It's a lie, but I need to try something. The one phone call they gave me was useless, since Knives didn't answer.

I don't know why I called him. When they read me my rights and said I get one phone call, the first person that entered my mind was him. He is a pain in my ass ninety-nine percent of the time, but if there is one thing about that damn annoying man is it's he's dependable. When the men call him, he drops everything, and he is there for them.

And for some stupid reason, I thought he'd be there for me, even though we don't like one another. Even though we fight more than we talk, I stupidly thought he'd come to get me out of this hell hole. After what happened at Christmas… oh, who am I kidding? I can't even recall what happened because it made no sense.

Because someone's first real kiss shouldn't be that good, right? Toe-curling, body aching, leaving my skin in a fever, good. A first kiss is supposed to be messy and gross, with too much tongue and too wet, wondering why people kiss to begin with, but no, that was not the case with Knives.

When he smashed his lips against mine, I knew what he was doing. He wanted to shut me up, but the firm grip on my hair loosened, and he sighed into my mouth as we both relaxed.

I bang my head against the bars, and the thud echoes in the small space. Am I hitting myself with the metal rods to help me forget the kiss or to remind me how stupid I am for speeding and then mouthing off to the cop to land me in here? Or to remind me how dumb I am for having a flicker of hope that maybe Knives and I like one another, and falling for that Christmas kiss?

All of it.

I'm just full of bad ideas lately.

"You aren't going anywhere, Miss St. James. Not until your bail is posted. This time you have a court date," Officer Daniels says as he bites into a donut and flips the page of the newspaper.

"Court? Come on! I was barely speeding."

"You're right. At first, your speed wasn't too far above the legal limit, but your *choice* to engage officers in a high-speed chase for nearly five miles was. Maybe think about that next time."

Oh, right. So I may have put pedal to the metal on the highway, attracted a bunch of cop cars, swerved off the road to try to escape, and cut across the lanes headlong into traffic to throw them off before finally getting pulled over.

Like I said, I'm not perfect.

He takes another bite of the donut, and my stomach grumbles, reminding me I haven't eaten since last night. I'm not going to ask for food. I just want another phone call. I let out a long sigh, push off the bars, and take three steps back.

My knees hit the metal cot, and I sit down, running my fingers through the inky strands of my hair. I hate sitting here. It gives me time to think about the things I'm doing and why I'm doing them, and the answer is, I don't know.

For the longest time, I was the perfect daughter. Straight A's and fake smiles, along with fake happiness and a fake family.

The only real experiences I've ever had are the ones the Ruthless Kings have given me, good and bad. I know how I got to the Atlantic City chapter. I know it was my own doing. It's my own fault, but I don't care to go back to that old life.

It was stale, lacking in love and life, and any type of excitement. Is that a reason not to go home? Probably not, but I know my family, and I doubt they are worried. They never were before, and Reaper says Badge checked for missing persons and found nothing. He found more, but I stopped him before he could tell me.

I don't want to know.

All that matters is what led me here, to now, to the present.

The past doesn't matter, and what happened to me is irrelevant because I didn't experience abuse from the bikers like the other girls. I have no reason to be afraid.

But you are.

I just don't know what I'm afraid of.

I like it here with the Kings, even if they barely give me the time of day because I tried to be a cut slut. I'm going to go ahead and mark that off my to-do list, because there aren't any sluts there now since two of them died.

I prefer to stay alive. Thank you very much.

Then why am I still with the motorcycle club? I should leave, get the hell away as far and as fast as I can, yet I'm rooted here.

And I have no idea why.

"Well, well, well."

I grit my teeth when I hear his mocking tone. I knew I should have called someone else.

"Looks like the little hellraiser is off doing what she does best, isn't she?"

I sigh when I see Knives standing in front of my cell, waving his phone in the air. "I got your message. Why am I not surprised to find you here?" he asks. He tucks his phone in his pocket and whips out a ninja star, scratching a spot under his chin. The cops see it and they don't even blink.

"He has a weapon!" I cry out, pointing at the man who drives me freaking bonkers. "Hello," I singsong. "He has a ninja star. He might kill me." I wave my arms in the air like I'm a person trapped on an island, waving my hands in the air, hoping the only helicopter I've seen in weeks saves me.

Freaking crickets. What good is law enforcement if they can't save me from Knives?

"It helps when you have the entire department in your pocket, Hellraiser."

"Stop calling me that," I seethe and then bolt to the bars, gripping them tight until my knuckles turn white. "I swear, you better be glad I'm in here, or I'd—"

"—You'd what?" He inches forward, and his nose touches mine between the bars. "Tell me."

The muscles in my cheek jump as I squeeze my jaws together. "I'd freaking choke you."

He chuckles; the sound is dark and delicious and travels down my spine like a shiver. When the tension has nowhere else to go, it seeps into the surface of my skin, creating goosebumps. "Oh, don't make promises you can't keep. You know how much I love a good time," he says, a teasing glint in his eyes.

I cross my arms to hide my hard nipples that his response created. I don't have control over my body. It's not like I want to be attracted to him. "Are you going to get me out of here or not?"

"Nah. I just wanted to come by and see you in here. Maybe being stuck in jail might give you a little perspective."

"Perspective! You can't be serious. Like you've never been in jail before?"

"Actually, I haven't. See, I'm a good boy, no matter what the lump of coal you got me says."

I'm fuming at this point. He is such a dick. I should have called Reaper or Sarah, someone that actually gives a damn and doesn't want to see me in here. "Just because I made a mistake—"

He slams his fist against the bars, but I don't flinch, even if my heart is drumming against my chest. "It isn't just this mistake, Mary. It's all of them. It's your reckless behavior. TJ here says it's the second time this week you've been

41

recklessly driving. Fourth or fifth time this winter." He slices the ninja star across the bars, and sparks fly when metal grinds against metal. "You're going down a dangerous fucking road, and you expect me or other members to pick you up along the way? To adhere to your carelessness?"

"Adhere? That's a fancy word for a guy like you," I nearly spit, rage shaking my body the longer I stare into his sky-blue eyes. They are cold and calculating.

I've heard people say the eyes are the window to the soul, but that doesn't apply to Knives. When I look into his eyes, I see nothing. His soul turned to stone eons ago.

"Hey, TJ. What is Miss St. James' bail?" Knives asks, never taking his gaze off me.

"A few thousand," the cop answers.

Knives hums as he thinks about what he wants to do; the right side of his mouth tilts up in a conniving smirk. "Perfect. Let her stew for a few days, will ya, TJ?"

"Anything for the Kings, you know that," he says to Knives, which leaves me baffled.

This can't be legal.

"Knives, you can't be serious? You're going to leave me here?"

"Guess you're going to have to see me walk away from you to realize that, aren't you?"

"Knives, don't you fucking dare leave me here," I growl low in my throat so he can hear the frustration. I grip the bars and try to shake them, which is pointless, because they don't ever move. It's called a jail cell for a reason.

He backs away slowly, flicking the ninja star over his fingers. His knuckles are so scarred from that trick, but he doesn't seem to care. He lifts his other hand and gives me a finger wave goodbye. "Hey, TJ, can I have a donut?" Knives asks, ignoring me.

"Knives!" I pound my fist against the bar. "Don't you fucking leave me here. I swear to god!"

"Mmmm, chocolate covered ones are my favorite. Thanks, TJ. I appreciate ya." He stabs the donut with his ninja star and takes a big bite of it as he watches me. "The real world is so much better, Mary. Oh—" he bonks his forehead with his hand, "—but you know that. Later, Hellraiser. See ya on the other side."

He really is walking away from me. He is going to leave me here. "I will never forgive you for this, Knives! Get your hairy ass back here!" I scream, slamming my fist against the cell bars one last time as I yell for him. The bastard only lifts his donut in the air and walks out the door.

I don't know if he has a hairy ass; I only said that because he has a hairy chest that I dream about running my fingers through. It's why they call them dreams. I'm not liable for what my brain likes to think about while I'm unconscious.

The exit door slams shut, and I'm left alone.

He really left me here.

This has to be some sort of joke, but as I'm standing here waiting for Knives to walk back through the door, the seconds turn to minutes. I pinch my lips together and try to control the anger. The members have done worse things in life, and Knives has their back; why can't he have mine?

"Looks like you pissed off the wrong guy, Miss St. James," Officer Daniels polishes off another donut and wipes his hand on his uniform, leaving chocolate smears on the khaki.

"Mind your own business," I mumble. Mouthing off to an officer, while I still can't make bail, probably isn't the best idea, but I'm shocked right now and disappointed. I can't believe Knives left me here.

If there is one thing I know more than ever right now, it's that the kiss we shared meant nothing to him. I had this bread crumb of hope that the dislike we shared toward one another was really passion just bursting at the seams to be released, but now that he left without giving me one last look, I know better.

If people really care when they walk away, they usually pause and give a parting glance over their shoulder, but I guess when dealing with a man whose soul is stone, I shouldn't expect much else.

But if that's the case, why am I so mad?

CHAPTER THREE

Knives

I paid her bail, and there isn't going to be a court date because I paid the new Chief of Police off too. He seemed very happy to be in business with us. Nothing like a large stack of cash to help pay for his daughter's college to get him on my side.

She's in there because the cops are following my orders. Mary needs to learn that what she is doing to herself isn't okay. I read the report. She was going 90mph in a 65mph zone, and then when she got pulled over, she veered off-road, nearly slammed into a bunch of cactuses, then gunned it to 110 mph while weaving in and out of traffic and crossing over into the other lane. Took a dozen cop cars to chase her down in the end. I don't know why the girl has a death wish, but I'm not going to let her die easily on my watch.

So she's going to sit there in jail and think about what she's done.

Oh, she's fuming.

Good. Let her boil in her mistakes, and maybe she'll come out of the slammer having learned something about herself.

I lift my leg over my bike and sit down, then pop a piece of bubble gum in my mouth. I chew it, letting the cherry flavor roll around, and blow a bubble. When it pops, I'm reminded of when I was around thirteen years old and Mason got us two packs of gum. He said we had to chew all the pieces, and whoever blew the biggest bubble won.

That's it.

We just won. There was no prize. It was just the ability to have bragging rights. I rub a hand over my heart when it begins the ache. I swear, the only time I feel pain is when I think about my brother. I lean against the backrest on my bike, watching the front doors of the police station. A lot of riders don't like backrests because it doesn't make the Harley look badass.

Listen, my bike is awesome, and I'm badass, so if I know that, then everyone else can go fuck themselves. I like to be comfortable, and when we're on long runs, I can relax while everyone else has a sore back.

I tap my fingers against the handlebars and debate if I want to go in the police station and get her. She can ride bitch behind me, but there is one problem: I've never had a woman on my bike, and I don't want the guys getting any ideas. Ol' ladies only on a member's motorcycle, and Mary is not my ol' lady.

No, she can't get off easy. Fuck that. She got herself into this mess; the least she can do is do a few days in jail.

I crank my bike and hit the throttle, waving to a few police cars as I drive by. It's a good day for a ride. It's cold, but the sun is out, and I need to clear my head. Mary fucks me all up. I'm a one-track-mind kind of guy. I know my duties and what I can bring to the table when Reaper needs me, yet Mary gets in my head, and I'm wondering if I'm a little more complex than I originally thought.

Maybe it isn't her I want; maybe I just want someone. All the guys are finding their ol' ladies, and it is making me want what they have. No one likes being alone. People choose to be because they feel like they don't deserve the love and happiness that comes with being with someone. Honestly, I think it all starts with yourself.

If I can't be happy and alone with myself, how can I be happy and alone with someone I love? It starts with the individual. I'm more than content with myself and being alone, I just know no one deserves to be pulled into my life. The MC life isn't for everyone.

And it isn't for Mary.

I don't know where she's from or why she doesn't want to go back, but someone out there has to be looking for her. She's too damn beautiful, too damn smart, too damn proper to be abandoned. There's a story behind how she got to Atlantic City before she came to Vegas, and I want to find out what it was, even if she doesn't.

"It's none of my damn business," I say to the wind as it blows in my face. "I need to stay away from her and let her figure out her own shit." I'm talking to myself, great. Isn't that what they say when you're going crazy?

She's made me insane. Perfect. The last thing I need is to be like Tongue, fucking stalking her with a damn gator strapped to my chest.

My phone vibrates in my pocket just as I come to a stop outside the tattoo parlor. A ride is what I need, but a different kind. I want to feel pain. I want to remind myself why I choose to stay alone, because anyone that enjoys pain can't enjoy love.

When I look at the screen, I see Seer's name flashing on the screen. "Oh, that's a big fuck no and fuck you, Seer. Sorry," I ignore the call and tuck my phone back in my pocket.

And then it rings again.

I groan and tilt my head back, staring up at the blue sky. "Why is this day fucking with me?" Just to make sure Reaper isn't calling, I bring my phone out again and see Seer's name. "I don't know what information you've got for me today, but I don't want to hear it, man." I ignore the call again, muting the vibration. Seer is one of a kind. He's good people, odd, but in the sense, he has sight.

He can see things before they happen. It doesn't bother me when it comes to someone else, but me? I'm not interested in what the future has in store. I'd rather take the punches as they come instead of dodging them, and if that means I die, then that's when I'm meant to leave this world.

My phone rings again, and this time it pisses me off. I throw the phone on the ground and step on it with my boot.

Again.

Again.

And again.

Until it's nothing but broken pieces and wires.

And the bastard still has the nerve to ring even if it does sound drawn out like a piece of machinery shutting down.

"You have got to be kidding me." I stomp the phone again, then dig my heel into the cracked screen, grinning when the ringer starts to die. "Yeah, take that, fucker."

"Tough day?" Luci's amused tone comes from the side of the building, as does cigarette smoke. He spins around the corner and stares at me with a playful grin, pulling the cigarette out of his mouth.

"You could say that." For good measure, I kick the pieces of the cell phone across the parking lot and breathe easier when it's out of my line of sight. I really don't mind Seer, but I don't want to know shit about something happening to me. His gift doesn't scare me; it's the truth of his visions.

"You shouldn't have done that. Reaper might need to get a hold of you," he says. "And you crush your phone too many times for the man to remain patient."

"Shut up." Damn, if Luci ain't right. I'm going to get my ass handed to me if the club needs me and I'm not available. "Come on—" I slap his shoulder and do my best not to inhale the cloud of smoke he blows from his mouth, "—I need a tattoo."

Luci flicks his cigarette to the ground and steps on it. "Let's do it, then. You caught me at a good time. I don't have an appointment for a few hours."

When I walk inside, my nerves settle, and the buzz of the tattoo gun eases me. The shop is nice, but what I love most about it is how classic Luci keeps it. It has American traditional flashes framed over the walls, and every artist has their own private room to tattoo their clients, but it's simple. There aren't any gimmicks. It's just a place where people come for tattoos and piercings, then get the fuck out. The walls are painted a simple color, beige because Luci doesn't like to make things complicated. He likes to keep things simple, but decoration is where simplicity ends.

He's the best fucking artist I've ever come across, besides Tongue. Actually, now that I think about it, Tongue would be a great tattoo artist. He can draw and make people bleed. Two things he loves most. I make a mental note to tell him my idea later.

"Well, well, if it isn't my favorite cock I pierced," Bobby-Jane greets me as she dries off her hands and snaps on a pair of gloves. The artwork on her body is more delicate, flowy, and feminine.

"Hey Bobby-Jane," I say and lean in to kiss the side of her temple. I've known her for a few years now before she became a tattoo artist. "How's it hanging?"

She cocks her head and stares at my crotch. "If I remember correctly, a little to the left."

I have a Jacob's Ladder, bars pierced right through my cock and two hoops on the crown, like horns, and Bobby-Jane is the one that pierced me. "You want to come find out again?" I ask her, remembering the few times we hooked up. The sex was good, but we both knew the deal.

It was just sex.

Maybe that's what I need. It's been a while because I've been so caught up with Mary that I've forgotten that I'm a single man. Mary drives me nuts, Bobby-Jane tugs my nuts. See the difference?

"Maybe, I'll call you later," she gives me a wink and heads into the room where her client is.

"Yeah, too bad she can't call you," Luci says, sitting down on a stool and pushes his feet against the ground to roll in front of me.

"Why not?"

"You destroyed your phone, remember?" he smirks, grabbing his notepad and a red pen.

"Fuck." I cover my face and let out a painful groan. A beautiful, missed opportunity, gone because I can't keep my head on straight.

"Your dick will live, but the time is ticking, Knives. What are we doing?"

"I want a pinup on my arm, a woman with long black hair and red lipstick." Once the words come out of my mouth, I nearly choke on my tongue and wish my swamp kitty carrying MC brother was around to cut it out of me. I just described Mary.

"How do you want her body?" Luci asks as he starts to draw on the paper in delicate lines.

I imagine Mary; she has fuller breasts and an ass shaped like a peach that I want nothing more than to sink my damn teeth into. My cock jumps, and I clear my throat and take a deep breath to get myself under control. How awkward would it be to get an erection while Luci tattoos me?

"Medium size tits and ass," I say to him, which he just nods as he starts creating the outline of her tits, and it's almost like he has seen Mary naked, because the body on the paper is everything I dream about.

I shouldn't be doing this, but as he draws her hair, long and wavy behind her back, I want nothing more than to finally close the distance between me and Mary. I think somehow... in some way; the little hellraiser wiggled her way into my heart.

I don't know when that happened, but as Luci places the stencil on my forearm and pulls it away, I know it's the only way I'm really ever going to have her. This picture is the only way I'll be able to have her close to me. "Can you add a leather jacket? Keep it unzipped."

"Yeah, I can freehand that on with a marker," Luci states as he starts putting the tattoo gun together and unwrapping a clean, sterile needle. "Come on. Come sit on my throne of pain," He laughs at his own joke, but all I do is roll my eyes. I flop onto the red leather chair, flip my arm over, and Luci shines the light on it.

I dig into my pocket for my ninja star and roll it over my fingers as the gun buzzes, and the needle hits my skin. Euphoria takes over as the pain hits. It's sweet, it stings, and it burns.

Just.   Like.   Mary.

CHAPTER FOUR

I'm going to kill him.

I cannot believe I've had to stay in jail for two days. I haven't showered. I have had to hover when I pee because there is no way in hell I am sitting on a stainless steel toilet that's probably never been cleaned.

When I see him, I'm going to wrap my hands around his throat, punch him in the gut again with that damn leg he bought me for Christmas, then scream in his face.

"Well, looks like you're a free woman," Officer Daniels slides the key in the cell and slides the door open.

Don't get sassy, Mary.

"You look familiar," another cop says, his blue eyes narrowing as he evaluates me.

I swallow, hoping he doesn't stare at me too long. Not a lot of people know who I am, but there are a few sprinkled about who recognize me. I zip up my leather jacket, and that's when he shakes his head clear, scoffing at himself. "Never mind, you can't be her. That's impossible." He tilts his head down and goes back to what he was doing.

Blowing out a breath, I start walking the green mile toward the exit when I remember I have a court date. "Officer Daniels? When will I know about the court date?"

"Oh, you don't have to worry about that. Knives took care of it when he paid your bail."

I freeze. His words encase me like an iceberg, and if snow could fall right about now, I'd be making snowballs and launching them at the cop. "You're going to have to repeat that. What?" I say with a bit of a bite.

"Oh yeah. You could have left days ago, but Knives wanted you to stay. We listen to the Kings. We know who really pays our bills." He walks around his desk, picks up a file, and doesn't pay me any mind as if what he just said doesn't make me plan Knives' murder.

"He's a dead man," I say through tight teeth. I cannot believe the bail was paid days ago. My fingers twitch, and the fury inside me is boiling over. I'm about ready to take his ninja star and stab him with it. I stomp toward the door and slam the bar against it, opening it with so much force it bounces off the brick wall and nearly hits me again.

The sun is too bright after being locked inside for two days. I lift my hand and block the yellow light out of my eyes.

"Hey, Hellraiser. Damn, you look like shit."

I scan the parking lot for the bane of my existence, and when I see him, I fly down the steps. He looks cocky sitting on his motorcycle, all leather cut, muscles, trimmed beard, the sides of his head shaved with a bit of hair on top, and a mischievous smile to wreck my heart. "You! Why would you do that?" I poke a finger against his chest.

His hard, broad, muscular chest. A real man's chest. It isn't shaved, not baby smooth, but hairy, all the way down his abs, and I itch to run my fingers through it.

53

Not that I'd ever admit that out loud to anyone.

"Here. Put this on," Knives says, completely ignoring the anger and the poke against the chest. My eyes land on the tattoo below his neck that says 'Judge Me.'

Oh, I'm judging. He doesn't have to worry about that.

"Did you hear me? Why would you do that, Knives? I am not a person you can fuck with whenever you want. I have feelings. Everyone makes mistakes, and you walked out on me when I needed you. You wouldn't have done that to one of your MC brothers."

"Don't for a second compare yourself to them," he says. "My brothers know when they make a mistake, but you don't. That's the difference, Mary. You're doing it for the good to fuck yourself over. My brothers land in jail because they are breaking laws for the better good. What the hell are you doing to better yourself or the world? Nothing."

"I—"

He stops me from saying anything else by pushing the helmet against my chest. "You, nothing. You have no reason to defend yourself. You're putting yourself in harm's way, and guess what? You were safer there in that jail cell than you were in your car. And guess who could sleep at night? Me. The club. The people that care about you. Shut the hell up, Mary. Put the helmet on and get on my bike."

If my ass wasn't burning from the spanking he just gave me, I'd sass him and tell him I'd rather walk, but the hard glint in his eyes tells me there is no room for discussion. With a nod, I slide the helmet on my head and swing my leg over to mount the bike. I'm squeezed tight between Knives and the backrest, my tits snug against his back. I inhale a sharp breath as my nipples harden from the contact. I dig my fingernails into my thighs to stop myself from wrapping my arms around his waist.

He revs the engine, but we don't move forward. He reaches behind his back and grips my hands, pulling my arms around his waist.

Just like I didn't want.

"You're going to have to hold on a lot tighter, Hellraiser. Lean when I lean, and don't distract me. You want freedom? You're about to experience it."

I have no idea what Knives means about freedom, but if it feels anything like his abs do clenching under my fingers, I want it. Once he feels like I have a good hold on him, he punches forward, and the bike jerks, which pushes me against his backrest more. I hold on tighter, my fingers toying with his shirt, and the motion, along with the air breezing by us, has his shirt inching up his torso. My fingers graze against his bare stomach, and the coarse hairs I love so much tickle my palm. I gasp and do my best not to move or explore, but being this close to him without fighting feels different.

It's just like that moment we kissed. Seems like we only ever get along when we're touching each other.

That's not a good thing.

The bike vibrates between my legs and tickles my swollen clit. Every bounce of the bike, every vibration from the bike speeding up, nearly makes me whimper and fall apart. With the throbbing between my legs, it is hard to figure out if the rumbling is actually coming from the bike or the man in front of me.

We zigzag through the parking lot until we are at the stop sign that takes us to the main road. He takes a right, passing the strip where all the fun is. Even though I've been in Vegas for almost a year, I have never been to the strip. Maybe I'll go and get a job; there are plenty of jobs I can do to put distance between me and Knives. Eventually, I'll move out of the clubhouse, and they won't ever have to worry about me again.

It hurts to think about, but I feel like the Kings got stuck with me. They aren't. I can take care of myself. It might not seem like it, but I can if I have to.

And I really think I have to, because something is changing between me and Knives. I'm not sure what it is, but it can't be good.

Nothing good can be built from hate.

And Knives hates me, that much I know.

We make our way to Loneliest Road, a long stretch of narrow pavement that cuts through four-hundred miles of the United States. There is desert on either side of us, mountains and forests. It's beautiful. Getting lost in the desert, the horizons of the sun, and the sand disappearing between my toes.

It sounds like heaven. A real break from life. I have been running from the truth for so long that I don't know what it's like to stop and think about what I want. I haven't pressed reset on my life since I've been here. I think maybe it's time I move on, somewhere, and do something.

I don't know what, but it's got to feel better than being a burden.

I hold onto Knives tighter when he speeds up, and the grumbling of the engine whips through the air.

I expect for him to slow down, but he doesn't.

The bike goes faster, quickly gaining more speed until I'm worried Knives is going to lose control and we're going to wreck. I squeeze his waist and raise my voice, "Stop it, Knives! Stop. You're going too fast!" I try to yell over the rush of wind we are slicing through as we fly down the road.

Most of my hair is flattened by the helmet, but the ends are slashing, dancing, stinging my arms. His hand twists the throttle again, and the bike lurches forward, gaining more speed, going even faster. "Stop! Knives, please!" I nearly sob. I'm scared. Everything is blurring past us. I can't see anything.

He slams on the brakes, and the bike fishtails. The smell of burnt rubber surrounds us, along with a cloud of smoke. He pulls off to the shoulder, the bike dipping from pavement to sand. I jerk off the helmet and toss it on the ground. I'm breathing heavily, inhaling dust and smoke from the tires. "What the fuck, Knives? What was that?"

He hops off his Harley, and his cold eyes hit me like daggers. "Isn't that what you wanted, Mary? Didn't you want to be free? Don't you like speed? Don't you crave the adrenaline pumping in your veins the faster you go? What, you didn't like it? Was it too much for you to handle? Is it so different from bursting past the cops at 110 mph, feeling the wind in your hair? When you aren't cozied up in a box of a car."

"Stop it," I sound pathetic with the emotion clogging my throat.

He kicks his helmet, and it flies across the desert, landing with a loud smack before it bounces again, this time stopping next to a dead bush. "Goddamn it, Mary!" he roars so loud, I can hear the gravel in his throat as he stresses his vocal cords. His voice carries, and a few crows down the road stop picking at a dead animal and fly away. "I won't stop it. I won't stop. You can't be doing shit like this; do you understand me?"

"I'm not a child. Don't talk to me like a child, Knives."

"Then stop acting like one. What the hell is your problem? Why are you doing this? Why act out? Why with the rebellion? Why do you have a death wish?"

"Why do you suddenly care?" I hiss, swinging my legs over the bike and sliding off. "Why do you care what I do? I'm a goddamn adult, Knives. I can do whatever I want. Stop acting like you give a damn when you'd be perfectly happy if I swerved off the side of the road and—"

Before I can say another word, he takes four long strides over to me and shoves his hand over my mouth. "Don't you dare say another word. Don't you dare sit there and say what I think you're about to say. I swear—" He removes his hand and screams in the air, takes out a ninja star, and scratches his beard with it. It's like the ninja star is his comfort. "You drive me fucking nuts, you know that? You drive me... insane."

"That's why you should be happy that—"

He flings the ninja star at me, and I jump. The metal lodges in the metal of his motorcycle right as I flinch. "I said, don't say another word. God, you think I'm that kind of man? To want you dead? Do you really think I hate you that much? Is that how much you hate me?"

"What? No, I don't think you want me dead, I care—" I catch myself before I say I care about him. "I would never want you, me, or anyone dead."

"Well, you know that isn't the case with me, right? You know that there are plenty of people I want dead, but you aren't one of them, Mary. Do you want to know why I don't want you speeding down the road? You want to know why I care?" He stomps toward me again and places his hand on the back of my neck. "This."

He slams our lips together in a fiery kiss, not giving me a second to think, a second to breathe, a second to figure out what the hell is going on. His palm is so wide, his fingers nearly touch as they wrap around my throat. Knives is telling me he is in control, the way he guides my head, moves his mouth, flicks his tongue.

I'm transported back to Christmas, where I felt his lips for the first time, and I can hardly breathe.

We are horrible to one another, though. I pull back to let him know I want to bring the kiss to an end. I don't, but I need to. The more I kiss him, the deeper I'm going to feel about a man that isn't good for me.

I'm not good for him either.

We're snakes coiling around each other, and the more we fight, the tighter we grip each other. And we are both too stubborn to let go. If we don't stop, one of us will get hurt beyond repair.

He pulls away and puts space between us, enough to where I can catch my breath without breathing the same air he is. Our chests are in sync as we grovel to breathe. My entire body is hot, his eyes are locked on my face, and his chin is nearly touching his chest. He's staring at me through ill intentions, wicked eyes, and long brown lashes. His shapely brows are drawn together, and his fists clench at his sides. The pinkness of his lips is heightened from our kiss.

I check out his entire body, slowly dropping my attention to his chest. His nipples are hard, and every time his lungs expand, the shirt stretches over the brute strength of his pecs. I swallow, coating my mouth with saliva as I notice things I tried not to notice before on his body.

Like how tall he really is. And how built and defined his muscles are. And how every time I see him, there's a new tattoo. And how about the erection tenting his black jeans right now? His cock is traveling down his left thigh, nearly poking out of the tear he has in his jeans. I can see the pale flesh of his leg, the coarse hair that is also on his torso.

"Why did you do that?" I find my voice, but it doesn't sound like me. It's hoarse with desire and uncertainty. I lick my lips, and I make my way up his body, but pause on his forearm. There's a tattoo there that wasn't there a few days ago. It's glistening in the sun from ointment, but the further I inspect it, the more I see a pin-up girl.

She's wearing my leather jacket and my red lipstick.

That has to be a coincidence. No way would he get me tattooed on his body when we can't figure out how to have a conversation with one another.

"Did you feel it?" he asks. "That moment where everything else faded away. All there was, was me and you."

I shake my head. I don't want to admit that I felt the exact same thing, just like I did at Christmas.

"You're lying," he says with a smile on his face, as if it doesn't bother him that I'm denying whatever... this is between us.

It's hate.

It's lust.

It's like.

But it isn't love.

And if it isn't love, if it can't be love, then I don't want anything to do with it. Nursing a broken heart isn't worth the tears over a man that can't commit himself to you, but you knew damn well he wouldn't be able to.

Yeah, I'm not about to fall down that hole.

There isn't much I know about Knives, but I know this, he isn't boyfriend material.

He isn't husband material.

But if I'm honest with myself, I'm not wife material either.

And what happens when the two clash?

Arguments. Fights. Yelling. He'll start drinking and call me a no-good, worthless whore. I'll tell him he doesn't know how to keep his dick in his pants.

What will we be left with?

Misery.

And my misery does not like company.

CHAPTER FIVE

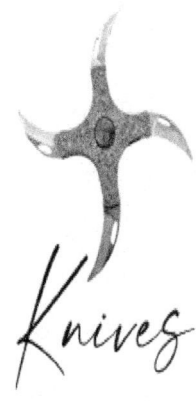

Knives

I wait for her to say something, anything, but she stares at me with round light brown eyes, frozen next to my bike. She's a pretty fucking picture standing next to my motorcycle, wind blowing her already fucked up hair from not being brushed over the last few days. The cascading strands fall to her ass, and the breeze picks them up, and they flow to the right, then left. Her lips aren't red from her lipstick since she isn't wearing any; they are swollen from our kiss.

She's lying if she says she doesn't feel anything between us. Because I see the emotion clear as fucking day as she stares at me. Don't get me wrong, I don't expect us to go skipping hand in hand across the desert any time soon, but damn it, she has to know there is something other than the constant arguing.

No, you know what? It isn't even arguing. It's bickering over little pointless shit because we get on each other's nerves.

"Knives, we don't even like being around one another—" she pauses, lifts her nose in the air, "—I smell gas."

"Don't change the subject, Mary. Slingshot isn't even here."

"Not... gross, no, not that gas. Like...gasoline," she coughs and fans her face.

"Jesus, okay, I should have known talking to you would be impossible. Maybe you're right. Maybe we just need to get each other out of our systems or something," I say, placing my hands on my hips.

"No, Knives—"

"—I'm going to go get the helmet. Let's just not talk for a minute, okay? I need to think." I need to find someone to throw my ninja star at, and since it can't be Mary, I need to figure out something, because I'm itching to fuck shit up. Maybe I can get with Tongue, and we can go to the Asylum. His brother is there; it's only fair that we pay a visit. Maybe draw a pound of flesh or two as revenge for all the shit he pulled on us this year.

I shield the upper half of my face with my hand as I look out along the endless amount of sand. The helmet is a good thirty yards away, not too bad, but enough to annoy me because I had to lose my temper. Stopping here was a bad idea. I shouldn't have tried to teach her a lesson because the only thing I learned is how I want my lips on hers again.

It's easier than fucking fighting all the time and for no damn reason. I don't want anyone else. I try to think of Bobby-Jane, her fake tits, and perky ass, but not even thinking of her hands on my cock does anything for me.

She doesn't have the sass, attitude, or the ability to piss me off like Mary does, and as much as that shit drives me crazy...

I fucking like it.

I want to bend her over my knee and spank her ass every time she gets mouthy.

I stop when I'm about halfway to the helmet and peer back over my shoulder to see Mary standing there, hands tucked in her pockets as she kicks the ground.

The woman is a damn mess, and because I'm an idiot, I want her to be my mess.

A red truck drives by, the window down, and I watch as the passenger flicks a cigarette out the window, which isn't a big deal.

Until a line of fire starts from the road and makes its way to my bike.

I've felt true fear a time or two. And right now is one of those times.

"Mary! Mary! Run!" I yell, but I don't know if she can hear me. She's fucking walking in a straight line and doing spins and twists, not paying attention to her surroundings. I pat my pockets for another ninja star because if I can throw one in the air and nail her in the shoulder, she'll fucking listen then.

Holy shit.

I check every pocket, but I don't feel another star. I always carry extra.

I pick up my feet and run, the sand making it difficult as my boots sink with every step. My heart is thundering under my bones as I pump my arms. I feel like I'm in damn quicksand with how much effort it's taking me to run.

"Mary!" I call out her name, hauling ass toward her. She finally hears her name, and when she jerks her head in my direction, the flames engulf my bike.

She gasps, jumping back, but the flames get higher. The hot red and orange fingers dance as they climb into the sky, black smoke billowing quickly.

Mary screams as her shoes catch fire.

Fuck. She said she smelled gas. Of course my bike was leaking. It was probably from the ninja star I threw. I punctured the damn tank.

She's probably been standing in gasoline, but the sand soaked it up and made the liquid hard to see.

When I get close enough to her, I tackle her to the ground and whip off my cut, patting her shoes until the flames are gone. When they are, luckily, her boots are a bit burnt, but I don't see her skin. That's good.

The roar of the fire is too loud. We need to get away before the bike blows up. I pick her up in my arms and begin to run anywhere that isn't here. We get far enough away right as the gas tank explodes, sending more fire into the air.

I should care more than I do about losing my baby. A man's bike is his treasure, but a bike can be replaced.

This headache of a woman can't be.

And I know I can never replace her.

"Are you okay? Are you hurt?" I check her over to make sure she doesn't have any burns. "How are your feet?"

"Warm, but I think I'm okay. Thank you." She tucks her hair behind her ear, and her mouth drops open when she sees the bike burning. "I'm so sorry—"

"What is it with you and not paying attention to your surroundings, huh? Are you fucking kidding me? Are you so reckless with your life you couldn't see a fire?"

She struggles as she gets to her feet since I'm sure they are sore, and I help her by grabbing onto her arms and stabilizing her, but she shrugs me away. "There wouldn't have been a fire if you didn't throw your damn ninja star and pierce the gas tank. I told you I smelled gasoline, and you didn't listen to me."

"Oh, so this is all my fault? All because I was trying to teach you not to kill yourself driving."

"Says the guy who threw a damn ninja star at me!"

"I missed you on purpose! I know what the fuck I'm doing with my ninja stars," I yell, needing to get the last word in.

"So you knew what the fuck you were doing when you aimed at the goddamn gas tank? Trying to teach me a lesson by nearly killing us both?"

"It was an accident!"

She throws her arms in the air and shakes her head. "You're impossible. Regardless of whose fault is—it's yours, by the way—we need to call for help."

I grind my teeth together when she blames me. "Okay, get your phone out."

"My phone is dead since *someone*," she glares at me, "left me in jail."

"You should blame yourself for that one, Hellraiser. You got yourself into that mess."

"Fine, whatever. I just want to get home. Get your phone out and call 911."

I squeeze my eyes shut because I know we are about to get into another fight. "I don't have it."

Besides the screeching of melting metal in the background, she doesn't say a word. "What?" she questions. "Don't joke right now, Knives. I'm not in the mood."

"I'm not kidding. I broke my phone days ago. I'm waiting on a replacement to come in the mail." It's been nice to get away from technology. It's put things in perspective. I've liked not having it in my hand constantly. I've read more, hung out with my friends more, and—

"Are you kidding me! I swear, you constantly pull this shit just to piss me off."

"Oh, right. I planned to blow up my bike for you, just so you can give me a migraine. Yeah, that's the dream, Mary. Nice one."

"Did you leave it at the poor girl's house?"

Do I hear jealousy? I should tell her I fucked someone. That would crush any...odd, slim, next to nothing chance she and I have together.

"I broke it when I got a call I didn't want to get." I'm starting to wonder if I should have answered that call from Seer. I wonder if this was what he was going to warn me about. There aren't many times I want to know my future, but I would have wanted to know this.

The last thing I want is to be stuck out here with Mary.

"Okay, someone will come. It's impossible not to see that fire from a distance," she sighs, sitting down on the desert floor again. "We wait."

I don't have the heart to tell her that there have been plenty of people on the side of Loneliest Road that never get helped. They eventually wander the desert for help, only to never be seen again. As long as we stick to the road and follow it, we will be fine.

Not many people travel this road at once. It could be hours before another car comes. I sit down on the desert floor too, wondering how the hell I ended up here.

It's not like this can get any worse.

Thunder rolls above us, and out of the corner of my eye, I see Mary's head tilt back on her shoulders to look at the sky just like I am. When did storm clouds roll through? Out of all the times it never rains, the weather has to choose today out of all days to show itself?

This is a cruel joke.

"Karma, for leaving me in jail."

I wish I had tape to keep her mouth shut. All of my torture supplies were in my saddlebag, which is currently roasting.

Stay. Calm.

Don't. Kill. Her.

Thunder vibrates the ground floor, and the first droplet falls on my face. "If it rains and puts out the fire, no one will come," she points out.

"Well, let's not sit here then, let's go home. We just have to follow the road." I hold out my hand to help her up, and she decides not to take it.

Independent woman and all that. Good for her.

Or she's as stubborn as a mule and needs a good smack on the ass.

From my hand.

Because even though she drives me crazy, her body makes me crazier.

In the next blink, heavy blankets of rain come billowing down, stinging my skin and soaking my hair. "You've got to be kidding me!" I roar to the sky, and in return, lightning cracks in the middle of the road in reply.

Mary grips my hand, then immediately lets go of me when she realizes what she did. My shirt is soaked, the water is flowing into my mouth, and I want to curse myself for not paying attention to the damn weather.

My damn bike is ash, and I'm stuck with a woman that pisses me off as much as she turns me on.

Another bolt of lightning strikes the middle of the road, and the clouds start to spin. "Oh, no." Whether she likes it or not, I grab her hand and start to run in the opposite direction toward the mountains. If I know one thing about tornados, it's that they need flat land to gain strength. "Come on. We need to go. Now." How can all of this happen in one day?

I'm starting to wonder if the Ruthless Kings are cursed. There is always fucking something we have to deal with.

Always.

"Hurry up," I tell her, dragging her behind me as we haul ass to the mountains.

"I'm hurrying as much as I can! My feet were on fire a minute ago, if you don't remember."

Damn it, she's right. Instead, I stop and swing her into my arms. "What are you doing?" she squeaks.

"Hurrying like I fucking want to." I throw her over my shoulder, wrap an arm around her legs, and check behind me to see if the funnel is being formed. My heart aches when I see the burnt pieces of my bike and the flames dwindling from the fire. The smoke will be there for a while. It's just as black as the sky is turning. I glance up to see the beginning of a funnel starting. The clouds are spinning, and I swallow, wondering if we are going to be able to get away in time.

"Why did we stop? Is everything okay?" she asks.

No. We are about to be tornado fodder. I turn around and look into the woods. The mountains are right behind them, and I know there are plenty of nooks and crannies we can hide in. I start sprinting toward the forest again, through the wind and rain. My eyes sting as the water bullets them. I don't have a free hand, so I can't wipe my face.

Small beads of hail start to fall next. The black clouds light up above us, and a second later, the thunder follows. I hiss when they pepper my skin, and as I enter the canopy of the trees, the only thing I can feel is the danger of the storm surrounding us and the whistling through the wind.

"Knives, I'm freaking out."

"Everything is fine. I just want to make sure we're away from the threat." I don't want to tell her that I'm freaking out too. Bad fucking omens everywhere. Maybe this is the universe telling me that if Mary and I get together, the world will explode.

Because not a damn thing has gone right since I've kissed her.

Damn, I should've answered Seer's call. I'll have to apologize to him.

Suddenly, the wind calms. The rain stops. I can't hear the hail against the leaves or falling against the ground.

"Fuck," I hiss when a realization hits me.

"What? What is it? I can't see anything other than your ass."

"Like that's a bad thing. I have a great ass," I say, trying to keep things light as I run away from the tornado.

Silence.

Even nature speaks the loudest when it's quiet.

I burst through the other side of the woods, and my feet dig into the rocks to stabilize us as we try to get to the top.

"I've seen better asses," she grumbles, and I know she's joking.

She better be joking.

I don't like the idea of her looking at another man, even if I can't stand her.

I want to be the only man she stares at in anger, frustration, annoyance, and love.

Love. Let's not get crazy. Let's start with like.

"Will you shut up? I'm trying to save our lives."

"You're doing a heck of a job."

The sarcasm. I want to spank her ass. "Yeah, I don't see you doing anything, fire toes," I say, digging my feet into the mud as I start to climb. My boots slide, unable to maintain a decent grip.

"Well, put me down, and I'll show you what I can do."

Yeah, I'm not stupid. She's going to punch me across the face. I ignore her because I have better things to do, like trying to find us shelter in two minutes before we are sucked up in a funnel. When I'm high enough up the mountain, I look over the desert to see the small bonfire created by my motorcycle just as the funnel touches the ground. It's slow-moving, barely spinning, but the funnel itself is growing.

I set Mary down and spin her around, pointing to the tornado. "Do you see that? Do you see why I'm trying to get us the hell out of here now? If you want to help, help look for a place to hide."

"Oh my god. I've never seen a tornado before," she whispers, her face losing all amounts of color.

"We are going to be fine," I say, wanting to give her hope. Desert storms are intense, sometimes quick, and come out of nowhere. Just like this one. A few miles away, I can see blue skies, but right now, that beautiful blue color is hidden by darkness. "Come on, let's go around." I take her hand in mine again and pull her toward the direction I want to go in. I'm keeping my eyes on our surroundings while also trying to keep an eye on the tornado. It's inching down the road, but tornados have a mind of their own. Any moment, they can change direction and shift.

When I get to the other side of the mountain, I let out a breath of relief when I see a farm about a half-mile ahead. I'd rather be in a barn than be out here in the open. "Okay, up ya go," I tell her as I swing her into my arms again.

She squeals, and her arms hook around my neck. This time, I'm carrying her like I would my bride, and something about holding her that way feels right. It's difficult to run down an incline with her in my arms, but I'd rather be in control and know she's safe than wonder if she is able to keep up.

Plus, her boots are still smoking. I bet her feet are hot, and the skin is sensitive.

My leg twinges where I got shot a few months back, and my knee buckles, slamming against a very well-placed rock. I groan, grinding my teeth together as pain shoots up my thigh.

"Are you okay? I can walk—" she says, placing a hand against my cheek.

"No, it's okay. It's the gunshot wound. I thought I was healed for the most part, but this incline sucks." I find myself leaning against her hand for a split second before I push myself back to my feet.

Mary buries her head in my chest as the rain starts to pour again. The wind gusts, sending water and sand against us in a whirlwind of fury. Alarms ring throughout the city, which tells everyone to take cover because a tornado has been spotted.

When we get to the fence, I lift her over the wooden post, exhausted, cold, drenched in sweat and mud. I place her down on the ground and hop over in one leap, then pick her up again. If I was that scrawny kid I used to be, I wouldn't be able to do this.

This is why I refuse to be weak. I wouldn't be able to protect the people I care about.

I run toward the rundown barn, and now when I see it, it isn't a farm, but an abandoned building. When we get to the barn door, the wood is nearly rotten, the lock rusted, but it's the best we have right now.

Right as I try to open the door, the wind decides to push against me. I lift my head to see the swirling of clouds, the rain blinding me, and I grunt, digging my feet in the sand. I would run over a damn mountain to escape a tornado just to have another one form on this side too, but I won't let this fucking storm beat me. I refuse to be defeated again.

I won't let any situation get the best of me.

Mary grips the edge and puts her back into it. With her help, we open the door, and I'm surprised. I didn't expect her to help me.

"Why are you standing out there? Get in here, you fucking mad man," she grips me by my shirt and yanks me inside where it's nice and dry.

I turn around, hiding the shock on my face, and close the door, sliding the wooden slab across the width to lock it in place. The inside is spacious, but there is hay and a few old saddle blankets for horses. I survey the room, looking for anything else we can use when I see a section of the barn where there is a white tarp covering something.

"Stay away from sharp objects."

"So I should stay away from you, since you always carry sharp objects, right?"

I don't say anything because I don't have the energy to argue with her or bitch about semantics. She knows what I mean.

The tin roof dings with the hail and rain pounding against it. The old bones of the barn shake from the wind, and Mary wraps her arms around herself. She's scared. I don't blame her. Storms like this aren't fun.

Before I walk over to the white tarp, I tilt her chin up with my finger, doing everything I can not to kiss her. Kissing her is a bad idea. Things turn to shit when our lips meet, and if that isn't a sign to stay away from her, I don't know what is.

"Everything is going to be okay," I tell her, locking our eyes so she can see the truth in mine. "I'm not going to let anything happen to you."

"You can't promise that. Anything can happen. We don't know how long this storm will last, and this barn is being held up by hopes and freaking dreams."

I smirk at her silly words and wipe a drop of water hanging off her bottom lip. I've tasted those lips, and they are just as delicious as they look. "I can promise I won't let anything happen to you, Hellraiser."

"I am not."

I snort and slide my thumb off her lip as I walk away. "You're a fucking train wreck, but that's okay. I wouldn't have you any other way." When I get to the corner where the tarp is, I grip the corner of the crinkled material and yank it off. Dust flies and my dumb ass inhales, causing me to cough. I wave my hand in front of my face and see what goodies we have here. I want to know if there is anything to get us warm.

Standing before me is a vintage bike, but the beauty is gone. It's rusted from the inside out, and the tires are flat. There is an iron bedframe that needs some TLC. There is a black chest with gold hinges, but it's locked, and if there is a key, it's somewhere in here. I don't care to look.

"I'll be damned," I mutter, wondering if I'm seeing what I'm really seeing. There is a wood-burning stove in the corner. It's small, but it's enough to warm up us. I know I won't be able to pick it up. These things are made out of pure iron.

"What is it?" Mary asks.

"Salvation," I say, cleaning the cobwebs off. I wipe my hands against my jeans and start pushing against the stove, but it isn't moving.

Looks like if we are going to get warm, we are going to come to the oven instead of the other way around. I grab the handle and open the mouth of it to see if anything is inside. It's too dark to tell.

I grab some hay and stuff it in there, then take the closest nightstand and break it into pieces.

"What are you doing! Those are antiques."

"Are you cold?" I ask, but don't bother looking at her. I keep two pieces of wood out and stuff the rest in the oven.

"I'm freezing," she shivers.

"Then hush your mouth and let me get a fire going."

"You're so—"

"Amazing? Handsome? Brilliant? Strong? Smart? I'm all ears." Do I think I'm all of those things? No, but I know when I sound cocky, it pisses her off.

"You wish," she says, then yelps when lightning flashes between the wooden slats of the barn. The loud crack makes her jump, and the howling of the wind gets stronger. I'm sure we are safe here, but I'm not sure for how long. All I can do is hope.

I place hay between the sticks of wood and start to rub. I learned how to make a fire when I was thirteen. I spent plenty of time in the streets, cold, and the only thing I had was survival skills.

"Holy shit," Mary says as the kindling starts to smoke.

"It's okay to be impressed by me." I roll my lips together to keep my smile hidden.

"I actually am impressed. I've never seen someone make a fire like that before."

I'm glad it's dark, because I can feel her watching me, and for some damn reason, the blood rushes to my face, and I blush. "Well, when you're on your own like I've been, you learn some things." I shouldn't have said that. I don't usually talk about my past, but luckily, she doesn't ask about it.

I carefully lift the kindling and place it in the oven, then blow, giving the fire the oxygen it needs to thrive. After a few seconds, I open the chute, and the smoke billows out the top.

Mary sits down next to me just as I whip off my shirt. "What are you doing?" she squeaks.

"I'm getting warm." I twist my shirt and wring the water out of it. I lay the shirt on the oven and hear it sizzle. Next, I stand, unzip my pants, and slide them down my legs. "And I'm getting my clothes dry." I throw them on the oven too, then sit down on the scratchy hay. I'm still in my briefs. They are soaked, but I'm not about to let my cock hang out right now.

She might cut it off.

I lean back on my elbows and enjoy the warmth. The rain against the roof would be soothing if it wasn't for the thunder shaking the barn.

"Come on, Hellraiser. You scared? Don't worry, it's nothing I haven't seen before."

"You have never seen me," she says with a bite of anger.

She's right. I haven't.

And if I do, I know hers will be the best body I've ever seen.

She   loves   to   call   my   bluff.

CHAPTER SIX

The man really likes to test me, doesn't he?

Well, joke's on him.

I sling off my leather jacket and hang it on the iron headboard. The barn shakes as another crack of lightning flashes outside, and the rain is hitting the tin roof so hard that I can't tell if it's raining or hailing. The sirens outside have stopped, but that doesn't mean the storm is over. Knives and I don't have a choice. We have to stay here unless we want to get caught in the rain.

I flip my hair over next, gathering the thick, unmanageable strands that I don't have the heart to cut, and squeeze out the water. Next, I twist, then wrap my hair in a bun, tying the strand in a way that keeps it up high and tight on my head, since I don't have a hairband with me. That's the benefit of having long hair. I can pretty much do whatever I want with it.

My heart hammers in my chest. I'm so nervous that I'm wondering if I'm about to have a heart attack. I've never been naked in front of a guy I've wanted to be naked in front of. I've never even really kissed a guy until Knives. Maybe that's why I'm so defensive about myself when it comes to him. He isn't the guy I imagined myself with. Knives is a biker. A killer. Tattooed and hot.

Crazy fucking hot.

And actually crazy.

When he gets in his violent streak, everything else around him fades. Something flips in his brain and a red haze takes over. He isn't the same guy. Does it scare me? No.

I've been in the clutches of bad men before, and I know Knives isn't one, no matter how much he likes to say he is.

He's a beautiful, unique man. The kind of guy I can't seem to wrap my head around, but he isn't hard to understand. I've never been allowed to like people like him, not with how I grew up. My household was religious. My father is a preacher.

And I don't mean a preacher of a little tiny church in the middle of nowhere.

He's The Preacher. He's on TV, in newspapers, and he even baptizes celebrities' kids.

But a religious man, my father is not.

He likes to put on a show every Sunday and puts on a smile for the camera, but behind closed doors? He's a monster.

My own personal brand of hell.

I've had bad shit happen to me my entire life. Underneath the cardigans and pearls that Knives likes to bring up is a girl afraid of the dark and what lurks in it.

"Hey, you don't have to do anything. I'm not trying to get you naked; I swear. Honestly, wet clothes—"

"—I know that, Knives." I take off my shirt next and lay it on the back of the oven, then wiggle out of my pants, but I forget about my boots. I unzip the backs and fling them off along with my socks. I have to dance a bit since my jeans are stuck to my skin, but I manage and lay them next to my shirt.

I got so lucky. Knives tackled me in time before the fire could eat through my boots and cause real damage. My skin is a bit sensitive, but it's not burned.

Knives doesn't hide how he checks out my body. His eyes linger on my chest, almost as if he is memorizing the lace detailing of my bra. When he is done, his eyes drop to my stomach, then legs, and then his eyes wander up again, pausing on my face.

Do you know what I like about Knives?

He doesn't try to hide anything.

I hate people that hide themselves, their true selves. I think when someone tries to hide their bad intentions, that's what makes a monster.

I should know; I lived with one for twenty-four years.

And he touched me for twelve of them.

I should be afraid of men after what my dad did to me, but having to stay quiet about what happened brought other things into perspective. I know not all men are cruel, but I know a lot of bad people are in the world.

Bad things don't happen to good people.

Bad people do.

And it's made me love and appreciate good people more. Maybe I'm different. Maybe I'm not crying every night or having nightmares. Maybe I'm not losing myself in drinks or drugs, but I have lost something about myself.

I'm just trying to find it.

"You give me a headache twenty-three out of twenty-four hours a day, but I can't sit here and lie to you and say you aren't beautiful," Knives says, honestly, meeting my eyes and keeping his hands to himself.

The flames dance in his cornflower blue eyes, and they are so damn bright. I've never seen irises like his before. They are unique, just like him.

77

"And the other hour?" I tease when I sit down on the hay, which scratches my ass and is very uncomfortable.

"I'm sleeping. It's the only damn peace I get."

"Shut up," I giggle, nudging his side with my arm. I lean forward and lay my elbows against my knees, watching the fire as it pops. The rain is slamming against the barn, and the door shakes when the wind carries around us.

"It's not letting up, is it?"

"No, it isn't. I can't believe it turned so ugly so fast."

"The way of the world is bittersweet, ain't it?" he asks, he stands and when I go to ask him where he is going, my eyes land on his package.

His very big, very long, very in my face, package. He has a tattoo above the waistband of his underwear, right above where I assume his pubic hair is, and it says 666.

What's that mean?

If a woman hops on top, does that mean she gets possessed by the devil?

Why does a part of me want to find out?

"You might give me a headache twenty-three out of twenty-four hours in the day, but I can't sit here right now and not tell you that you're beautiful too," I sling his words back at him as I take my turn to check him out. He is a hairy man with thick hair on his chest and legs. His tattoos decorate parts of him that enhance his body, something I can tell he works hard at keeping in the best condition. Strong shoulders, a thick neck, and while he is lean, he has just the right amount of bulk to his body.

"What about the other hour?" he grins, being cheeky.

"I'm cursing you."

He tosses his head back and laughs at the same time a loud burst of thunder rolls, trembling the barn and everything inside it. "Look at that," he sighs. "We just complimented one another. Looks like we can be civilized after all. I'm going to go get those blankets for our asses. I'll be back." His hand falls to my shoulder and grazes my back as he walks

78

away, awakening my skin in goosebumps and leaving me shivering.

Only I'm not cold.

What the hell is happening between us? Figuring that out causes me a damn headache.

"Alright, stand up. Let's get comfortable." He lays the blankets on the chest and unfolds the first, then shakes it out on the other side of him. Knives lays the blanket down, then does the same to the other. "There," he says.

Gosh, if I didn't know any better, I would think this moment was romantic, but that would be ridiculous because the series of events that led us here were not.

I sit down and do my best not to think about the last time these were washed. We are lucky to be alive. "Thank you," I tell him, feeling warm and flushed.

I don't think it's from the fire, either.

Knives being so close, and how the shadows curve the muscle of his arms, abs, and legs make him seem like he is from another world.

"I wonder if there is anything to drink in this place," he muses, looking around in the dark.

"You're kidding, right? Whatever is here would be deadly."

He plops down on the blanket and covers his legs. "You're probably right," he says, just as the alarm bells sound again.

I hold my breath and wrap my arms around my legs, hoping the tornado is nowhere near us. I hope the clubhouse is okay. I hope everyone is safe. Knives throws his body over mine when the walls start to shake violently, and I hold onto him, ready for us to get sucked up in the tunnel of the tornado.

And then it stops, and Knives pulls away from me, taking the cloak of bravery and strength with him.

"I think we are fine," he tries to reassure me, rubbing soothing circles on my back. "But I'm going to try to look for some alcohol in this place. Farmers always hide booze, and I'll be damned, if we are going to be stuck here, we are going to do it right." He pops up again, and he seems jittery and restless, like he has to be doing something. I mean, now that I think about it, he always is. He's always working out, always making ninja stars, always practicing his aim, or he is in the garage or at Kings' Club helping Tool.

He's always doing something, and I'm sure resting isn't something he is used to.

"I'll be back," he says again, grazing those calloused fingers along my back again. My skin prickles again, moving down the knots of my spine.

"Sure," I whisper, watching him dart into the darkness. I can see the outline of his figure every time lightning bursts outside. It's like a show. When I do see him, he is standing somewhere else in a new position. And with a flash, the outline of his body appears again, and even from here, I can see the square, cut jawline slicing through the sudden night.

"Ah-ha!" he cheers, holding up a bottle. "Told you." He runs back over to me and sits on the blanket, wiping the dust off the label to see what it is. He whistles. "Damn, this is fifty-year-old whiskey."

My nose scrunches at how horrible that sounds.

"Not a whiskey drinker, huh? Could have fooled me before we got rid of the booze at the clubhouse. I saw you turn up a few bottles."

"—Of vodka, or tequila, but not whiskey. Bleh." I shake my entire body as if just the word grosses me out.

"Do me a favor and try it," he says, twisting off the cap and taking a swallow. He doesn't flinch, but my eyes are burning from here from the strength of the whiskey.

I bet this whiskey could start a lawnmower. Makes me wonder what the hell it will do to my body. The bottle is heavy in my hand, and I can still feel the grime on the glass from years of being in this barn. "I have a feeling I'm going to hate you for this," I say to him.

"You already hate me, remember?" There is a teasing note in his tone, but in the depths, there is this breach of pain that makes his words crack.

I turn the bottle up like I have a dozen others and wince, cough, then somehow manage to swallow. The liquid burns, just like I thought it would. My stomach warms, and my eyes water, but the after taste isn't that bad.

"Hair on your chest?" he asks, taking another swing.

"Well, I'm sure I'm sprouting hairs, but nothing like yours." I wipe my mouth and chuckle when he falls to the side, grabs his stomach, and laughs. It's deep, like it's stuck in his gut and can't seem to find a way out. It's raspy, a larger than life kind of laugh, which is curious to me, because when he is around the guys, he's more serious.

He hands me the bottle, wiping his eyes as he gains control of himself. "Well, don't let me stop you from being a man."

I snort, and the air rushes inside the glass, causing a whistle. "I'm better than a man," I inform him, taking another large gulp. After the first one, the second isn't so bad.

"Oh yeah? How might that be?"

"I'm a woman." I take another drink for dramatic effect.

"A pain in my damn ass is what you are," he jokes, taking the bottle away from me.

Out of habit, I tuck my hair behind my ear, forgetting that I have it up in a bun. Knives and I fall into a comfortable silence, the white noise of rain comforting instead of threatening. The worst part of the storm must be over.

"I'm sorry about your bike," I say, playing with one straw of hay. I repeatedly tie a knot in it until it's nothing but a ball, toss it into the fire, and grab another.

"Yeah, me too. Shit happens, right?"

"Today it does," I grumble, stealing the whiskey from him.

"Yeah, today was a shit show. I can't help but wonder if that's why Seer called me the other day."

"You didn't answer?"

"No. I'm not the kind of person that wants to know their future. I want it to happen when it happens."

"I don't know. If someone would have told me I would be chained in a basement before it happened, I would have wanted to know." I keep my voice light and playful, but Knives doesn't find it funny at all.

"Don't do that. Don't joke about what happened to you like it doesn't matter. It matters."

"I'm not saying it didn't. I'm saying if someone had the ability to tell me something horrible was going to happen to me, I would want to know, but that doesn't stop other terrible things from happening, does it?" The fire in front of me mirrors how angry I am.

Maybe that's why I'm so reckless. Because I have this rage inside me burning away at my humanity every moment I'm awake.

"Want to know something?" I ask right after, not really giving him an option to say no. "When I found myself chained up in that basement in Atlantic City, a damn collar wrapped around my throat and my hands bound, you know what I finally thought?" My eyes begin to water, but the last thing I wanted to do was cry in front of Knives.

Must be the whiskey.

I take another drink and sigh, swirling the bottle until the amber liquor creates its own funnel. "I thought, finally, a break. I went from the hands of one monster to another, but what's even more disgusting is when I looked at the bikers that wanted to use me, I didn't care. I was happy to be away from home, away from the man that numbed the part of me that's supposed to care. The Atlantic City chapter were assholes and horrible people, but at least they weren't family. Isn't that sad? I almost looked forward to their touch, Knives. A part of me welcomed it. I'm not like the other women

82

Boomer saved. I'm more haunted over what happened to me before I ended up in that basement."

He steals the bottle from me, twists the cap on it, and sets it to the side. "I'm going to need you to clarify that, Mary. What do you mean you didn't care? You knew what they were going to do to you, right? They weren't the kind of men that were going to tell you they loved you or fluff your goddamn pillow at night."

"I know. They were going to drug me, keep me loopy, use me up, and spit me out. I know. Yeah, that didn't scare me. Like I said, it would have been a good change from the norm."

"And what was the norm?" he asks.

I turn to him when I hear the murderous rage. His jaw ticks, and the Knives that is about to flip the switch and disappear from this moment is close to the surface.

"It doesn't matter."

"It matters to me. No one knows anything about you."

"I don't know anything about you either," I point out, then reach out to steal the whiskey from the side of him, but he snatches it away from me in time.

"I'm an open book."

"With a damn lock on it that no one has the key to," I sass, and my words take him by surprise, so I hurry to grab the bottle. "Got to be faster than that!"

And then he jerks it away from me right as I take the cap off. "Gotta have a tighter grip than that!" he winks, and the way his lashes curl at the tip and fan over his cheek, heat floods me.

My nipples bead, and I pull my legs up to my chest to hide the traitors. The way he says, 'I need a tighter grip' sounds like there are implications in it, like he is giving me a dirty secret.

Maybe he likes a tight grip?

"So, what's the story with Mary St. James, Hellraiser? What has her wild?" he asks, eyes glittering with humor.

Being wild isn't new.

My wild just isn't being suffocated.

I'm free.

The moment I could, I unleashed what's been hidden inside me for so long. It isn't about being untamed or a rebel.

It's about living, and that's all I've ever really wanted.

I've only ever wanted to feel alive.

Not just to wake up every day, thankful for the heartbeat in my chest, but the electricity in my veins and the wild thump of my heart when something exciting happens, *that* kind of alive.

I've been searching for it, and I've found it.

And   I   fight   with   him   every   day.

CHAPTER SEVEN

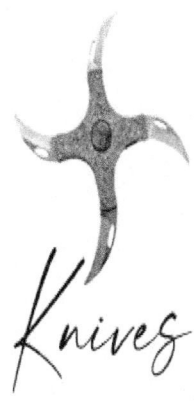

Knives

I want to kill the man that made that kind of abuse a norm for her. How the fuck can she sit there and tell me she was looking forward to what the Atlantic City chapter had in store? They were monsters. A girl like her with the pearls, the class, the riches, she isn't supposed to know the hardships of life.

I guess it doesn't matter what walks of life people come from; shit happens that will change you forever.

"I feel like all we are doing is talking about me," she says, her voice smooth with a hint of vintage. Like if I asked for whiskey on the rocks, her beauty would be the whiskey, and her voice would be the ice.

It's the only way I know how to describe it

"What do you want to know?" I look up just as another piercing crack rings through the night.

"I want to know your real name."

"You don't? It isn't like it's a secret. I'm not like the other guys. A name is a name."

"I don't know it," she answers.

"Thomas."

She blows a raspberry with her lips as she cackles, nearly falling backward in fits of fucking giggles. I can't help but smile. "What?"

"Thomas? I don't know what I expected. Tyron or Zeke, maybe Loch or something badass, not something nerdy."

"Knives is badass," I protest, shocked and almost offended. Almost.

"Exactly. You're this badass guy. You have tattoos and muscles. You're a biker. But to call you Thomas, I can't," she snickers. "Thomas is a frat boy who wears khakis."

"I fucking hate khaki," I mumble, remembering the time when my mom made me wear them. I only wore them once, and that was the day I lost my entire family.

"I didn't mean to make you mad; I'm sorry."

I grab her hand, and it's warm from the fire. "You didn't. It's me. Bad memory."

"A penny for your thoughts?" she asks, scooting over to inch closer to me. I expect her to move her hand away, but she doesn't. I should move my hand away.

I don't know if I can. Fighting her is too exhausting.

My entire life has been a fight. There comes a point where someone in my position has to accept that something I thought might be bad for me will be the best thing for me. I'm not used to good things. I'm used to pain, marveling in it, soaking in it.

I don't want Mary to turn to pain. I can't handle the idea of something happening to her to add any more agony to the loss I've already experienced. What if I fall for her, which, as crazy as it sounds, I can see myself falling fucking hard, and something bad happens? I'm left with picking up the shadow of myself again.

86

I've done that too many times, and I don't think I can do it again.

I don't talk about my past, but since she's shared a little bit of herself with me, and since we are stuck in this barn for who knows how long, getting to know one another seems to be the only option. We could fuck, but I need to earn getting between those legs, and I'm not going to do that on a stack of hay in the middle of a storm.

First off, it's cliché, and second, we aren't fighting, and that needs to last more than a damn day.

I want to earn her trust. I want... hell, I want her.

I must want a headache for a damn lifetime.

"What do you want to know?" I lean back, prop myself up on my elbows, and hope I don't have to dig too deep.

"Where are you from?"

"Here. Vegas."

"Mom? Dad? Family?"

Damn, she has to hit all the spots I don't want to talk about, doesn't she? Makes sense, since she loves to drive me crazy.

I shake my head. "No, my family died when I was a kid. I grew up in foster care." I take another swig of whiskey, but it isn't enough to burn the pain from my chest.

"I'm so sorry, Knives." She squeezes her hand around mine. "Can I ask what happened?"

"Car accident," I whisper, thinking back to the best memory I had. "Remember Halloween? When I nearly drowned because of Tongue's brother?"

"Yeah, I still can't get over that detail," she says. "And yeah, I remember. That was terrible. I was so worried about you."

"Oh, I bet."

"Hey, we might fight, but I care. I don't ever want to see you hurt."

"I don't want to see you hurt either." My voice deepens, and the air between us sparks, crackling just like the lightning outside.

I trace her knuckles with my index finger, loving how soft she is and wondering how anyone could hurt someone like Mary. "People say that your life flashes before your eyes when you die, but I didn't have that experience. I relived one day." I smile when I think about my sister running after me, me running after her, and mom yelling at us to stop. "It was a regular day, beautiful, and the sun was out. Dad was grilling, and my sister and I were as thick as thieves. Mom was watching us to make sure we didn't hurt ourselves, but I remember laughing. We decided to go to a movie that night, and out of nowhere, a truck ran a red light and smashed right into us."

She gasps, holding a hand over her lips. "Oh god," she says, squeezing my hand even tighter.

"My parents died on the spot, but my sister…" my throat clogs up when I remember the moment as if it happened yesterday. "She had this piece of metal, right here—" I rub the side of my neck, a spit right under my ear. "She couldn't breathe. There was so much blood. I was the only one that came out with no injuries, can you believe that? I was safe. What crock of shit is that?"

My eyes blur, thinking of my sister's young face and her long hair coated in blood. "She looked at me, unable to speak. She tried. She kept trying to talk to me, but her throat was crushed. I held her hand and waited for help to arrive, but by the time they did, she had already died."

Mary is crying, big tears wetting the sharp edges of her cheeks. "Knives, I'm so sorry. I'm so sorry that happened to you." She throws her arms around my neck and buries her face in my shoulder. It takes a second for me to react, because I can't remember the last time someone hugged me.

I wrap my arms around her, too, pulling her tight and enjoying the way she feels against me. I inhale her scent, getting lost in her comfort, and a tear falls, dripping down my cheek until it lands on her shoulder. I haven't cried in a long time, but Mary brings me to my knees. She opens me up, and I think she always has. It's one of the reasons why we fight so much. She makes me vulnerable.

I hate being vulnerable.

I hate... feeling. I'm not used to it. With Mary around, it's like the walls I built around me crumble and welcome her home to heal me.

But I miss what my life could have been. I miss my family. I miss my best friend. I hate what my life turned into after my parents died, but now, my life isn't so bad. It took too long to get here, though. Way too long, and I've pushed the pain away, locked it inside, thrown away the key, and lost hope that my beat-up heart can be anything other than rundown and tired.

Mary is breathing life into me, and it terrifies me more than death itself.

Death is easy.

And I think I've been waiting for it to come back around for me.

I'm not afraid of a lot of things. I love making people afraid of me, but emotions bring even the strongest men to their knees.

She pulls away and sits back down in her spot, sooner than I was ready to let go, but I don't want to make her stay in my arms. I want her to *want* to be there. "I need a drink," she says, taking the bottle and taking a gulp. "No one should have to experience that."

"It didn't stop there," I say in a small whisper, hoping she doesn't hear me, but at the same time, hoping she does. "Foster care sucked. I bounced around a lot. I wasn't the kid that everyone liked. I was a loner, a weirdo, scrawny—"

"—You were scrawny? No way, I don't believe that for a second."

"Believe it. I was short too. And the damn butt to everyone's joke. I ran away for a bit when I was thirteen. That's when I learned to build fires." I can't believe I'm telling her this. No one knows this about me, but she makes me want to talk. She makes me want to heal. "Most of the foster parents I had, they were in it for the paycheck. They would have so many kids and all of us shared a room sometimes. We could only bathe once a week, eat certain times during the day, so I was skinny and smelled a lot of the time."

"That should be illegal. The system shouldn't allow that to happen."

"System fails everyone all the time, but there was one good thing that came out of it." I smile when I remember his face. "Mason. Reaper knows about Mason, but only because Mason hung around the club when we were teenagers. When he aged out of the system, he was going to prospect, but that never happened."

"Why?"

"Because of me," I admit, hanging my head. I deserve the shame and guilt to wash over me. "I wasn't always fit. I wasn't always six-foot-three. And there was this group of kids, three of them, and they loved to beat the hell out of me every chance they got. Mason, even though he was a foster kid, no one gave him shit. He was big for his age, strong, nearly looked like a man, and was only a year older than me. He was my protector. My brother, when I had no one else."

Her hand slides over my thigh and squeezes, telling me that she's here and listening. How long has it been since I talked to someone and they willingly listened? I can't even remember.

"He was all I had, and at fifteen, that's a big deal. Especially when it seemed like the entire world was against you. He tried to protect me all the time, but he couldn't always be there, and I'd get the shit kicked out of me."

90

"If they only saw you now..." she says, letting it be known that I'd be their worst fucking nightmare.

Rain continues to pound the tin roof, and I open the oven to shove another piece of the nightstand in there, along with hay, to keep the fire roaring. "I was walking home from school one day, and I decided to take a short cut. It was this old back road, I'm sure it's still there, but I haven't checked. I haven't been able to go back. They called it Miscellaneous Way because that's where people dumped anything and everything. If I had just gone the other way home, everything would have been fine, but I didn't, so Mason came looking for me." I let out a big exhale until I have no air left in my lungs and wrap my arms around her again and pull her close. Our knees touch, and her hands fall to my legs. It probably isn't comfortable for her, but I need to be close to her. I fought it before by fighting with her, and I hope tonight gets us past it.

"I protected myself with a few old knives, stabbed one kid, and right as I was about to attack the others, Mason was there, saving me like he always did. Only this time, he didn't use threats to scare off the kids. He had a gun, and he shot all of them. He told me to run, but I wanted to take responsibility, yet, he wouldn't let me. He said, 'always take responsibility for your actions,' and the police came. I ran into a shed and watched as the officers drew their guns. When they asked him to drop the weapon, the barrel was pointed to them, and they fired."

Pow. Pow. Pow. Pow.

I can almost hear the ringing in my ears still.

"I watched him die and fall on the guys he killed. For me. It was always for me, and that pissed me off. Before he died, he told me to go to the biker bar we always passed by, and that's where I met Reaper's dad, who was the President, and Reaper was only a few years older than me. They've been my family ever since, but it still hurts like hell thinking about the family I've lost."

91

Her hands lay on my chest. My heart thumps with the sad memories coursing through me and the way the warmth of her soaks into me, wrapping around the ache in my soul like the fire coming from the stove or a blanket.

I never thought sorrow could be thawed and warmed until it reached relief, but here we are. I lay my hand on top of hers and rub the top. I'm cut open, raw, and I feel weak.

A feeling I never wanted to feel again, but she's here, and the weakness isn't so bad when she's touching me.

"That shouldn't have happened to you," she whispers, lifting her eyes from the middle of my chest to meet mine. She's trying not to cry, but tears spill anyway. "Bad shit happens to everyone."

"And what about you? What made you think the Atlantic City Chapter was a fresh start?" She shakes her head, and the tears reflect off the glow of the fire beside us. One falls, then another, and I'm trying to catch them and wipe them away, but I'm not quick enough.

"I'm from a very religious family," she whispers, cutting her eyes to me. "My dad is a preacher."

"I know," I say, thinking back to when Reaper called for Church and Badge gave an update on the girls we rescued. Mary St. James was a preacher's daughter, a famous preacher who makes a ton of money, but Mary doesn't seem like the religious type to me. Now that I'm getting to know her, I'm starting to realize her rebellion isn't new but hidden.

"You knew? And all the times we fought, you didn't try taking a dig at me?"

"I'm an asshole, but that was your family; I wasn't going to slap that in your face. Especially since you're so adamant about not going back to them, so I kept quiet. As did everyone else. Pretty funny though, the Preacher's daughter hanging out with bikers. I bet your dad would have a heart attack."

"I doubt it," she says, a flat, monotone grip to her throat. "He isn't very religious either. He's a fake. He's horrible."

Her fingers dig into my chest, her nails pinching my skin like she wishes he were in front of her so she could rip his heart out. "He's the reason why Atlantic City wasn't so bad." Her gaze meets mine, and hatred, holy hell, hatred unlike anything I've ever seen before, flashes in her eyes.

I thought she didn't like me, but that wasn't the case at all. Now that I see what her hate looks like, it is safe to say I'm on her good side.

"For twelve years, he molested me. Twelve. Long. Torturous. Years."

And just like that, the peace I felt disappears. I lift her off me because somehow, she found her way to my lap. I start to pace, feeling the need for blood pumping through my veins. I pop my neck, grab the sides of my head, and snarl.

I'm breaking.

"Knives?"

"He did what? For how long? I'm going to kill him. I'm going to fucking kill him!" I yell so loud, someone up above must hear me, because thunder grumbles the ground and lightning booms overhead. I'm fucking pissed.

Twelve years of being caged.

Twelve years of being in her own prison.

Twelve years of being silent.

Twelve years of acting normal.

No wonder she is how she is.

She's free now. It's no wonder she's a fucking hellraiser when praying got her nowhere.

And then I've been kissing her, throwing my lips on her because I couldn't wait another second. Did she even want it? "I'm sorry, Mary. I didn't know. I wouldn't have... I would have respected your space and not kissed you."

"Don't do that; don't take that away from me. I'm not someone who is ruined by her past. The only thing I don't want is to go home. I never want to go there again, but I want to move on with my life. I want more than what I had. That's

93

why I was okay with Atlantic City; at least there would have been variety—"

Hearing her talk like that, about being raped and abused by different men, has a possessive beast swelling inside me that I've never felt before. Barely breathing, I cup her face and hope she can see the cold in my eyes as I make a promise, "I swear, I promise, I'll kill him. He won't even have to be in the back of your mind anymore. I'll hunt him down. I'll—"

She hushes me by kissing me this time, and her lips are lava soaking into my veins, warming me from head to toe in the middle of this desert winter. My hands go from soft to hard along her jaw as I take control, slipping my tongue between her lips. This isn't good. We're nearly naked, her breasts are rubbing against my chest, my cock is hard and leaking, but I know the last thing I want to do is have sex with her here.

Mary deserves more than some haystack fuck.

No, she doesn't even deserve to get fucked; she deserves better than that.

How the hell do I give it to her? I've never experienced anything like that before. I've never felt like this for anyone before. It's consuming me.

Her hands slide down my chest as mine drift down her back; the smooth lines and the curve of her delicate spine have me growling low in my gut. Her fingers tease the waistband of my briefs, but they don't slip under, so I take her lead.

I don't grip her ass, I don't cup her tits like I really want, because I want her to be able to call the shots.

And I'm not going to lie, having her fingers tease me like this is the hottest fucking thing I've ever experienced. My stomach clenches, and the touch feels… intimate. My brows pinch together, trying to understand what intimacy is.

I don't love.

I break people.

I'm not a person someone takes a chance on because I don't let them.

I suck her lip into my mouth and groan as her nails sink into my hip bones. This is a bad idea. Just because we are getting along now doesn't mean we always will. What if we aren't constructed to love the way other people do?

Then I'll deconstruct myself and find a way to build the foundation of who I am again. She deserves the effort for me to try.

"Knives," she gasps, saying the only name that I've ever really felt like matched my soul. My cock jerks from how wispy my name sounds, falling off her lips. I lay us down on the blanket, fall to the side, so I'm not nestled between her legs like I want to be and keep my hands on her waist.

My balls pull against my body when she sucks my tongue into her mouth and strokes me like I'd imagined she would my cock. My eyes roll to the back of my head and a dollop of precome slides down my shaft.

"Mary," I rumble her name, laying my forehead against hers as I try to bring this to a stop. "You have no idea what I want to do to you." I slap my hands on either side of her head and grip the blanket in my fists, trying to squeeze out all the desire into the hay under us. My entire body shakes from roping in the control, nearly smothering me.

"I...we can..." she tries to find the words, but I interrupt her.

"I don't want us to be here in this barn for the first time, Mary. I'm a fucking asshole, and I've done a lot of questionable things, but I won't take you and claim you before you're ready."

"Claim me?" She lifts a curved brow at me, a questioning and challenging tone. She doesn't like the idea of being owned.

That's too fucking bad.

"Claim you," I lower my voice. "Fucking show you who owns you and this body, show you that the only fight you're going to give me from now on is the one you relent when I'm ten inches deep."

Her mouth drops open, and the flames allow me to see the blush staining her cheeks. "Knives... I—"

"—Not now, or tomorrow, but when you're ready. You can act like the cut sluts all you want, Mary, but I know better. You aren't the kind of woman to give yourself up like that."

"Maybe I don't want to be claimed. Or owned. Ever think about that?"

Her sudden reversal has me defensive.

"Mary, it's not—"

"Maybe I should be the one claiming you. Maybe I want to make you mine."

That throws me for a loop. I look down at her, then look back up, totally at a loss for what to respond.

"Does that bother you?" she asks, crossing her arms over her chest to hide herself. I haven't seen her like this before, naïve, but I guess she is. The only person she's been with is her father, and that makes me fucking sick.

I wrap my fingers around her wrists and gently lay them on either side of her body so I can see the mounds of her tits hiding behind that bra. "No, Hellraiser. You're making me learn a lot, that's all."

"Is this a joke? How can we be at each other's throat one minute and laying here the next? I want nothing but to kiss you again, but if we are going to fight all the time again, maybe we shouldn't do this."

"I'm not going to let it stop me." I don't care if we fight, if she screams, or if she punches me in the stomach with the fake leg I got her for Christmas. Headache and all, temper and all, fights, screams, and everything else in between.

I don't care what comes with this.

I realize what I want—no—what I need is her.

CHAPTER EIGHT

I have no idea what I'm doing or why.

All I know is Knives is more than I thought he was. No, that isn't true. I always thought there was more to him than meets the eye, but he hid behind his ice-cold demeanor, the frozen tundras of his eyes, and his ninja stars.

We fought each other because we were fighting what we felt for one another. Things still might not be perfect. From the sounds of it, we don't know how to have a good thing when we have been surrounded by bad.

He grew up poor and lost everything.

I grew up rich and had nothing.

We are cut from the same cloth.

"Can I watch you and you watch me? Because I need to take the edge off, Knives."

I barely have the question out of my mouth before he seals his lips on me again. He slides between my legs, his hard cock rubbing against my clit, and his hands slide down my shoulders, cupping my breasts, and he groans into my mouth. Every inch of me is lost in the touch he gives. I've never been touched like this.

My dad stole from me.

I've never been explored, and Knives wants to. I can tell he is trying to respect me at the same time, and it only has my heart falling for him even more. I whimper and cry out when something hard like metal slides over my bundle of nerves again. My eyes widen, and my entire body tenses. Knives backpedals and sits on his knees, staring down at me. His chest booms with every breath he takes, and he inches his briefs down until his cock bobs free.

"Holy mother of…." I pinch my lips together and sit up on my elbows, a gush of heat leaving my center and wetting my panties when I see the beautiful, erotic sight in front of me. Of course, his cock is magnificent, just like the rest of him is.

Long.

Thick.

And pierced.

He has a Jacob's Ladder and two hoops on his crown, reminding me of horns. My eyes drift to the 666 tattoo, and it makes sense.

The plum-colored head is nearly purple with how hard he is and how much blood is pumping through. I can't tear my eyes off him. He has a slight curve to the left, and I have to dig my fingers in the blanket to stop myself from reaching out.

I lick my lips, watching the palm of his hand wrap tight around the thick shaft and pump. My breaths leave me in tiny bursts. I lift my hand, trickle my fingers down the middle of my chest, slide down the bumps of my ribs, and tease the edge of my panties. "Kiss me," I tell him, but he shakes his head.

Does he not want to do this anymore? Disappointment slams through me, and I look away from him, tearing my eyes off a man I'll never be able to forget.

"If I kiss you, and I want to, I'm going to push those panties to the side and slide into that hot cunt, because I'll be able to feel the cushion of your lips against me. I'm only so strong, Mary."

"Oh," I say, locking our eyes together again.

"Oh, is right," he says as he tugs on the rings attached to the crown of his cock. He groans, continuing the tease. A bead of precome leaks off the tip and drips down the vein protruding along the ten inches. "Do you know how beautiful you are, my little Hellraiser?" he asks, using not one but both of his hands to grip his cock and jack it. "What you do to me, what you've always done to me?"

I shake my head, keeping quiet as I dip my finger below the waistband of my panties. My fingers slide through my wet folds, and I moan in my throat, dropping my jaw when I feel how hot I am.

"That fucking mouth, that temper, every time you fought me, you have no idea how bad I wanted to bend you over..." he can't finish his sentence because he speeds up his thrusts, moving his hips, so he fucks his palms. He tosses his head back, the tendons on his neck tensing, and just like the rest of him, his cock seems so mad, so intense, and all I want to do is show him how fucking unique he is.

Unique because I'm going to assume there are not a lot of men with so many piercings in their dick.

Knives must like the pain, which also helps me understand him a bit more. The scars on his knuckles because of how much he plays with his stars, the tattoos all over him, the piercings... does he truly like pain, or does he think he deserves it?

His chin drops to his chest as he looks at me. "I thought we were going to watch each other?"

"Sorry, I got caught up in watching you," I say and sit up, becoming eye level with the intimidation of his cock. I don't have the courage to take him in my mouth. I've never done that before, but I also don't want us to do things we aren't ready for, only for me to be disappointed when we walk out of this barn to the real world and go back to who we used to be.

What if this barn is all there is? What if when we are home, the bickering and slight frustration comes roaring back? The last thing I want is to have sex with a guy who winds up treating me like everyone else he has ever been with.

I trust Knives with my life. I know he'll protect me, but my heart? The heart is another matter, a delicate one, something that can break without being put back together again.

Life has room for fault, but the heart does not, or the fault line makes it fracture.

I purse my lips and blow on his throbbing cock, getting a good view of the piercings decorating his length. I'm in awe that I like it so much. I never thought I'd be into something like that, but my tongue twitches to flick out and tug on the silver loops, then lick the ladder.

His knees buckle as I tease him. My nails scratch along his legs as I move up his body and grip his hips. Knives has a V-shape of muscle on either side, leading to the thick patch of hair settling around the base of his cock. He is more than I could have imagined.

I lean down, staying away from his cock, but I can feel the heat of it as I lay my lips on the delicate skin of his V, right along the V. I move to the other side, kissing him there too, grabbing onto the lust I've been feeling for him all this time. It feels good to let go of the anger and just be.

Keeping my nails stroking his thighs, I blow air on his cockhead again, watching a bead of precome drip from the slit. I want to lick up and taste him. Does he taste sweet?

Salty? Maybe he tastes like nothing. I kiss my way up his ribs, and he is panting, his stomach rising and falling as he struggles to take in a lungful of air.

"Jesus Christ, if you keep doing this, I might come," he admits, taking me by complete surprise. He acts as if no one has explored him either. What kind of woman would do that when a man like Knives is with her?

"Good," I tell him, making sure to keep a distance from his groin. I graze my nails up his sides and around his back, staying away from his ass as I drag them up his spine. I move around his shoulders, dragging the blunt edges of my fingers down his chest. I kiss his right nipple, lick it, then blow on the bead too. I watch as the pink bud tightens, reacting to the wet and cold. Grinning, I move to the other one and do the same before I kiss my way down his other side, loving the scratch of his hair against my palm.

I'm level with his cock again, staring at the beast before me. I can't help but wonder how he will fit in my mouth when the day comes. His hands land on my shoulders, and as a quick goodbye, I kiss the head, letting the bead of precome drop onto my lower lip before I lay back down on the blanket.

Licking him off me so I can taste his flavor, I moan as my taste buds awaken. I tug my panties down, remembering what I said about watching each other, and spread my legs so he can see me.

All of me.

Sitting back, his eyes hood when he watches me slide through my folds, the wet sounds mixing with the rain falling to the ground outside. Like Knives, I use two hands. One to plunge two fingers inside me, while I use the other to circle my engorged clit.

My back bows as my thighs tremble, and Knives growls. "Fuck, you're killing me. No one has ever teased me like that before. You're going to be the goddamn death of me, Hellraiser. I knew you were fucking trouble."

101

I remember that I need to watch him, so I bring my head down to see him furiously fucking his fist, his stare locked onto my cunt. "Knives, it feels so good." I want to tell him to touch me, but I'm already addicted to his kiss. I'm afraid if I give in, then I'll always want more from him. Reality is different than being locked away alone.

I should know.

For too long, my mind was bent and shaped by my father, a man who made sure he was alone with me every chance he got.

No, I can't think about him right now. I don't want him ruining this.

"I'm close," I say to Knives, feeling the trembling warmth of an orgasm brewing in my body. "I'm so close." My toes curl, and Knives tugs on the horns again, stretching the tip of his cock in rhythm with his strokes.

"That pussy looks delicious. You have no idea how bad I want to taste you; how bad I want to slide in and fill that cunt to the fucking brim until you're dripping with me. I'm close. Goddamn it, I'm so close." His hand jerks faster, and I move my fingers at the same speed, circling my clit in desperation, so we fall over the edge together.

"Knives," I breathe. "Oh—oh, yes!" I shove my fingers as far as they can go until my knuckles stop me from going deeper. My body ignites in an array of fireworks and sweat. I'm rocking against my hand, hoping the friction will prolong the sensation.

"The death of me," he whispers before grunting my name, "Mary!" And hot streams of cream land on my stomach. I don't know what to expect, but I don't expect so much. I gasp when a sixth line coats me, landing on my inner thigh.

I don't know what's gotten into me, but he said he wanted a taste. I sit up, get to my knees, swipe his come off my stomach with one hand, and at the same time, shove one hand in his mouth and the other in mine.

His salty seed slides down my throat, and Knives grips my wrist in a tight lock with his fingers, keeping my fingers in his mouth for as long as he can. He sucks and licks, moaning when he tastes me. He makes me sound like a five-star meal, a gourmet dish he can never get enough of.

I fall backward, exhausted, and high. I never thought it could be like that, sex without the sex. Well, was this sex? I don't know. Foreplay might be a better word for it, but it was better than anything I've ever experienced.

"Holy shit," he huffs, falling to his side.

We chuckle at the same time as we notice how hard we are breathing. He turns my head and traces my jaw as he stares at me with...I don't know... adoration?

"You're pretty fucking amazing, you know that? I've never experienced that. I usually..." he stops himself, and I roll over, tucking my hands under my cheek, and I stare at the tattoo on his chest.

"I know you've been with plenty of other women, Knives. You don't have to stop yourself with me. You aren't going to insult me or anything. Just because I don't have much to compare it to doesn't mean you don't. I know that. You probably are used to just having sex and—" I'm about to launch into why I didn't want to compare, but he kisses me, it's quick with no tongue, but his lips are soft and passionate against mine.

"You're right. I am used to it. I'm used to fucking whoever I want, whenever I want. I bend them over and get down to business, but there is no comparison, Mary. What we just did, it's number one for me."

"Yeah?" I ask, not wanting to sound so damn hopeful, but I can't help it. The way the annoyance for Knives morphed makes me hope.

"Yeah, Hellraiser." He wipes my stomach off with the edge of the blanket, then folds it, tucking it under the sheet, so we don't roll in wet goop. "Come on, let's get some sleep, and tomorrow we can see if we can get home." He kisses the top of my shoulder before pulling the blanket up.

I expect us to roll over and go to bed, but Knives surprises me again by yanking me against his chest and spooning me. His chin is on my shoulder, and his leg is thrown over mine.

He likes to cuddle!

I bite my lip to stop the squeal of excitement. It's right there, bubbling in my throat, needing to be released. I swallow it down and let the beat of his heart against my shoulder lull me to sleep. The fire has died down, just a few crackles and pops every now and then, but I'm warm since Knives is against me.

Right as I'm about to be dead to the world, a hand falls over my mouth. I snap my eyes open, and it's Knives. He lays a finger against his lips, brows drawn in concern as we remain as quiet as possible. The barn door opens up, and two masculine voices are arguing.

"No, I don't know, okay? You have to let Natalia go. I'll give you money. I want my niece back."

"Not until I get what I want!"

"I don't know where your daughter is, Mr. St. James. I swear, but I want Natalia. I did what you asked last time—"

I grip onto Knives as hard as I can, knowing I'm leaving bruises, but it's the only thing stopping me from screaming when I hear my dad's voice. What the hell is he doing here?

"And look how well that turned out. You're useless."

Bang. Bang. Bang.

Knives covers me with his body, just like he did when he thought the tornado was about to take us, and when the barn door slams shut, he lifts his head. "Are you okay?"

I'm shaking. I can't form words. "That was my dad. I…"

"I know. I know. Fuck. Okay, this is a mess. I need to go check on the guy he shot."

"No! Knives, please," I whisper and try to hold onto him, but he kisses my inner wrist before running to the middle of the barn.

"Holy shit, Maximo. What the fuck did you get yourself into?"

There isn't a reply.

I should have known my dad would come back for me. I should have known he would come back to ruin my life the moment I found happiness. And if I know my father, I know he will kill anyone and everyone in his way to get what he wants.

I've brought the Kings more trouble, something they don't deserve. Knives will be a target now; everyone will be in danger because of me.

Maybe I should disappear, but the thought of leaving hurts more than death. I'd rather my father kill me than take me away from the home I've built here.

And just when I thought I was living the dream…

My monster had to come emerge from the dark.

CHAPTER NINE

Knives

Nothing can surprise me much. I've experienced pretty much everything there is to see and feel that would drive a man to kill himself, but being in a remote, abandoned barn with Mary and having the best night of my life? That surprised me.

Drinking with her surprised me. The depth of how much I wanted her surprised me.

Finding Maximo Moretti in an abandoned barn, shot twice in the shoulder and once in the thigh? That surprises me.

And knowing it was Mary's father who pulled the trigger? That fucking shocks me.

Two men that have a fucking death warrant on their heads.

"Maximo? Long time, no see." I pat his sweaty face, and his eyes open. "Yeah, your injuries aren't deadly, so don't play the dead card on me." I slap his face again, and a painful wheeze leaves his chest. "Where have you been, buddy? You know who has been looking for you?"

His eyes snap open then, and he gulps when he knows exactly who I am talking about. "I—I have my reasons. I swear, I'd never hurt any of the ladies who belong to the Kings. You have to understand—"

I wrap my hand around his throat and pull him up by his neck. Maximo fucking Moretti. The man Tongue has been salivating for after what he did, not only pinning Skirt and him in the same ring but for holding a knife to Daphne's throat. Tongue is a maniac, a fucking unstable, sick, and twisted man, but no one fucks with his woman.

"We require payment for your actions," I whisper, letting my breath cross his face so hopefully he can smell the fucking threat in the air. Once I get him back to the clubhouse, I'm going to make sure we drain every bit of information from him.

He turned his back on the wrong men.

"Knives?" Mary asks from our dark corner, our spot, and disappointment rears its head when I realize our fucking moment is ruined because, for some reason, her father and Maximo decided to bust in here. Out of all places they could fucking ruin, they had to ruin this.

Mary and I already don't have the most stable relationship without jumping down each other's throats. We made progress. More than progress. I got to see her come, and I wanted to see that a hundred times over and more.

"Get dressed, Hellraiser."

"Mary? As in Mary St—"

I squeeze Maximo's throat and sneer, "You don't get to fucking ask questions about her. Do I make myself clear?"

"Crystal," Maximo says, groaning when I dig my knee into his shoulder.

On purpose.

107

Mary comes out from behind the old furniture, dressed in her tight jeans and T-shirt with her leather jacket in hand, then tosses me my clothes. They are dry, luckily, since it's been a few hours, and the storm has seemed to pass with just a mist of rain peppering the metal roof.

"I need a hospital," Maximo struggles to say.

I lift my knee off his shoulder and get dressed. Mary stays away from Maximo, leaning against the wall of the barn, right underneath a damn hook that looks like it held pigs or cows for someone to butcher. After I tug on my shirt, I walk over, move her to the left because all I can think about is the hook falling and slicing through her neck, just like my sister. I kiss the top of her head, hating that the happiness we shared is now gone.

I want to kill Maximo for ruining my goddamn night.

Her eyes are red and swollen, her cheeks flushed with fear, and tears fill her beautiful chocolate eyes. I want to kill Maximo for making her cry, too, and her dad.

Oh, I really want her dad's blood on my ninja stars.

"I'm going to fix this. You're going to be safe. I don't want you to be scared, okay?" I tell Mary, needing her to see that I'm going to protect her. She has nothing to worry about. Her father isn't going to lay his hands on her again, not as long as I am alive.

And history has proven, killing me is not easy.

Maximo tries to get up by placing his weight on his hands and knees. "Oh, I don't fucking think so." I slam my foot into his back, and he shouts as his body bends, and he falls to the ground. "You don't get to try and get out of here. You're coming back with me." I grip him by the back of his hair and yank his head off the floor, hoping he is uncomfortable. I could break his neck right now if I really wanted to.

Tongue would cut out my tongue and feed it to Happy if I did. This is his retribution, but I'm allowed to be angry for my brother, and I'm allowed to be angry that Maximo is friends with Mary's father.

108

Nothing good can come out of that.

"What are you doing here?" I ask him.

"I live here."

I push his head against the ground, my fingers twitching for a ninja star, but I don't have any on me. I don't have my backup gun either.

What a fucking shitshow.

"You aren't exactly in the position to get smart with me. You have no idea how deep of shit you are in with the Kings. After everything we have done for you and Moretti, your own fucking brother, you turn your back on us."

"I'm doing this for my brother!" he hisses, but whimpers when I push my knee into the exit wound on his back.

I want to know everything, but it's pointless to get the story out of him now when I know he will go to the playroom at the clubhouse with a few of the guys, and they will get every drop of information out of him. "What's in this barn? Why is Preacher Man here, huh? Didn't know you were the religious type."

His eyes roll to the back of his head, and for a minute, I think he is pretending, so I kick him for the hell of it. But he doesn't make a sound. He's completely passed out. "Damn it. They always pass out right before I need information." I turn around to see Mary folding up the blankets and making sure the fire is out; she's still crying, and her hands are trembling, but she's trying to pull herself together.

I want her to fall apart.

I want her to realize she doesn't have to be strong anymore, or runaway, or feel caged. She can fall, and I'll catch her.

And I'll put her back together again

Mary isn't the kind of woman that can be hidden. She needs her freedom, and I can be that for her.

"How are we going to get back to the clubhouse?" Mary asks, looping her arms through her leather jacket when she shivers.

109

"Mafia boss has to have a phone on him, right?" I flip an unconscious Maximo over on his back and see blood spreading over his suit and dripping on the floor.

Uh.

He might be dying.

And I couldn't care less.

I search his pockets and pull out his phone and dial Reaper's number. As it rings, I glance around the barn and wish we didn't have to leave. This place was a little getaway for us; it healed me in some ways and opened me in others.

And it's ruined because if a man like Maximo and her father are here, it means this is a place that holds bad intent.

I won't bring Mary to a place that is a meeting ground for men like this.

"Maximo," Reaper answers with a dark growl. "You better hope I don't find you because when I do, I'm going to rip your heart from your chest, crush it with my fist, then shove it down your throat."

I'm really fucking glad I'm not Maximo right now. "It's me, Reaper. It's Knives."

"Knives?" he sounds shocked, and the threat in his voice vanishes and is replaced with confusion. "What the fuck are you doing with Maximo's phone? And where the hell have you been? The guys have been trying to call you."

I really need a phone. "I don't have my phone yet. It's been a hectic twenty-four hours. Mary is with me—"

"I thought she was in jail."

"I picked her up yesterday. My bike blew up. The tornado happened. We are in an abandoned barn off Route 50. Maximo is here."

A rumble comes from the other end, and there is a flurry of sounds in the background behind him. "You're going to have to tell me what happened in more detail later. We are coming to get you, don't fucking move, and don't you dare lose Maximo."

110

"We have more issues to worry about than him, Reaper. Shit is brewing, and I'll tell you everything later. Bring my ninja stars."

"Why?"

"Because I don't have them, and I feel naked," I say, suddenly feeling defensive. I crack my neck, annoyed that I even have to defend myself.

"I should have known something like this would happen. Seer called me and told me to tell you that you're an idiot. What's the deal with that?"

A loud bang pulls me away from the conversation, and I see the bedframe fell over, and Mary mouths, 'I'm sorry' to me.

"Another long story," I say, pinching the bridge of my nose. "Can you just get here, please?"

"Yeah. Be there in ten."

The line goes dead, and I stuff the phone in my back pocket. When I stand, I try and find something about this place that rubs me the wrong way, but it's just a barn. I stare into every corner, evaluating the stacks of hay, but nothing stands out to me besides a bunch of cobwebs and the musty smell of horse and rain.

Reins hang on the hook against the beam, and I step over Maximo, yanking the leather straps off. I flick the cobwebs away and flip Maximo on his stomach, pull his arms behind his back, and tie the reins around his wrists into a knot I know he can't get out of. When I'm satisfied, I take a step away.

"They are on their way," I say to Mary, who is still in the same spot as she was in before.

"Good."

I don't like how she said that. I don't like that she's putting distance between us. She won't even look at me in the eye. I'm about to show why we fit when a dozen Harleys grumble outside. This time, I do give her space, because I'm

111

not sure how to be with her in front of the guys. Or maybe I do.

I shouldn't care.

But I'm in unknown territory here. She doesn't seem like she wants me around, but if I act the same, I'm damned. If I out us to the world before she's ready, I'm damned.

What the fuck? Relationship business sucks.

I expect a knock on the door.

I should have known better.

The door is kicked down, and Tongue is standing there in the entryway, his shaggy hair hanging in front of his face and his fists clenched at his sides. He has a knife in his hand and the urge to kill in his eyes.

Hay particles and dust zoom around us, and Tongue looks from left to right, staring at Mary for a few seconds before stepping inside the barn, breaking the downed door even further as he walks across it. The wood creaks and splinters from his weight.

"Tongue! Don't you dare kill him. I want answers." Reaper comes into the doorway next, rubbing his chin when he sees Maximo tied up on the ground.

"I want his tongue."

"That isn't shocking." I pat Tongue's shoulder with my hand, and heat is radiating off him in waves.

Tongue kneels on the ground, snarling like a beast, ready to rip the man's head off. He digs his knife into the ground and drags it in the dirt and straw. His fingers hold the blade tightly, and he doesn't look away from Maximo. He doesn't blink.

He barely even breathes as he holds onto Reaper's order. Tongue wants more than Maximo's ability to speak.

He wants his life.

"Load him up, Bullseye," Reaper says, turning his cheek to his shoulder as if he is talking to someone behind him.

Bullseye comes through the doorway next, twirling a dart in his hand, which makes me wish for my stars. Bullseye

112

must have seen the longing on my face because he pulls two stars out of his pocket, and they gleam in the early morning light.

So pretty.

He flings them in the air, and I catch them without hesitation. One star is one of my newer ones, but the other is one I haven't touched since I made it.

"Sorry, we were in a hurry, and I grabbed what I could," Bullseye says, jerking Maximo up to his feet. "What did you do?"

"He passed out. That's not my fault."

"The bullets. Doc needs to—"

"Leave them. His pain is far from over." Reaper steps out of the way when Bullseye throws Maximo over his shoulder with a grunt and walks outside.

"Maybe tie him to the back of the truck and drag his ass home," Tongue says, perking up when he mentions the options. His eyes stop frowning, and the darkness in his head spins with the idea. He is probably imagining what Maximo would look like rolling around on the ground, losing limbs, becoming bloody. He groans, closing his eyes and licking his lips. He grips his cock, which is hard, and I jerk my eyes away to stare at the ceiling, then drop them to Mary. For the first time in an hour, she has a smile on her face because my discomfort amuses her.

"Stop getting off on getting your revenge, Tongue," I mutter and stalk my way toward Mary. I need to close this distance between us. Now that I've had her, I don't want us to go back to the way we were before.

Why fight something that comes so easy and feels so good?

"I can't help it. The thought of him dying is turning me on. I need Daphne," he says without shame, without blinking that he just admitted that death makes his cock hard.

"Well, stop your moaning, literally, and let's go home. I have a feeling it is going to be a long night. Bullseye? Tie

113

him up in the playroom. Knives and Mary, you're going to Church when we get home."

Ah, what a horrible choice of words.

"I hate church," Mary says low, so only I can hear.

"You can worship the ground I walk on later, then," I tease her, hoping to make her smile.

"Like I'd even want to get near your feet. Gross," she jokes back, and my chest flickers with happiness. I had hoped the teasing nature wouldn't go away in our relationship, just the fighting.

When everyone walks out the door, Reaper backtracks and tosses me a set of keys. "Bullseye is leaving his bike for you to take back. I'll call up Pocus and Seer and see if they can't get a price on a customized one down in NOLA for you. Their hogs are beauts," he says, just as I catch the keys in the air. "We saw your bike. It's fucking toasted. Nothing was salvageable, Knives. I'm sorry."

"It's all good, Prez. Shit happens."

"Story of our fucking lives," he says, stomping outside in the muck the rain left behind.

Before we leave, I lay my hand on Mary's shoulders and notice she is looking away from me again. Her lip is trembling, and she keeps wiping the tears that fall on her cheeks. I want to fix this. I don't want her to cry again. It... it makes me feel things I haven't felt in a very long time. I doubt this will be the last time too.

I bet every day I'll wake up and experience an emotion that has been in hibernation for twenty years. She's awakening me from a coma, and I nearly don't recognize the world I'm seeing or myself, but I like it.

That's new to me too. Liking something. I've been so focused on rage and harm, so lost in violence, that I've forgotten how to *be*.

"You okay?"

"I don't know," she answers honestly. "It's not a good thing if my dad is here, Knives. He isn't here to talk about God."

"I know." I wrap my arms around her and pull her close, kissing her forehead as if I do it every day. The other day, I wanted to tape her mouth shut, and now the thought of silence brings pressure to my chest.

But if Preacher Man wants to talk about God, I'll make sure that before he leaves Vegas, he gets a one on one meeting with the man upstairs.

No one is going to take what's mine.

And if they do, it's nothing a ninja star to the throat can't fix.

CHAPTER TEN

"Tell me everything, start to finish. I don't want you to leave anything out. Mary, sit down, please."

My ass hits the seat so hard, I slide backward. I would have hit the wall if Knives' arm didn't stop me. Reaper makes me nervous. He always has. He can be the reason why I stay or go. He holds the power.

Power can be a scary thing when it is in the wrong hands.

"You're okay, Mary. No one is in trouble. I need details before we go downstairs."

"Down…"

"Don't worry; you don't have to go and see what is about to be done—"

"—I know that Knives, but I can handle it," I snap.

"I didn't say you couldn't," he defends himself, digging his fingers into the table.

"I'm sorry. I'm stressed out. I shouldn't take it out on you. I don't want us to fight." I find his hand and grab onto it.

"Aw, you two kissed and made up. I knew that would happen after what happened at Christmas. Bullseye and Tank owe me fifty bucks."

"You've been betting on us?" Knives pulls out a ninja star and slams it into the table. I think he is about to throw one at Reaper he is so mad. "No one could have told me what was happening between us? I figured she was just a pain in my ass—"

"—Hey," I say, pretending to take offense. He's right. And for all I know, he is still going to be a pain in my ass.

"You know I'm right," he says, tugging the star from the table.

"We figured you two would figure it out. Glad you did, I'm a hundred bucks richer." Reaper leans back in his chair and lays his hands on the armrest. "Catch me up. What the fuck happened?"

"Well…" Knives starts. "I went to go pick up Hellraiser here from lock up—"

"—After you left me there for two days!"

"Anyway," he drawls. "We were on our way back when I tried to teach her a lesson about speeding…"

"Nearly killing me."

"Did you die?" he grins.

"Might as well have," I huff, crossing my arms.

"I pulled over, and we fought…"

"You yelled at me, and then you flung a ninja star at me."

"Semantics," he says.

"Semantics!" I nearly come out of the chair I'm sitting in and strangle him.

"She wasn't listening."

"Oh, you want to talk about listening. He hit the gas tank to the bike with the star, trying to prove a point, and guess what? A man tossed a cigarette out the window."

"And you wouldn't move," Knives drones, slamming his head against the table.

"Yeah, keep doing that. Maybe it will knock some sense into your head."

"Like how you would have been knocked on your ass if I wouldn't have gotten you away from the explosion," Knives counters. "You were kicking fucking rocks."

"Pretending they were your head at the time."

Knives growls at me, and if it were possible, I know steam would be rising from his body with how angry he is getting. He flips the star over his knuckles, something he does when he has something on his mind.

"And the tornado happened," he grits out. "We had to hightail it out of there. I carried her because her shoes were on fire. We found the barn. Maximo came into the barn a while later, early morning, I guess. We were waiting out the storm, and that's when her dad came in."

Reaper is rubbing his temples and taking deep breaths. "You two are going to give me an aneurysm with your bickering. So much damn bickering."

"Sorry," Knives says at the same time I do. "I guess there are a few things that won't change."

The words cut deeper than they are supposed to. I set my jaw, reminding myself that this is why I didn't take it further with him in the barn. "My dad came in next and shot Maximo. I didn't hear much. Something about a woman named Natalia. My dad was looking for me."

"Do you want to go back with him—"

"No!" Knives throws both of the stars against the wall, then slams his fist on the table. "She cannot go back with him."

"That isn't up to you, Knives."

"The hell it isn't," he sneers at his Prez, and then realizes his mistake when Reaper stands tall.

"Watch yourself. You don't control her. Sit your fucking ass down before I tie you up next to Maximo."

Knives lowers himself into the chair, then grabs mine and rolls it closer to him. His hand falls on my knee, his fingers playing with the frayed hole in my jeans. "Sorry, Prez. She can't go back."

"He's right, Reaper. Please, the last thing I ever want to do is go back home. My dad isn't who he says he is, and I think Maximo knows more."

"Why don't you want to go home?"

"Prez—"

Reaper lifts his hand in the air, silencing Knives on the spot. "I won't ask again."

"Um…" the table blurs as I stare at it, and I realize I'm on the verge of tears. I don't want to say this again. Knives' hand finds mine, and he locks us together by intertwining our fingers.

His hold on me grounds me.

"He molested her for twelve years, Prez. He isn't a man of God," Knives speaks for me, and I'm relieved just as much as I am disappointed that I couldn't find the strength to say it to a man that wants to help. When I talk to Knives, it's easy.

Anyone else, I want my secrets to stay my own.

"Is that right?"

I can see Reaper's fingers folding around the gavel and the bone creaks.

"I think we need to go see what Maximo wants. We will find your dad and take care of him, then figure out what the hell Moretti's daughter has to do with this too."

Take care of.

I'm not stupid. I know exactly what that means.

And I don't care.

"I won't let him take her, Prez. No way in hell."

"I'm sorry," I say to Reaper. I stare at the stone-cold expression masking his face. He looks so mad, and this time, I can't stop the tears falling onto the table. "I didn't want to bring you trouble. I don't know how he found me. I thought I got away when I ran—" I gasp and zip my lips shut. I have never, ever been that close to saying those words.

A chair creaks when Knives leans forward. He spins my chair, and his eyes analyze me, confused, but then his brows do a little jiggle as they reach his hairline, and the blue irises become even brighter. It's like a light bulb turned on in his head as he stared at me.

"You ran away," Knives says in horror. "And you ran right to them, didn't you? You wanted to be with the Atlantic City chapter. They didn't steal you, no one sold you, no one trafficked you, you went to them willingly."

Words catch in my throat, and shame crawls up my neck. I trace the groove in the table with my finger and try to think of an excuse, a lie, something that didn't make the truth sound so bad, but nothing came to mind.

"Yes."

"Why? Why would you do that? Out of all places, you could have picked to save yourself, and you picked them? It was as if you were asking to die."

Reaper clears his throat when the awkward tension heightens.

"You...you went there to die?" Knives whispers in realization. "You knew exactly what you were doing when you ran away."

"I couldn't do it myself," I admit. I rub my palms on my thighs when they start to sweat. "I wanted to die, but I knew I needed someone else to do it."

Knives stands, picks up the chair, and with an agonizing cry, he throws it over the table. It crashes against the wall, and I jump, closing my eyes as the chair falls to the ground. "How could you do that?" he yells at me. "How could you give up on yourself? How could you?"

"Knives, that's enough," Reaper says.

"No. It isn't. It's far from being enough. How could you do that? What about me? You were just... you were going to leave me? You would have left me. Everyone always fucking leaves," he continues to scream at the top of his lungs, which starts to gather a crowd outside. "You would have chosen to give up on me."

"I didn't even know you," I say to him. "All I knew was what I felt, and after what my dad did, I heard about the Atlantic City chapter, and I knew that life had to be better, and if I died, I died," I shrug.

"Death. Is. Not. That. Simple," he bites out each word and pulls his ninja stars free. "Death leaves behind everyone that loves you."

"Don't you get it, Knives?" I asks. "No one loved me."

He hangs his head, flipping the ninja star over his knuckles as he thinks. Bullseye comes into the room and tries to guide Knives out of the room, but Knives pushes him away.

Knives throws his star, and it whooshes by me, landing so hard against the wall, it disappears into the crack. "I would have missed out on you," he says, patting his chest. "I never want to miss out on anything again. I've lost, and I've lost, and damn it, Mary, I would have missed you if I never met you." Knives starts to walk out the door and slams into Bullseye's shoulder. "Get out of my way."

The guys part to let Knives through, and I want to go after him, but the stomps of his feet going down the stairs tell me he does not want to be bothered since Maximo is down there.

"I didn't know," I sob, whipping my head to Reaper. "I didn't know about him. I just... I felt useless after what my father did to me and... I wouldn't do it now. I'm sorry. I didn't mean to bring you trouble. It's always on your doorstep. It's the last thing I wanted." I bury my face in my hands and sob. Knives' heartbroken face is all I see.

I would have missed you if I never met you.

The words play on repeat in my mind, dissecting what he meant and didn't mean. I need to know more, but I decide to give him space instead.

"Listen, I've known Knives for a long time. He doesn't handle emotion well. He's had a lot happen, and he tends to put his feelings in a box and shove them away. You kind of open that box for him. He hasn't felt in a long time; let him have his space." Reaper pushes on the table to help him stand, and he gives my shoulder a comforting squeeze as he walks behind me to make his way out.

"Yeah, okay," I nod, staring at the ninja star embedded in the wall. I wipe the tears and decide to sit in the room alone to gather my thoughts.

This church is so much better than the other kind. Truth is spoken here, love is here, pain is here.

The Ruthless Kings are a religion.

Or at least, they have the qualities that religion is made up of. The right qualities.

Like my father, a lot of people use religion to fuel their hate.

After everything that has happened, I don't know what I believe in. I find it hard to believe that my path in life has always been set in stone to lead me here.

"You okay?" a soft voice comes from the doorway, and Reaper's sister Delilah is standing there, tapping on the trim with her knuckles. She surprised everyone when she showed up a few weeks ago. They look so much alike, but it is obvious Reaper is older.

"I don't know."

"Been there," she sighs, slinking into the room. She's so small, like if a stiff breeze blows, she'll float away. Her dirty blonde hair is in a Dutch braid hanging over her shoulder. We don't know much about her. Her stories are hers to tell when she's ready, which I can relate to. Everyone knows my truth now, and I don't want to see how they will look at me now.

"Everything will be okay. It might not seem like it now, but it will be. Knives cares about you. That's been obvious since I've been here, and I'm sure it's been obvious before that too."

"We bicker a lot. I don't know. Maybe it's just sex." The words don't sound right as they leave my mouth. They leave a bad taste, because I know it isn't just sex. It's more.

"Maybe you're bickering to stop what you really want to do. Maybe you're bickering because that's what you two have been doing for so long, you don't know how else to be. It takes time to learn. Or maybe it is sex. Would that be so bad?"

My body turns to fire when I think about what happened in the barn. Sex with Knives wouldn't be bad; it would be out of this world.

And it could never be just sex, because I know I'd fall in love with him if I'm not already there.

Maybe that's why we fight

It's because we might love each other after all.

Except he doesn't want love. And I don't know how to love.

CHAPTER ELEVEN

Knives

"Tell me!" I swing the star and cut a gash on Maximo's cheek. I'm fucking pissed off. Ever since Mary told me the truth, I've had this burning in my veins to kill someone. I need to inflict pain. I need to figure out where her father is so I can throw a dozen stars into his body.

Maximo groans in pain, but not once has he tried to beg for his life or pull on the straps in the chair. It's like he has given up. "I swear," his Italian accent slurs. "I swear, I don't know much. Preacher St. James isn't the kind of man that drops by for a visit. I've never met him before tonight."

"It sure seemed like you knew each other," I spit, wondering why we are prolonging this mother fucker's death.

"I say you let me slice his tongue out and feed it to Happy," Tongue says from the corner. "I want payback for what you did. You touched Daphne!" Tongue unsheathes his knife, and Reaper blocks him from trying to come closer.

"This is bigger than you. Stand down," Reaper orders, and Tongue blows out a breath through his nose. He's barely hanging on to his restraint, and he starts to pace, never taking his eyes off Maximo.

Reaper sighs and stretches his arms before coming over and pressing his finger in one of the gunshot wounds on Maximo's shoulder. "I suggest you tell us everything there is to know about this Preacher Man and why he wants Mary."

Maximo's entire body trembles from the pain Reaper is inflicting by digging his finger inside the wound. "It has everything to do with Natalia. I swear, I'm not trying to get involved in his plan. He wanted information. His people came to the casino. They asked questions. I said I hadn't seen Mary, but then Natalia was gone, and he sent me a picture of her. It isn't a prostitution ring. It's an auction. I would do anything for my niece, and I'm not about to let her get sold to some fucking asshole! So if it means throwing Daphne or Mary under the bus for my own flesh and blood, then I will!"

I throw a ninja star at him, and it lands between his ribs. He tosses his head back, gritting his teeth through the pain. "You act like you wouldn't do the same," he says, spittle flying from his mouth. The veins in his neck jump as he gathers himself. "I know all of you, and there isn't anything you wouldn't do for one another."

He has me there. I'd trade Natalia for Mary in a heartbeat.

"How did his men find you? How did he know to come here?" Reaper digs his index finger in the bullet wound again, and Maximo shouts, tugging on the straps at last.

I pluck a freshly made star from its packaging and roll it over my knuckles. It's one of the reasons why I'm so scarred along my hands. It took a lot of practice to throw, catch, and play with them like I do, and I messed up.

A lot.

And now I'm a fucking pro, and it all started with my first one made of knives.

"I don't know, Reaper. I swear I don't know."

"That isn't good enough," Prez says.

"It's all I've got. Natalia is all I have. My brother, he doesn't even know me. I can't let his daughter disappear. You've met her, Reaper. This is Natalia."

So Preacher Man auctions women off. I guess praying doesn't pay the bills. My stomach rolls when I think of Mary and what her father did to her. Was he grooming her for future auctions? Or was she his own deviant secret that he always wanted to keep?

For the hell of it, I throw another star, and it lands right under the one lodged in his ribs. Fuck, that feels good. I roll my shoulders, then wipe the sweat off my mouth and forehead. "He's here, though. In Vegas? For how long?"

"Until he gets Mary." Maximo's normally perfectly styled hair is messy, dripping with sweat. His shoulder rises as he wheezes. There is no doubt he is in pain.

I grip his jaw and squeeze as hard as I can, wishing I could break every bone in his fucking body. "There is no way he is getting her. You hear me? Sorry to disappoint you."

"What did Daphne have to do with it?"

"He said he wanted a brunette. Daphne was perfect—" a blood-curling scream fills the room and leaves the open abyss of his mouth.

Tongue has cut three fingers from Maximo's hand. He stares at them in disgust as he examines them and plucks the gold ring off the pinky that's still twitching. Damn, Tongue moved quickly. I didn't even see him bring down his knife across Maximo's hand.

Reaper doesn't reprimand him because, at the end of the day, you fuck us, you get fucked in return. An eye for an eye.

"I'm feeding these to Happy. No way in hell you're getting these back. Be glad you have your tongue." With that, Tongue scoops up the fingers and leaves the room, kicking the door open with his foot. It slams against the wall, and in his departure, he didn't close it.

And Moretti steps inside.

"What are you doing to my brother?" Moretti asks, his accent just as thick as his brother's. Something about him feels familiar like he is in business mode. "I suggest you stop."

"Why do you care?" Maximo heaves, blood dripping onto the floor from where his fingers used to be. "You don't remember me anyway."

Moretti comes out of the dark, and the burns on his arm aren't as bad as I thought they were going to be. "But I feel it. What did you do?"

"I betrayed them, for good reason, just believe me. Okay? Fuck! He took my fingers. That crazy bastard!" Maximo tries to get out of the restraints again, but it's pointless. He is at our mercy until we say otherwise.

"Why?" Moretti presses. "Why would you do that to them?"

Bullseye interrupts by throwing a dart, and it lands right in the muscle of Maximo's calf. Everyone turns to him when Maximo curses. The dart isn't as bad as getting your fingers cut off, but I'm sure it's uncomfortable. "Oops," Bullseye says, shrugging his shoulders. "My fingers slipped."

Moretti pulls out a gun and aims it at Bullseye's head.

The only sound in the room is the drip of blood coming from Maximo's hand.

"I'd think twice if I were you," Tool growls, pressing his screwdriver against Moretti's neck.

"I'd get a bullet between his eyes before you had that shoved in my throat."

I reach around and pull out a new gun, aiming it at Moretti's head. I cock it, and the click of the bullet sliding into place always gives me the same feeling a ninja star does.

Almost.

"Mine's bigger," I say with a smirk, noticing the small handgun he has. Mine will blow his head off and paint the fucking walls with his brains.

"Drop it," I say to him, and when he doesn't listen, I move the aim from him to Maximo. "I said drop it, Moretti. You know we aren't afraid to make you both gator food."

"What did you do, Maximo?" Moretti has a desperate edge to his voice. "What did you do?"

"It's Natalia. Your daughter. She's been taken as collateral."

Moretti drops the gun and backtracks. "No," he says, shaking his head. "No! Not Natalia. Why? For what? Give the man whatever he fucking wants!"

"He can't." I lower my gun next, pointing it directly to the floor. "What her captor wants is something he will never have again." If he is in Vegas, I'm going to search every hotel, every corner, every house, apartment, shack, and whatever else I can find. I'll look under every rock, look in every hole in the ground, have Badge look into his credit cards, his life, and I'll fucking ruin him.

"But Natalia—" Moretti asks, rubbing the middle of his chest.

"I'm sorry, Moretti. I can't risk Mary for you. I won't. This your problem, you fucking figure it out." I step forward and yank the five stars out of Maximo's body. I have no idea what to do with him. If this had been anyone else, he would be dead. I almost don't understand why we don't kill him. Sure, we have a working relationship, but he ruined that when this shit happened.

I believe that Maximo doesn't have all the answers that I'm looking for. For instance, how did Mary's father find her? Why did they go to Maximo? And how the hell can I make sure they never come here again? I want answers. Maybe Mary has them, by some off chance.

"I'm sorry," Maximo whispers. "I was only doing what I needed to do for my family."

I get that. I've done a lot for my family, been through a lot, seen a lot, and I think that's why I'm so mad. In a sense, I thought Maximo and Moretti were a part of this fucked up family. I thought we could count on them.

"Why didn't you come to us, Maximo?"

"Because he asked me not to," he says.

Reaper, Tool, Bullseye, and I all share a look. "So he knows about us?" I ask, the hairs on the back of my neck standing up.

Maximo closes his eyes, sweat dripping down his temple, and there is a smear of blood on his lip from when I punched him in the face about twenty times.

The man has taken his beating like a champ, I'll give him that.

"A lot of bad men know about you. How can you be surprised?" he mumbles through a wince as he tries to readjust himself to get comfortable.

Yeah, that's not happening.

"How can a Preacher know so much about us?" Bullseye asks, plucking his dart from Maximo's leg, which earns a sudden pained shout. Bullseye lifts the dart and clicks his tongue when he sees a chunk of flesh on the fingers of the dart. "It hurts more coming out. I should have warned you."

Maximo doesn't miss the sarcasm dripping in Bullseye's voice and curls his lip to show his teeth that are glistening with blood.

Thanks to me.

"Maybe he didn't know about Vegas, but he knew about Atlantic City," I say as information starts clicking into place.

How did Mary know about the Atlantic City chapter? Maybe her father knew what happened, and he didn't care, and now that he wants her back, he has gone and examined all resources—including other chapters.

Which led him here.

Reaper's phone rings, and when he pulls it out of his pocket, he sighs. "It's Seer."

129

And I bet he saw everything the day he fucking called me. All of this could have been avoided.

Reaper slides his finger across the touchscreen. "You're on speaker, Seer."

Tool digs his screwdriver into Moretti's neck but doesn't break skin before tucking the Phillip's head behind his ear. It clearly was a warning not to make any sudden movements.

Seer's cajun accent fills the room, and I smile, forgetting how much I enjoy listening to him. "Mon Amie, it's about time one of ya'll answer my fucking phone calls. I'm going to assume now isn't the best time considering Maximo is tied to a chair, three fingers less. Hi, Maximo," Seer greets.

Maximo stays quiet.

"You have any new information now that we are listening?" I ask, needing every detail I can to keep Mary safe.

"Oui. You've got the fight of your life ahead of ya.' I wish I had better—" but it sounds like betta' coming from Seer "—news. But the man you're at war with, he ain't a good man. A son of God, he is not, more like the Devil's spawn. His Preachin' is a set-up, a cover. He's in Vegas. A tall hotel."

"They are all tall, Seer," Reaper sounds exasperated.

"Oui, but this one has an M on it."

"That's better detail, thank you. That it, Seer?" Reaper rubs his eyes, no doubt exhausted and annoyed that all this shit keeps happening.

"Knives, I know ya' ain't one to want to know what happens with your future. It's why you kept breaking ya phone when I called."

Tattletale.

"Ya gonna lose Mary, Knives."

Everyone sucks in a breath, even Maximo, but that's probably because he can't breathe.

And I can't either. I shake my head, dropping the stars in my hand, and they clatter against the floor. The rings of them trying to fall to their sides goes on and on; they twirl, like a penny spinning until it finally loses momentum.

"No," I mutter. "No. I just got her, Seer. I just realized—" I rub the ache in my heart, the one I've felt twice before when I've lost someone I've loved. It's why I'm so closed off from everyone and everything. It hurts too damn bad to feel anything other than what I need to be for the club. "No. I can't lose her too, Seer. Your visions, you said they can change, right? They change. They aren't set in stone."

"Most of the time, they are."

"Not this time. I've waited too long. I've lost too much. I won't lose her too. You hear me, you sight-seeing sonofabitch! She's mine. I finally have something that's fucking mine, and none of you fucking assholes are going to take her from me. I don't care what I have to do, where I have to go, she'll be safe."

"That's not how it works, Knives, and ya know it," he says sadly. "I'm sorry, Knives."

"When?" I place my hand on my hips and tilt my head up, staring at the ceiling as if it has all the answers, but it clearly doesn't. Only Seer does.

"Two weeks from today."

"What happens?"

"Ya really want to know?"

"Yes." Because I'll do everything in my power to save her.

"She saves you." Seer takes that moment to hang up the phone, leaving me staring at a blank screen and a dial tone.

She saves me.

I now understand why I didn't want to talk to him, because nothing he has to say to us is a good thing. I'm sick of it. I'm sick of always fucking fighting. I'm getting tired. How much bullshit can a club take before it falls apart?

"Knives—" Reaper starts to say, but before he can get a word out, I turn on my heel and walk out the door.

131

I need to clear my head. I need to go for a ride; only I don't have a fucking bike because it exploded.

I have to be cursed. The universe loves to take everything from me. Why not just kill me? Why torture me consistently? I slam the door behind me and run up the steps, getting away from Maximo, Moretti, and Reaper. I'm getting away from the pain they want to inflict.

I'm the one that came out afflicted. My heart is in tattered pieces. When I get to the top of the stairs, I lean against the door and take a minute to myself. I feel dizzy. Memories bombard me: the sound of metal crunching, bullets flying, blood, fear. Before I know it, I'm that little kid again, wondering how I'm going to make it through life without my person at my side.

I'm not meant to be with someone.

I'm meant to be alone.

I'm   always   alone.

CHAPTER TWELVE

I creep out of my bedroom in the corner of the clubhouse. It's in the back. A newly renovated room near the gym. I think Reaper wanted to give me space from the guys, but I want to be close to everyone else. As much as I wanted my father to leave me alone, I hate being alone. Sometimes, he would sneak into my room and hold me, and I was so afraid; I didn't want his touch, but I wanted the company.

How sick is that?

It's why I'm on the couch right now, sleeping with Tyrant at my feet and Chaos by my head. Tyrant is Juliette's dog, and Chaos is Skirt's. I fell asleep watching reruns of Friends, but the sound of the front door opening and closing has me stirring. I glance out the window right as the motion light comes on outside, and that's when I see Knives. He is leaning against the porch rail, the puffs of breath fogging in front of him as he breathes in the cold air, and he hangs his head.

Something is wrong.

I rub my eyes and get up. The dogs groan, not too happy to be jostled and roll to their backs at the same time. The only dog missing is Lady. She's been hanging on to life, and the vet doesn't understand why. It's killing Poodle. He barely leaves his room so he can be with her. It's sad.

"Good boys," I say to them, patting their heads, so they know they are loved. I wrap the fluffy blanket around me and make my way to the front door. I open it and carefully close it behind me.

Knives hears the door click and turns around. My breath catches from how beautiful he is. The scalding blue eyes sear a brand on my heart in the shape of his name. The mug he has in his hand drops to his crotch to cover the bulge, and that's when I notice he is wearing a black onesie.

That hugs everything.

Yeah, the mug doesn't hide a thing. And as funny as it should be that this badass biker is in a onesie, I find myself wishing I could unclasp the white buttons to reveal the hair on this chest.

"I… uh… it's laundry day. This is what I wear when I need to wash clothes," he says, bringing his fist to his mouth as he coughs. "No one usually sees me in this."

"I like it," I smile, keeping my hand clutched on the blanket. My feet are freezing, and the deck is just as cold as the air. I sit down in a rocking chair, and he forgets that he is covering his bulge when he brings his mug to his lips, taking a long sip.

My eyes drop to his crotch and widen. It's impressive. I can see the outline of his piercings too.

"Knives—"

"—No, let me." He sets his cup down on the rail and kneels. It's funny to see him in something other than his cut and jeans, but something about this onesie brings out his vulnerable side that he keeps hidden away. Like he is dying to feel comfort, so he does this because no one can see it.

He thinks no one can see him, but I do. I see him.

I see right through him.

Knives isn't made of ninja stars and blood. He's made of onesies and aches to feel the warmth of being secure.

I won't ever say it out loud, but I'll be his onesie if he allows me to be.

"I can't... I don't know how to do this." There is a pain in his eyes, the same pain that was in them when he threw the chair. "I don't do this. And Seer..."

"What?"

"Nothing," he says, but I know it's something. He is hiding it from me. Seer told him something that spooked him.

"Tell me."

He takes my face in his hands and shakes his head. "No. There isn't a time that's more important than right now, and I want to enjoy every moment I have with you." He presses his lips to mine, soft, slow, and deliberate. He takes his time prying my mouth open to make room for his tongue. I deepen the kiss and lean forward, wrapping my arms around his back and pulling him into the warmth of my blanket.

The cold hasn't affected him. His skin is warm, but his tongue is cold. I don't know how long we sit there and kiss, but the crickets are in the background, and heat lightning flashes across the sky.

I'm starting to wonder if Knives is the reason why I didn't die. There were so many chances for me, but none ever came, no matter how hard I tried.

And he was there every time.

At first, I thought he was a nuisance, but he was the saving grace I had no idea I needed.

"I want you," he says against my lips, not breaking the kiss or breaking us apart. "I want all of you." He slides his hand down my jaw, caresses the curve of my neck, and lays

135

his hand in the middle of my chest. "I've never had it before."

I've never freely given it before.

Not that I ever planned on giving it to him. Knives kind of wiggled his way in and stole it without me noticing. He's had my heart for a while now, and I've fought him to get it back; I just didn't know what I was fighting so hard for until now.

The heart is fickle.

It breaks, it mends, but it is never the same after being welded together.

I don't want to have to weld myself together. I don't want Knives to wreck me. I don't have the energy to pick myself up after that.

And I don't think he does either.

"Take me then," I say.

We pull away from each other, but not by much, just so we can look each other in the eyes. I could look at his eyes forever and not once get tired of their depths. He holds so much behind those blue prisons. I used to think he was cold, but really, he is an inmate in his own body, and he is begging to be released.

He lifts me up into his arms, the blanket dragging along the porch, and he takes the steps carefully. I don't know where we are going, but I trust him. He walks around the building and heads toward the back entrance to the gym. I almost want to stay outside, but we might get caught, and I don't want anyone seeing us.

"What's wrong? Change your mind?" he asks.

"Not when it comes to you." I drag my finger through his beard. It's thick and coarse, just like the rest of the fur on his body. "I just wish we could be outside for our first time. I loved being alone with you in the barn."

He nuzzles my cheek with his, and his breath ghosts over the shell of my ear. "I did too." He lifts up and stares out toward the back of the property. "I'll make sure to build us our own barn."

"You'd do that for me?"

"I'd give my life for you, Hellraiser. You want the barn? I'll bring it here. You want the stars? I'll fucking bottle them for you. You want the moon? I'll find a way to give it to you. I'll find a way to give you everything. I hate that we didn't realize what we felt for one another sooner. I lost out on so much time. I'm afraid I won't be able to give you all the things you deserve."

"Knives, I'm right here. I'm not going anywhere anytime soon."

The look in his eyes tells me he doesn't believe me. I'm not sure what has him spooked, but I'm sure it has something to do with Seer. I'm not going to ask because I don't want to know. I just want to be with Knives.

"Take me to bed," I say, tugging on his beard while snapping my fingers.

He smirks and opens the door. When it is cracked, he bumps it open with his hip so we can fit through. "So fucking sassy. You and that mouth."

"What are you going to do about it?"

"Tape it shut."

"I'd like to see you try." I lift my chin in a challenge, and when he steps foot on the gym floor, his boots echo.

That's another thing I love about him wearing this onesie. He has his damn boots on, and the laces are untied.

He's a mess, and he only lets it show through at moments like this.

Onesies and unlaced boots

My new favorite combination.

He stops in the middle of the gym and sits me down. He takes the blanket from me and lays it in the middle, fluffing it, so it's an even square along the slick floor. "Stay here. I'll be back." He brings his lips to the top of my head, and his boots scuff with every step he takes. He presses a few buttons, and that's when the roof opens.

I gasp. I had no idea it could do that. The stars are out by the millions, surrounded by black and blue hues.

"I know it isn't the barn, and I know I didn't bottle them, but maybe this can be a close second."

"It's perfect. Come here. Come look at the stars with me," I say, holding out my hand, telling him silently to come back to me.

His boots scuff again as he crosses the floor. When he gets to the blanket, he takes off his shoes and lays down. I nestle against his side, staring up at the vast sky that seems to hold more questions than answers.

"Seer told me you were going to die in two weeks. You die saving me, Mary. I can't... I can't lose you too."

I roll over on top of him, wishing he hadn't told me, but I'm not mad. I push my hair out of my face and stroke his cheek. "I can't think of a better way to die than protecting the person I—" Am I about to say love? It's too soon for that.

Is it? How long have I really been in love with him and denied it, fought it? Too long, but I'm too afraid to admit it. "If that's what he saw—"

"Death really doesn't scare you?" he asks.

"No, but just because he saw it doesn't mean it will happen."

"He said one of us."

"Let's prove him wrong, Knives. We've fought for so long, and now we have something to fight for. Let's not stop fighting now."

"As long as I'm fighting for you and not with you, I'll be a happy man," he says, bringing his lips to mine, kissing me under the stars. He brought me the outdoors, just like he said he would. He might not have bottled the constellations or brought me the moon, but he brought me a memory that will last forever.

He whips my shirt over my head, and he unhooks my bra with a flick of his fingers, freeing my breasts. He never breaks the kiss, and when he tugs the straps off my arms, Knives gathers my hair and lays the thick strands over my chest to hide my tits.

Leaning back, he admires his masterpiece. "I've been wanting to see this dark hair covering your tits for so long. You're so fucking gorgeous, Mary." He tweaks my nipples, and I gasp. "But I want to see you like this completely naked." He smooths his hands down my body until his fingers hook in the waistband of my shorts and tugs them down to my knees, taking my panties with them.

Time stands still as I'm laid bare before him.

And I get lost in the silence as he becomes speechless, staring at me so hard it is like he is burning me into his memory. He fluffs my hair just right, covering my tits, and the ends of my hair stop at my hip. I love how he looks at me like I'm the only star he sees.

CHAPTER THIRTEEN

Knives

I don't know how she can be so calm about death. I know I've killed dozens of people, but when death is close to home, it scares the hell out of me. When she said we had to keep fighting, I knew she was right.

No matter what, Seer's vision cannot come true.

I'll fight, tooth and nail, skin and bone, blood and guts, until I've given all of me to make sure she has breath in her lungs. I won't stay silent and watch her die. I won't be the guy on the outside looking in and watch his world pass him by.

She looks fucking hot with her hair cascading over her breasts. It's better than all the dreams I've ever had of her. My cock is throbbing, pulling against the thin material of my onesie. I should be embarrassed for her to see me like this, but for some odd reason, she likes it. She sits up, her long luscious strands of hair still covering her round tits, and her pink beads poke through, hard and waiting to be plucked. Her hands skim down my arms, tracing the outline of my tattoos, pausing on the one that looks exactly like her.

She doesn't ask.

She doesn't need to.

Her nails tickle as she gently rakes them up my arms before coming to the middle of my chest. A shiver runs down me. She works with the buttons, unclasping them one by one. With every inch of skin exposed, she kisses my chest. She works her way down, her lips getting lower and lower until she's at the last button.

My hand moves on its own accord, taking one side of her hair and throwing it over her left shoulder. I want to see her. All of her. When her breast is exposed, I have to hold back a groan. Of course, they are fucking perfect. Round, perky, nipples that are red and remind me of those candy Jolly Ranchers I love so much.

Her skin is soft, creamy, and flawless. The light from the stars is so bright, and the half-crescent moon hanging in the sky shines, giving Mary an ethereal glow.

Reaper spent a shit ton of money on the retractable roof because Sarah mentioned something about stargazing with him, and of course, he went all out.

I'm glad I get to use it for my benefit.

She traces the ridges of my abdomen, lifting her lashes so her eyes meet mine. She's turned me into a goddamn sap just like the rest of the guys that are in love with their ol' ladies. Her hands grip the lapels of my onesie and slide them down my arms. The material hangs on my hips, and Mary kisses her way up my stomach, my muscles bunching from the softness of her lips.

When she's almost eye-level with me, she tilts her chin up, so our gazes catch. It has me sucking in a stunned breath. She is so gorgeous.

I've only ever fucked before. It was only ever about getting in and out, a temporary relief for the permanent pain I felt, but I don't want that with Mary.

She's the permanent fix.

And I'll fight like hell to make sure this love isn't temporary. I won't let it die in two weeks. I finally have my chance at happiness. I'm no longer alone.

I grip her chin and bring my lips to hers. It's almost painful kissing someone so damn perfect because, at any moment, I know that I might not be able to feel perfection again. Our kiss is lazy and languid. We take our time exploring each other's mouths. Our tongues fight for dominance, which has me smiling against her mouth. I don't expect anything less from her.

My cock throbs painfully, keenly aware of what is about to happen. I push her down against the blanket, never once breaking the kiss. She pushes the onesie down my legs, and my cock slaps against her leg, heavy and dripping with precome.

"Do you have a condom?" she asks, making every fucking ounce of lust I'm feeling screech to a halt.

"Where would I put a condom? In my onesie pocket? I didn't know this was going to happen."

"You should always be prepared."

I pin her against the floor, the bickering turning me on more than it should, and I decide a condom would have never mattered. "I'm not fucking you with a condom, Mary. We've had a barrier between us for far too fucking long, and I'm not about to feel this cunt for the first time with latex. I'm going to own you, raw. And you know what you're going to do?" I press my hand between her legs and roll my thumb over her clit. I can't wait to bury my face between her legs.

"What?" She has a hard, defiant glint in her eyes as she meets my challenge.

"You're going to lay back and get the fuck over it." I plunge three fingers inside her channel, not bothering to stretch her or get her used to me.

She'll never be used to me.

And no amount of prep will change that.

Her nails dig in my shoulders, and she whimpers, relenting to me, giving me control. Fucking finally. Is that all it takes to get her to listen to me?

What a hardship.

"You're so tight, Hellraiser. I can't wait to feel you wrapped around my cock," I say, watching her tits bounce, and I continue to finger fuck her.

Her eyes squeeze shut as if she's in pain, and I stop. "Are you okay?" I should have thought about how sex with me would feel for her. I'll be the first after her father. "We don't have to—"

"—No, I want you so much. You feel so good. I've never felt so good before. Don't stop."

I pull my fingers out of her warmth and bring them to my mouth, licking the sweet nectar. I nearly fall on my ass when her hand wraps around me, giving me a tight pump. I groan, closing my eyes as she has her way with me. Her fingers slide up and down the Jacob's Ladder, and I'm trembling with how good it feels. Not a lot of women play with the piercings, which is a shame. The bars heighten the sensitivity. I get they can be intimidating, but Mary doesn't fucking hesitate. She tugs on the hoops, and the cry that leaves my mouth bounces off the gym walls, singing my pleasure back to me.

"Did this hurt?" she asks, rubbing me with one hand while pulling on the hoops with the other.

I can barely breathe. I think I could come just like this. "Yes," I answer.

"Do you like pain?"

"Yes."

143

She twists the hoops, and the skin screams for her to stop, but my balls pull tight. I grip her shoulder and hold my orgasm back. I don't want to come. Not yet.

"Do you think you deserve it?"

"Yes," I answer honestly, and her hand leaves my cock. "What? No, come back. Keep doing that." I grab her hand, but she yanks it away, and right as I look down, she's kissing the head, dipping her tongue through the hoops. "Oh, fuck." My head falls back onto my shoulders, and I stare at the starry night, enjoying her soft kissing on each bar she finds.

"You don't deserve pain, Knives." Her words are soft puffs of air that dance over the sensitive flesh. "If you want pain because you like it, that's one thing, but I won't give you pain because you think you deserve it. That's not pleasure, Knives. That's torture. I don't want to torture you."

"You are. Right now, you're torturing the hell outta me—" my words are cut short when she sucks the tip into her mouth, lapping her tongue along the slit. "Oh, fuck. Sweetheart, you feel so goddamn good." She's trepidatious as she takes me to the back of her throat. It's obvious she's never done this before, and hell, if that doesn't have me wanting to spill down her throat and watch my come drip from her lips.

She gags, chokes, but then hums, then grips my ass to pull me closer. Her nose is buried in my trimmed patch of hair as she sucks me, her tongue licking and playing with the piercings like she's experimenting with a lollipop.

I'll be her goddamn sucker anytime she wants. "Fuck, Hellraiser. Is this what I've been missing out on this entire time? I thought the only thing this mouth could do was bitch." I bury a hand in her hair and close my eyes, enjoying the hot mouth taking me better than anyone ever has before.

She bites down in response to my words, and I grunt, getting the picture that it is her way of telling me to shut up. "Do that again," I say, surprised that I liked getting my cock bit.

I can tell she's confused by the wrinkle appearing in her forehead, but she does it anyway, and the bars rub together from the pressure, then her tongue twirls around me, and I'm fucking lost. Tingles spread down my spine, and the threat of pouring down her throat is becoming a real possibility.

But I want to be inside her.

I pull out of her mouth and shove her to the ground, covering her lips with mine. Her mouth is red, swollen, and spit is everywhere. It's a sloppy kiss, but knowing her mouth is wet from sucking me has me manic.

I nudge her legs apart and settle between them, pressing my cock between her folds, I rock. She cries out as the piercings rub over her clit. I can't help the smirk that appears on my lips. As much as I want to be inside her, I want to feel the slickness of her lips hugging me while I bring her to orgasm fucking her clit.

"Knives. Oh my god." Her body jerks, and her hands fly above her head. It's like she doesn't know what to do with her body.

I glance down, watching the tip peek from between her sheath with every rock. I speed up, needing her to orgasm before I slide inside.

I'm not ashamed to admit this, but I'm not going to last long. I've never felt this intensity before with someone. It's always been about sex, never about anything else, and with Mary, it's everything else.

"Knives!" My name reverberates in the room. It's music to my ears to hear her voice crying out for me over and over again while she comes. Her back arches, her mouth falls open, and her legs shake around me as the hold she has around my hips weakens.

"Fucking finally," I growl, and this time when I rock back, I thrust inside. The balls from the piercings rub against her velvety walls, and I have to give myself a minute to calm down. If I move, I'm going to come.

And there is no fucking way in hell I'm going to have this end that quick. I want this moment to last all fucking night. Or for the next two weeks. If she's in bed with me for fourteen days, then nothing can happen to her, right? Just mind-blowing orgasms.

"Move," she begs, her fingers digging into the flesh of my ass.

"Not yet." I lower myself onto my elbows and steal another kiss.

"I said move, damn it."

"And I said no," I huff.

"I want to feel you."

"I'm going to come. Do you want that? I don't want this to end so damn fast, but you seem to have a negative effect on me!"

"Then fuck me through it!"

God, she really pisses me off. "You want to be fucked?" I flip her over onto her stomach and hold her head down. "Then I'll fuck you." I pull out and slam home. Her ass shakes from the constant pounding. "You want to feel me fill you up? You want me to lose control?"

"Yes! Fuck yes, I do," she moans, thrusting her ass back.

Her pretty puckered hole winks at me, and without a second thought, while I'm driving into her vise of a cunt, I stick my finger into my mouth. I let it go with a pop, rim her hole with my fingertip, and her hips stutter.

I'm not going to give her time to give me any more of her mouth. She's going to shut the fuck up for once in her life and take what I give her. I shove my index finger knuckle deep. "I'm going to take this ass too. Every fucking hole, Hellraiser. I'm going to stretch you out and ruin you for everyone else." Sweat drips into my eyes, and my hair falls over my forehead. I stare down at where we are connected and love how my dick is shining with her juices.

She rises up and hooks her arm around my neck. "You feel so good. I love your cock. I love the piercings," she gasps on a heavy breath.

She's out to kill me.

I spin her around, keeping us locked together, and bite her bottom lip. I'm fucking angry with how much I want her. I'm not close enough. This isn't enough. I growl as I let go, then, like a savage, seal our lips. I fall to my haunches, grip the meat of her ass, and use the new leverage to grind her against me.

She whimpers, and I moan; her sounds are a symphony playing down my throat. She groans with every rock, every thrust.

And I come.

My body becomes rigid, and I toss my head back and shout, relishing in every spurt coating her insides. She falls against me just as her inner muscles spasm, and her teeth lock onto my shoulder as she stifles her own cries while she orgasms.

I don't stop either.

I fuck her through it and hold onto her tightly, letting my forehead fall against her chest with every up and down motion of her pussy.

I can't lose this. I can't lose her.

CHAPTER FOURTEEN

Mary

I wake up in my bed, and if it wasn't for the soreness between my legs, I would have thought last night was a dream. I can't remember how I got here, but I'm not going to question it because the night I had with Knives is something that can never be explained, just felt. The intensity we shared, the passion, the sweat…

I've never been so slick in my entire life

I yawn, stretching my arms over my head, and groan when certain spots on my body hit me with a pinch of pain. I'm definitely bruised.

It was worth it.

I sit up and notice I'm alone. His side of the bed is cold as I lay my hand against the pillow. He's been gone a while, then. I'm not too sure how I feel about that. Waking up alone after the night we shared, I don't want it to be devastating, but it is. Maybe I was just another girl to him, after all?

"So stupid." I fall backward and sink into the pad of my mattress. My eyes burn, and I press my palms against my eyes to hold back the tears. I should have known better. A biker like Knives doesn't do relationships. He has club whores and anyone he wants, really. Not that the club whores are something to be worried about right now, since none of them are around. It's been too dangerous, and they don't want to risk getting killed like their friends.

I thought they were my friends too, but the moment things got rough, they bolted, and I realized I'm nothing like that. Sure, I ran away after dealing with my dad, but that's different. I would never run away from my family. My *real* family. Whores aren't family, are they? That's why none of the guys ever touched me. I was more to them than that, and it makes me happy knowing I had a place to call home this entire time I was trying to find a home.

The only person that's been missing is Becks. She has been gone a while now, but at this point, I'm starting to wonder if she's ever coming back. She seems like the nomad type, not to stay in place for too long because she gets restless. I miss her, and I hope she's doing well since I haven't heard from her.

"Hey, what's wrong?"

I put my arm down from my eyes and gape at Knives, who is holding a tray of food. The smell of coffee and bacon has me sitting up, clutching the blanket to my chest. "I thought you left."

"I did leave," he says, tilting his head in confusion. "I wanted to make you breakfast. I can't say it will be good. There might be an eggshell in the eggs, but I tried."

I love him. He's so different from what I thought he was. "You didn't have to do that," I say, scooting over to make room for him on the bed.

"I wanted to," he says, placing the tray on my lap. "You deserve breakfast in bed." He pushes my hair off my

149

shoulder, then tucks it behind my ear before tapping the tip of my nose with his finger.

"Well, if I eat an eggshell, I'm sure it will taste so good."

"Aw, I hope you choke on it."

I gasp, taking the fork and pretending to stab him in the arm. "Brat."

"I'm kidding. There is only one thing I want you to choke on, and it sure as hell isn't breakfast," he lowers his voice.

I shove his shoulder, and he slips off the bed, landing on the floor with a hard thump. "Oh my god, Knives. Are you okay?" I move the tray to the side and slip off the edge of the mattress. I land on his lap, straddling him, and lean down to give him a kiss. "I'm so sorry. I didn't mean to shove you off."

"Sure you didn't," he grunts, laying his tattooed hands on my hips.

"I really didn't. What can I do to make it up to you?"

He opens one eye, the intense color of ice freezing my veins as he deliberates. "Well," he starts to say, before rocking against my sore center. I moan suggestively when I feel his erection, right as my damn stomach grumbles.

"That's embarrassing. Way to ruin the moment, right?"

"No. My woman needs to be fed. I think we might have skipped dinner last night, but make no mistake, when you're done, I'm fucking you, Hellraiser."

I bite my lip, then slide off his lap and climb back on the bed, swaying my ass in the air to drive him crazy.

"Don't tempt me," he growls, slapping my ass to get me to sit down, but that only makes me hotter. "You're going to be the death of me. Eat your food." He picks up a piece of bacon and shoves it in my mouth. I moan in appreciation as the salt bursts over my tongue, along with a hint of maple.

"There you go again, making those fucking noises. Is the bacon really that good?" He takes a bite and nods. "Okay, it's debatable."

I laugh, scooping up a spoonful of eggs, and just swallow. I don't want to risk biting into an eggshell. If I do, I might not be able to eat the rest of my breakfast. We fall into a comfortable silence, eating our food, and enjoying small touches between each other. Every now and then, he will place his hand on my knee or feed me a grape, and those little gestures, the small ones that everyone overlooks, are everything to me.

A man like Knives doesn't give his touch away to anyone, not like this.

"When you said you thought I left, you really meant that you *thought* I *left*."

I take that moment to bite down on a damn eggshell. But I don't make a face, I don't gag, I hold my breath and swallow, because he took time out of his morning to make me food. I grab the coffee and sip, washing down the hard bits and pieces of the shell. I nod, then push the eggs around the plate. "I know, I shouldn't have, but I woke up, sore and happy, then I felt for you, and you weren't there."

He places two fingers under my chin and forces me to turn my head. "Listen to me," he says, his hair wet from a shower. He is out of his onesie now, dressed in faded blue jeans, a t-shirt, and his cut. "I'm not going anywhere. I need you to believe that." He slides his hand over mine, and I love the differences. My skin is naked compared to his. He has a large red flower on one hand; his knuckles are decorated in traditional stars and letters.

He's so different from me on the outside, but we are the same on the inside, and that's all that matters.

"You're used to a certain kind of woman, Knives," I tell him.

"No, I'm not. I'm not used to any kind of woman, because I never got to know a woman like I've gotten to know you over the last few months. No woman drives me crazy the way you do, and no woman turns me on like you do. No woman has ever brought me to my knees so fast. I'm

151

not someone who gets scared, Mary, but what Seer said scared the hell out of me."

"Nothing is going to happen to me."

"Everything he said has come true so far."

"Remember what we said last night," I say. I want to change the subject. I don't want to talk about this anymore. If I die saving Knives, then I died for someone that matters. What better way is there to die? "How is Maximo?"

"He's still strapped to the chair. His brother, Moretti, is there too. Even if Moretti doesn't remember Maximo and his daughter, he says he remembers how he feels, so they are talking about Natalia."

"Is it really necessary to keep him down there? He is three fingers less," I point out. "And it isn't like he is truly the bad guy. He isn't my father. I feel like that's where the attention needs to be."

"He turned his back on the club. Reaper isn't sure what to do with him."

I hand him the tray, and Knives places the empty plate and tray on the dresser. "I know what to do with you," I say in a low purr, rubbing my hand over the bulge behind his zipper.

"Is that right?" His hands fall to my ass and grip the cheeks. "How are you feeling?"

"Sore," I whisper, licking up his neck. "But in the best way."

"You want me again? Is your pussy greedy for my cock, Hellraiser?"

My aching hole flutters with need, wanting nothing more than to be stretched by his cock. I want to feel the piercings rub against that spot inside me. I want to feel him pour inside me again. I rock my bare pussy against his jeans, wetting them with the liquid lust he causes to erupt from me.

"Fuck. This is going to be quick. I need you too fucking much," he says, dipping his hands between us to free himself. The heavy head slaps against my clit the moment he is free, and the hoops leave a slight sting behind. I toss my head back and moan and rub my slit over his flesh, similar to what he did to me last night.

I don't know what it is about it but feeling him against me like this turns me on so much that I know if we only did this, I could climax. "Oh, you feel so good, baby." I quicken my speed, chasing every spark that ignites through my body after his cock rubs over my clit.

"I need more. Fuck this," he growls, and when I'm about to slide down, he shoves himself inside me, pushing in to the hilt, sending an electric surge all the way up my entire body.

"Look at you," he admires me by sliding his hands over my breasts and stomach. Every scratch of his hands, every glide of his cock, every breath heating the skin of my neck from his lips, I fall.

I fall into him.

I fall in love with him.

I fall for him.

"I'm going to come, Hellraiser," he growls, fucking me so hard the bed slides across the floor and the mattress groans. "Come with me." His fingers twist and pluck my clit, electrifying me, and my arms spread out just as my back bows and my orgasm possesses me.

He groans deep in his throat, a sound of pure pleasure as he feels my release dripping down his shaft. In three more thrusts, he plants himself inside me, emptying his warmth as deep as biology allows him to go.

"Nothing feels better than you. You've fucked me up, Mary. You got me all tangled up in your web."

"I understand your demon dick now," I gasp, shoving my hair off my sweaty face as I fall onto the bed.

My body shakes as he laughs. "My what?"

"Your demon dick. 666. It possesses me," I gasp, swallowing to coat my dry throat.

His laugh his loud, shaking my breasts as he lays his head on my chest, his fingers digging into my sides. "Demon dick, huh? I've never heard it called that before."

"I thought you named it that because of the tattoo."

"I just wanted the tattoo, but now that I think about it, it makes sense, and you're inflating my ego, so please don't stop talking."

"Shut up."

"You shut up," he says with a smile, then starts tickling my sides. "You."

"No! No!" I scream, shouting with laughter as he tickles me from my armpits to my hips. His cock is still inside me, and every time I try to get away, he hardens again. "Oh my god, I give. I give."

"Tell me you love me, and I'll stop."

"Wh—" my words are broken as I come down from the tickle high. "What?"

"Tell me you love me, and I'll stop." His face gets serious, the fun expression is gone, and the serious mask falls over him. His blue eyes aren't as inviting. Like if he doesn't hear the answer he wants, he might kill me instead.

Loving him might kill me anyway.

"I love you," I say to him, pressing my hand to his cheek.

"Really? You aren't just saying that because I asked you to say it?"

"Well, yeah," I pluck a few hairs on his chest when the excitement falls from his face. "Hey, you know I do. I think I have for a long time. Why?"

"I've never been loved before, so I wanted to know if you did. I love you too, you know. And if you didn't, I'd make you love me."

"You wouldn't ever have to make me. I simply, just... do."

A knock comes from the door, ruining the sweet moment we are having. I was ready to jump on that demon dick again and go for another ride after he admitted he loved me.

"Go away!" Knives says, licking his lips as he pulls out of me, only to slide back in, which steals my ability to breathe.

"Knives, Mary, you're going to want to come out here."

Knives' head falls on my stomach and mutters something I can't understand.

"Slingshot, we will be out in a minute," I holler.

"Knives, you're going to want to load up," Slingshot warns, and that gets Knives' attention.

He lifts up and pulls out, grumbling in discontent, and if I'm not mistaken, whimpers when he stares at my pussy. "One of these days, we are going to stay in bed all day. I'm going to fuck this mouth—" he rubs his fingers over my lips, "—this pussy," he slaps between my legs and my legs tremble, "—and this ass." His finger rims the forbidden hole, teasing me. "I want to own every inch of you."

"You do, Knives. You do. More than anyone ever has."

He brings my knuckles to his mouth and gives me a kiss. "Come on, let's go see what is in store for us and why I need to pack heat."

"Oh, you're packing heat."

He swats my ass as I get up, and my cheeks hurt from grinning so much. He stands up and tucks himself in his jeans, careful as he zips. "Why don't you go without me? I'll catch up," I say, opening a drawer to pull out a simple yet sexy black pair of panties.

"You are not wearing those out there."

"I wouldn't just be wearing these," I say with a roll of my eyes. "I'll be wearing pants."

"Yes, but then I'd know you're wearing them, and then I won't be able to focus on being the big bad man they want me to be, because all I'll be able to think about is the sexy underwear you have on."

"You'll live."

He crosses his arms and watches me get dressed. His eyes stay heated as I slide on a pair of jeans, taking my sweet time, so I torture him. I throw on a shirt, then my leather jacket, put my hair up, and go brush my teeth. When I'm in the restroom, I spray on perfume and apply my red lipstick. I'm not sure what it is about it, but it makes me feel empowered.

I walk out of the bathroom, and Knives' fists clench. "You do this just to test me."

I rub a finger down his chest as I strut away from him and head toward the bedroom door. "I have no idea what you're talking about."

Oh, but I do.

I love testing him.

CHAPTER FIFTEEN

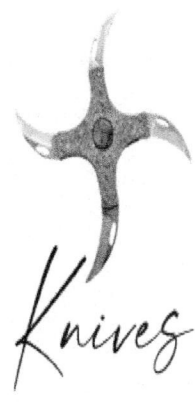

Knives

I stop by my bedroom and grab a few ninja stars per Slingshot's request. Mary is behind me, safe and alive, and it's hard not to think about what waits for us in 13 days. She's so nonchalant about it, and it irks me.

I don't care what we have to do. I don't care if I have to lock her in jail 13 days from now; she isn't going to be anywhere near me. I'll make damn sure of that. "You ready to go see what the fuss is about?" I ask her, noticing how I don't like that her leather jacket doesn't have my property patch on it

Holy shit.

The pain in my ass is the love of my life.

Go fucking figure.

I want my name tattooed on her too. I want there to be no doubt who she belongs to. Everyone here knows, but everyone out there in the world doesn't. One look at the woman tattooed on my arm, and then one look at the woman by my side, makes it obvious I belong to her. I want it to be obvious that she belongs to me.

"Yeah, the voices are getting louder, so that can't be good," she says.

I wrap my arm around her shoulder as we walk down the hallway to the main room, and saying the voices are getting louder is an understatement.

Reaper and Mercy are going at each other's throats.

Whistler is behind Mercy, gripping someone by the back of the neck that has seen much better days. One, Whistler's righthand man, has a gun aimed at the stranger's head.

"Go in the room with the other girls, Mary. I'll get you when it's safe."

She nods at me, giving me big round Hershey's kiss eyes when Reaper turns around and points at her. "She stays!" His booming voice has her flinching.

Mercy shakes his head and says something, but I can't hear it since Tool shoves him from behind, which starts a fucking brawl. Mercy rears his fist back and punches Tool, which dislodges the screwdriver from his ear, and it clatters to the floor. Tyrant latches onto Whistler's arm, and Yeti is in front of Tool, growling so deep, drool starts to drip off his canines.

Another one of Whistler's men, Socks, according to his patch, gets a hard hit from Skirt. Socks stumbles back, and before I can pull Mary back, he slams into her, knocking her off her feet. Her head bounces against the wall, and her eyes roll back.

"Mary!" I dive for her, gathering her in my arms before she can hit the floor.

Okay. Now I'm fucking pissed. "Enough!" I yell, flinging a star across the room until it lands right in Whistler's shoulder. I throw another before anyone can think, making sure the next one lands in Socks. The fucker.

Everyone stops yelling, and Doc comes from the kitchen, wiping his hands off after dealing with Maximo, and squats down to check on Mary. "I've got her," he whispers.

I stand slowly, wanting to kill everyone in the room. "What the fuck is going on?"

Something hits me on the forehead, and I see Slingshot across the room, hiding the slingshot behind his back, pointing at Patrick, who then throws a bag of skittles in his face. One annoying MC brother at a time.

"You fucking got me with a ninja star," Whistler groans, leaning against the couch. "I knew you were good with them, but holy shit." He cups the star and has to let go of the guy he has a hold of, but he stays right where he is, so he isn't a prisoner. "Someone get this fucking thing out of me."

"Not a chance in hell," Bullseye says from behind him, then moves to the side and flicks the star, pulling a hiss from Whistler. "Whoops."

"Knives, Mary is fine. She's just knocked out," Doc informs me.

"Just knocked out? She wouldn't be knocked out if everyone in the room could act civil."

"Knives, that was before Mercy came to our doorstep and said he had information on Mary's father. Apparently, the FBI has been investigating him for a while now," Reaper says.

I stomp forward and press a star under Mercy's chin before he can blink. "Are you even good at your job? He abused her for twelve years. Twelve. Where were you and your agents?"

"I'm sorry, I didn't know that," he says, the crinkles around his eyes not only showing age, but sorrow. I hate that I know he is sincere. "I hope we can take him down. He has really built a name for himself over the years." Mercy looks toward the guy they brought in, who has a black hood over his head. "He can help."

159

"Why is he hooded?" Patrick asks, popping a peanut in his mouth. Ever since he stopped drinking, Patrick has been eating his weight in peanuts. I think it helps him stay off the bottle.

"That's One's doing. He said he didn't like how 'sad' the guy looked."

"I don't like sad people. They freak me out," One says, shrugging a shoulder as he holsters his weapon.

"This fucking star hurts! Get it out," Socks yells.

"No one help him. He is the reason why Mary is knocked out," I say.

"Yeah, suffer, asshole," Bullseye grumbles, and he and I tap knuckles.

Mercy rips the star from Whistler's shoulder, and the guy's knees buckle while he rolls his lips together to hold in the pain. "Thanks," he says on a held breath.

Mercy side-eyes me and tosses my star to me, then rips off the black hood from the guy. "I believe you know each other," Mercy states. "Thomas, this is your brother. Mason."

Blood rushes to my head. My heart beats so fast; I'm positive it is about to pump right out of my chest. "That's impossible." I stumble, and Reaper catches me. My world tilts as I become dizzy, memories flood my mind, and his death plays over and over again in my head at the speed of light in this very moment.

"Thomas," Mason says my name with a familiarity that only a brother would. He struggles to get out of One's hold, but he can't. "Let go of me. Thomas, it's me. It's Mason. I swear to god, it's me."

"No," I shake my head. "No!" I yell. I can't breathe. I can't fucking breathe. I gasp for air, pressing my hands to my head when the pressure becomes too unbearable. "You can't be. You can't. I watched you die! I saw it."

"It's me. You always take responsibility for your actions," he says, tilting my crooked world back into place.

160

Only Mason would know the very last words we ever said to one another.

"You can't be real," I whisper, my hands shaking. I glance over to Mary, needing her more than ever right now, but she's still unconscious. "You died."

"Yeah, that's a long story," Mercy says. "He's been an FBI agent for a while now. He's been undercover for Mary's father."

There are so many questions.

"Who is Mason?" Slingshot asks, popping a skittle in his mouth. Everyone turns to him and stares from his poorly timed question. "What? What'd I say? Oh, please. As if no one else is curious?"

"Mason was my foster brother. I watched him die when I was fifteen, after he killed three guys that constantly bullied me. That's how I know this is wrong." I point to the man calling himself Mason, then to Mercy. "You have it wrong. This man no longer exists. And if he was safe, why is he zip-tied?"

"That's Zip-tie's doing," Mercy says. "No one trusts anyone." He snatches my ninja star from my hand and sliced the thick plastic, so the stranger's hands are free. The guy that says he is Mason.

"I need to go. I need to clear my head."

"Thomas—"

I silence Mason with a quick punch to the jaw, then another, and once he is off-balance, I slip a star into my hand from my cut pocket—the one I made out of the knives I found on the road all those years ago—and throw it as hard as I possibly can through the air. I've never thrown a star so hard in my life, but I'm so fucking mad.

So fucking hurt.

The star veers to the right, away from harming his heart, which is too fucking bad. It lodges deep into the muscle of his shoulder. Mason stumbles back and holds his hand to the wound. Blood is spilling, but he'll live.

161

"I deserve that," he says, as if we haven't gone years without talking. As if I haven't gone every day without mourning my brother. As if I didn't visit his grave every single fucking day and wish like hell I had been in his place instead.

"You deserve that?" I ask, taking a step toward him, then back, because I don't want to be anywhere near him right now. I still don't believe it's really him. "This is a fucking joke, right? You expect me to believe my dead brother has worked for the FBI all these years? What... he faked his death and wasn't allowed to tell anyone? And then, boom, coincidence, he works for my ol' lady's father? Get the fuck out of here."

"It's all true. Every last bit of it," Mercy says. "It's a long story about how we found him, but—"

"—There are no buts," my throat burns as I yell. "And I don't give a fucking shit. You've been dead to me twenty years. You can be dead for another twenty." I stalk forward and yank the star from his shoulder and start to walk out the door, then pause. I turn back to Mercy. "How long have you known? Have you known the entire time?"

"No, just recently. When I got put on the case, they gave me the file," he says. "I'm sorry you had to find out like this, but Mason is our best lead to bring down her father."

"No, Seer is."

"We checked all the hotels with the letter M, and he wasn't there Knives. Mason might be our best bet," Reaper acknowledges.

"I would rather die than ever ask for his help. A person that would lie to his brother about being alive... all this time, knowing he was all I had, and still chose to leave me alone?" I lock stares with him, and Mason steps forward, holding his hand to his shoulder.

I hold up my hand and shake my head. "Don't. Nothing you say will ever make me forgive you. Any information you have for Mary and about her father, tell Reaper. They will update me. I don't want to hear a thing from you. And fuck you, Mercy," I add for the hell of it.

Fucking, fuck everyone.

"Doc, call me when she wakes up, and I'll come right back. I need to clear my head. I don't want her to think I left her. I'd *never* leave anyone I care about. I'll always be back." I run out the front door, ashamed to admit that not only am I angry, but I have tears in my eyes. I am feeling a hundred emotions.

A part of me is happy that he is alive. Holy shit, my brother is alive, but a part of me feels stupid. I feel like that little boy again who knew nothing about the world, and I hate it. I have worked my ass off to not be that boy, yet here I am. Once again, Mason is showing up to be the knight in fucking shining armor, and I'm left to watch him save the day from a distance.

I pause at where I usually park my bike to see the spot empty. I'm confused for a second, wondering where the hell my bike went, only to remember it's burnt to a crisp on the side of the road, so I can't go for a ride.

"Sonofabitch!" I scream at the top of my lungs. I don't need to ride like this anyway. Riding angry is never a good thing; that's how accidents happen. You become more careless and not as aware of your surroundings. I need to be here for Mary when she wakes up anyway.

"Everything okay, Knives?" Braveheart pops his head from the security shed where he controls the gate.

"Does it sound like everything is okay, Braveheart?" I snap at the kid, feeling bad. None of this is his fault. I rub a hand over my face, trying to get my bearings. "I'm sorry, Braveheart. I didn't mean to snap."

"It's okay," he says, his large Adam's apple bobbing as he gulps. He is wearing his glasses today, which reminds me of when he first started to prospect for the club. He usually wears contacts these days, so seeing him wearing the black frames makes me remember a doofy kid who had no idea what his strengths were.

He is a lot like Skirt, more of a scrapper than a professional fighter, but holy hell, Braveheart has the heart of a lion. It surprises me because he is tall and lean, a bit awkward too.

"Well, if you ever want to talk…" He lets the words hang out as bait, and I wonder if I should take him up on it. I'm still riled up from the tension in the clubhouse. It might be good to talk to someone who isn't pissed off either. "I have hooch," he says, holding out a bottle of whiskey.

"You dog. What the hell are you doing with that?" Warmth firing down my throat is just what I need.

"We can't have any near Patrick, which is fine, but out here, I get bored and cold. Whiskey helps."

"You know you don't have to stay out here, right? Please, tell me someone told you that."

"Um…" he pushes his glasses up the bridge of his nose and twists the cap off the whiskey. He gulps it down and coughs from the spice of the whiskey. "No…" he admits, and his blatant oblivion has me tossing my head back and laughing. Oh my god, the poor bastard.

I take the whiskey from him and shake the bottle at him before sighing and take a swallow. "I needed that. Braveheart, man, you don't have to protect the gate at all times."

"Yes, I do. Too much shit has happened. Too many people have hurt us. I'm here. Night and day. I watch the road. I watch the gate. I don't want anyone to hurt my family again."

He feels guilty. He doesn't look at me. He doesn't have to. I see it in his profile as he stares down the road. Braveheart's jaw is tight, and he stuffs his hands in his jacket pocket. It's cold out here, lonely, and he feels obligated to protect us.

164

"You haven't done anything wrong," I tell him, setting the bottle on the shelf in front of him. "These people, they come at us from all angles, from every aspect. Whatever happens here, it is not your fault. You should be inside with everyone. Believe me when I say, there is no obligation here to waste your life away in a fucking shed when there are people who care about you inside, Braveheart. Tank is in there, bless his damn teddy bear soul, he jumps when Happy is near. He doesn't have a brave bone in his body."

That makes Braveheart smile. "And what about you?" he asks. "Why aren't you inside?"

"Because someone is in there that's been dead to me for a long time. I need a minute to wrap my head around it."

"Oh, the guy Mercy brought in?"

"Yeah. He has information on Mary's dad, but how can I trust him? How did he get into the FBI? Why didn't he tell me? What if he wasn't on our side? Does he know anything about Maximo and why the hell he is working for Preacher Man?"

Braveheart blows out a breath, and frozen particles fill the air as he thinks about what to say. He lifts his feet up, placing them on the shelf to get comfortable. "Those are a lot of questions, Knives. Questions only he knows the answers to."

"I don't want to talk to him, Braveheart. I don't think I can."

"For Mary?" he asks me. "Maybe don't do it for you. Do it for her. After all this is said and done, you don't have to talk to him again."

And the thought of that hurts like hell too. "Give me that." I steal the bottle away from him again and take another swig. "Don't let Patrick see this."

"No, I keep it locked up like Prez says to do. If Maximo went behind our backs, if he's as slimy as I think he is, what would happen?"

"War," I say, the word causing my stomach to turn. A lot of lives would be lost. "Moretti needs to remember. If he can get his memory back, I think we would know a lot more than what we do. Right after our partnership solidified, the hotel explosion happened, and we weren't able to grow like we wanted to. Maximo came and changed everything."

"Something is up with him, Knives. I'll be honest, and I've never said this out loud, but I don't think he can be trusted. Every move he makes, every time he speaks, I don't understand how Reaper can look past the obvious. He has to know Maximo is not on our side. He has to."

"Reaper has a lot to think about right now. He is trying to keep the peace. We have families here."

"Either way, they are in danger until the threat is neutralized."

"Yeah," I agree. The more I think about his words, the more they resonate with Mary. The club isn't my only family anymore; Mary is too. Until her threat is taken care of, she will always be in danger.

"Oh, before I forget." Braveheart ducks back into his shed and grabs a package, handing it over to me. "This came in the mail for you."

I raise an eyebrow in curiosity and rip open the package. It's my new phone. Finally. With everything going on, at least something went right today.

"Thanks, Braveheart." I don't just mean for the phone, but by the look we give each other, I'm sure he understands what I mean.

"Anytime, Knives."

I turn on my heel and head to the clubhouse, sucking up all my pride and all my pain to go take care of Mary.

Mason is dead. My past has no say here.

It's all about Mary and how I can make sure she's safe.

CHAPTER SIXTEEN

Ow.

"Holy crap," I say on a held breath as I start to rouse. My head is killing me. I feel like I got hit with a bat.

I did see Whistler...

But no, that's not what happened.

"Hellraiser."

I wince as I look left to see Knives sitting in a chair, and he looks so relieved to see me awake. "What happened?"

"Someone ran you over, and you tripped and hit your head."

"You worried us," Sarah says from the bed next to me. "Sorry, I'm down here for monitoring for the little chipmunk, since I've been having some pain."

"Oh no, is everything okay? Is the baby okay?" I ask her in a hurry.

"I'm fine. I have to take it easy. The muscles in my stomach never healed properly after being shanked—"

"—Don't say it like that. It isn't funny," Tongue says out of the darkness… somewhere. And his statement is followed by a hiss.

That is terrifying. I'm glad I woke up to Knives next to me.

"Anyway, he might be hard to carry to term because I won't have the muscle strength for my stomach to grow, and it will mess with my hips and pelvis."

Tongue comes out from the far corner and walks by us, head down, and heads upstairs with Happy strapped to his chest.

"Tongue! I'm going to be—" but Tongue shuts the door before she can finish her sentence. "Okay." She lays her hand on her stomach, which is still flat. If I remember correctly, she isn't that far along, and she's already having issues. I'm sure she's scared.

"Okay, Sarah. Everything looks good. No exercise," says Doc.

Sarah purses her lips and narrows her eyes. "Define exercise."

Doc rubs his temples and then places his hands in a steepled position under his nose. "No rough sex. Nothing that will strain the muscle in your stomach. Keep it vanilla. Extra vanilla. I'll have a talk with Reaper."

Sarah groans dramatically and falls back on the bed. "Vanilla? No one likes vanilla here, Doc."

"Oh, me so sad for you," Doc pouts.

"You're mean."

"You'll thank me when you're holding your baby for the first time."

Sarah gets this wistful look in her eye as she lays her hand on her belly, but the moment is ruined when loud, pounding steps hurry down the basement stairs. It's Reaper. His eyes are wide, and he seems scared. "Doll? What's wrong? Why are you down here? What happened? Is the baby okay? Are you okay? Why didn't anyone come and get me!" he roars, and the stainless steel walls vibrate from the loud boom.

"Oh my god, no," Reaper leans against the wall, defeated, broken, and his eyes water. "We lost the baby? Sarah..." He turns around and punches a hole in the wall, and everyone is so shocked from the quick conclusion that he made that no one speaks up to calm him down.

"Reaper, no. Oh my god, no. The baby is okay," Sarah says, swinging her legs over the bed to stand. She pulls the stickers that connect to the monitors off her stomach and tugs her shirt down and runs over to him. Her hand lands in the middle of his back, and he pulls her in front of him to where we can't see her anymore because his body covers hers.

"You're okay. The baby is okay?"

I turn away from them, my heart breaking for Reaper and Sarah. The relief, fear, and tremble in his throat has my eyes burning.

"I was having some pain, and you were in a meeting. It wasn't the same kind of pain as before," Sarah explains. "The muscles in my stomach didn't heal like they should have and carrying can be complicated and dangerous. Doc wants to keep a close eye on me. Very close. But the baby is healthy. And... Doc found something I think you'll really like. Want to hear it?"

Reaper doesn't say anything, and I watch as Sarah drags him to the bed where she was sitting moments ago. I squeeze Knives' hand, and for some reason, I feel really lucky to be a part of this moment with them. Knives kisses my temple and brings his lips to my ear, "I want that with you."

"Really?" I say, holding back from tackling him to the ground and getting to work on a family. I never thought this would happen. I thought I'd always be at my dad's mercy, but I ran, thinking I was running toward death, when really it led me right here, to freedom

"Really."

I'm about to ask what changed when Doc squirts the jelly on her stomach and rolls over an ultrasound machine.

Reaper is holding her hand, his entire body shaking. It's hard to see this big bad man, the President of the Ruthless Kings, become emotional and afraid. Knives leans over and slaps Reaper on the back, giving him an encouraging nod.

A gesture that everything will be okay, but I can tell Reaper doesn't believe it.

Doc places the wand on Sarah's stomach and points. "Okay, Reaper. Do you see this area? It's grey."

"Yeah," he chokes.

"That's the muscle. It's fragile, but it isn't in the worst shape. Down here—" Doc sides the wand further down and searches for something specific. "Where is it…" he continues to try, and then a fast whoosh takes over the speakers.

Thumpthumpthumpthump.

"That's your baby's heartbeat, Reaper. Strong and healthy."

Reaper stares at Doc with watery eyes, and his cheeks turn red. "Yeah?"

"Yeah, Reaper. You want me to record it for you?"

Reaper nods, squeezing Sarah's hand so hard, I'm afraid he is going to break it. "Please, please, please. I want to hear it every day."

Even Doc is getting emotional.

"Sure thing," he says, pressing a few buttons. "And that little bean right there is your baby." He points to a little blob on the screen, and I can't tell it's a baby, but I believe Doc.

Reaper can't stop staring at the computer. He lifts his finger, grazing it over the white dot. He peers down at Sarah and lays his hand on her belly, cupping it with protection. The width of his palm covers her midsection, but it makes me hold my breath.

"Thank you," Reaper's voice breaks. "I love you so much, Doll." He pulls himself forward and kisses her senseless.

I can't help it. I'm a crying mess, and I start clapping. "Congratulations. I'm so happy for you guys."

"Mary," Knives rolls his eyes but keeps a smile on his face as he tries to lower my hands, but I shrug away and keep clapping. "They don't want a round of applause."

"Don't tell me what to do," I say out of the corner of my mouth, and Reaper takes a bow. "Yay! You did it."

"Yeah, we did." He doesn't say it in a cocky way, but a proud reassuring way. "Hey, Doc. Do you care if we stay down here for a while and watch the screen? I just... I'm not ready to leave yet."

"I'll say you two deserve it. Take as long as you need."

"When can we find out the sex?"

"I don't want to know," Reaper says. "It doesn't matter. Happy and healthy, that's all I want the two of you to be."

"Aw."

"Okay, Doc. I think she is having concussion symptoms," Knives says about me.

"I'm allowed to be happy for them. And aren't you supposed to be..." A pain shoots through my head when I think about the fight upstairs. "Isn't there something important you need to be doing? I can't remember what it is..."

"You missed all the important stuff," Doc says, flashing a light in my eyes to check my pupils. "You wouldn't have remembered it, so don't strain yourself. Knives' brother came back from the dead, and apparently, he worked with your dad because he is undercover FBI."

"What?" I stare at Knives, who is flipping a star across his knuckles. I snag it from him and hide it under my butt. "Mason is back? I thought you said—"

"He is. He was. I didn't know he was alive. I don't know if it is him."

171

"Would I know him?" I ask. "If he worked for my father?"

Knives' eyes go dark, and the clear crystal color replaces the bright blue, something that happens when he is pissed. "He better hope like hell he never ran into you, because I'll kill him all over again."

"Why aren't you talking to him?"

"Because you're more important. He can wait. Your dad can wait. You were hurt, and I want to be by your side. I want to make sure you're okay. When I know you're safe, I'll talk to him."

Moretti walks out of the playroom, and as he walks to a nearby bed, he leaves bloody footprints behind him.

Doc closes the playroom door right as Maximo screams.

"I don't think my brother is a good man," Moretti says. "I can't remember why, but I don't believe him when he says Mary's father took Natalia. Something in my gut tells me, Reaper."

"We will find out. I think tonight, everyone settles. Relax. Tomorrow, we try and get everything out of the way. We'll make a plan. Mary will be safe, and maybe, we can save a few others from his clutches too. It won't be easy, but nothing worth it ever is." Reaper rubs Sarah's stomach and closes his eyes to listen to the song of the heartbeat on the monitor.

"Congratulations, Reaper. I am happy for you," Moretti says, trying to smile, but his eyes are sad.

"I'm not going to let anyone hurt my family, and that includes your brother. I think he is trying to play us. I'm starting to wonder what else he is behind if he has his hand in this."

"I wish I could tell you," Moretti says, dropping his elbows to his knees. "I wish I knew."

I can't imagine not being able to remember anything. Every memory Moretti makes is one of his firsts. We are all he knows, and I'm wondering if that is why he has stayed here. I know Doc said he could leave, but he chooses not to.

"I swear, Reaper. If I remember anything, one tiny thing, I will let you know, but my head is dark. There is nothing. I want to protect him. He is my flesh and blood. He's my brother."

"I know," Reaper says with understanding, not only for his MC brothers but for his sister that surprised everyone for Christmas. "It isn't you I doubt, Moretti. Okay?"

Moretti nods, stands, and leaves. He is light on his feet as he climbs the steps to head toward his room.

"Seems like all the issues revolve around family," Knives says, tracing the spot where a ring would sit on my left hand. "Family can be a real pain in the ass, can't it?"

"You need to talk to him before getting information out of him," I offer, hoping he chooses to be put next to his issues and make himself a priority. "Talk to your brother before you talk to the agent side of him. You won't be able to talk if you don't ask the questions I know are rolling around in your head."

"You come first."

"Knives—"

"You come first. End of discussion, Mary. I love you, but please, do not push this. Mason might not be dead to any of you, but he is to me. The sooner we figure this out, the sooner he can leave."

I know Knives doesn't mean that. He is angry, and he has every reason to be, but we won't be able to move on. Knives will regret having Mason leave his life again. I can't push him though.

"And don't get me started on if he knows you. What if he helped your dad get to you every night?" Knives shakes his head and gets up from the chair, then lays down next to me. "It's something unforgivable. I'll kill him myself if I find that out."

I want to say Mason had nothing to do with me, but I don't know that, and I can't comfort Knives if I don't have the whole truth. Instead, I run my fingers through his hair and take Reaper's advice.

Tomorrow is a new day, but a voice in the back of my head whispers: Only twelve more.

CHAPTER SEVENTEEN

Knives

It's eight in the morning. Everyone is in Church. I've never seen every chair taken up before, but here we are. I sip my coffee, unable to bring myself to look at Mason, who is sitting right across from me. He's staring at me too. I can feel it, that invisible cloak blanketing me and the energy warping the hair along my arms, taunting me to look.

But I won't.

I won't give in.

He left me hanging for twenty years; he can deal with the fact that I've moved on from his death.

"Thomas," he says my name to get my attention, but I ignore him. Is it childish? Maybe. I feel like I have the right to be fucking mad. No. Mad isn't the word.

Devastated.

He was my only friend in the world, a person I thought would never betray me. He did what he said he'd never do: he betrayed me.

"Thomas, please, you have to talk to me. I know—"

Tongue slams his knife between Mason's index and middle finger. "He doesn't have to do a damn thing, Mason-jar. Keep asking him to talk; I'll feed your tongue to Happy. Your voice is fucking annoying."

Tongue yanks the blade from the wood and sneers at Mason. "And I don't give a damn that you know Knives. I stabbed my own brother, right in his tongue. If I can do that to him, imagine what I'll do to you." Tongue rubs the onyx blade against Mason's cheek, but Mason doesn't flinch.

A few other members trickle into the room and shut the door. My thoughts are on Mary. She's still downstairs recovering from the concussion Socks gave her. I'm worried about her, but instead of being there with her, I have to be here, because somehow, someway, my formerly dead brother is connected to Mary's father.

Small fucking world.

Too small.

If Earth had a twin planet, I'd take Mary and get the hell out of dodge because the way people are connected here makes me unsettled.

The gavel made of one of our first enemies slams on the table as Reaper calls Church into session. Everyone has a cup of coffee in front of them; the room fills with the aroma. Sips are the only thing that fills the silence.

I hate the quiet anyway. It's too loud, with endless bouts of possibilities and leaves me alone with my thoughts.

Can't have that.

"Okay," Reaper says, already pinching the bridge of his nose. "Before we start. You bastards are going to listen to something, and hopefully, some of the tension will be gone." He pulls out his cell phone, and I smile around the rim of my mug.

176

I know what he is going to do, but I'm not going to say anything. This is his moment, and he is proud and excited. He presses play, and the biggest, cheesiest, happiest fucking smile blooms across his face as his baby's heartbeat sounds in the room.

"That's my fucking kid. It's beautiful, isn't it?"

Everyone sitting around the table bangs on the wood, then cheers, all except for Mason because he isn't a part of this life and doesn't know what to do.

Now who's the outsider?

"Reaper, congratulations, man," Mercy says, holding out his hand.

"Thanks, Mercy."

"Way to go, Reaper!"

"Happy for you, Prez."

"I hope it is a girl, so she drives ye nuts," Skirt says from the back. For the first time in weeks, he doesn't have Joey strapped to his chest, and he seems a bit lost. Out of habit, his hands go to his chest, as if he feels her there, but then when he feels air, he scratches his pecs to play it off.

"Don't you dare, Skirt. I can't handle a girl. I'll kill all the boys."

"Aye, the boys," Skirt's voice darkens, becoming threatening. "I'm going to make them fight me to take Joey out on a date."

"You'll kill them, Skirt. How is that fair?"

"Ye don't fight fair, ye fight to win, and if they are smart boys, they will figure that out."

"Jesus, okay," Reaper says, pressing the mute button on his phone. When the heartbeat stops, he frowns, plays it again, and takes a breath.

I think Reaper is more afraid than he lets on. Losing their first child in a miscarriage fucked with him. It would mess with anyone, but now that Sarah is pregnant again, if he isn't listening to that heartbeat, for a moment, it's like he thinks it will vanish.

177

It's how he was all night. I don't think he slept.

"We need to get on track. We should hear from the FBI agents. They're the reason why we are all here, right?"

Mercy stands beside Reaper and gestures for Mason to get up. Tongue snarls in Mason's ear as he stands, trying to scare him, but Mason still doesn't react. I know Tongue is on a mission now. He will have to scare Mason, or he will be a nightmare for us all.

"Thomas—"

"Don't fucking talk to him," Tongue says, pushing Mason forward.

None of my MC brothers correct Tongue for what he did. Mason has found himself in the wolves' den, and I don't know if he will make it out alive.

Mercy clears his throat. "Okay, I know there is a lot of tension in the air. There are a lot of issues that need to be addressed. The first place to start is with you, Knives."

I finish off my coffee and smack my lips together, then throw the mug right as Mason's head. He dodges it, green eyes wide with shock. "I'd rather not, Mercy. Let's talk about how to save Mary."

"No. You'll be too pissed off. This needs to be addressed," Mercy says, "in order for this to go smoothly. Mason, explain."

Mason pulls out an extra chair from the corner, turns it around, and straddles it. Looks like some things don't change at all. It's the only way he sat in a chair when we were kids. Always too cool for school. "My name is Mason Fletcher. Thomas Underwood is my foster brother."

"Was. This isn't a fucking soap opera, Mason. Get on with it so we can move on to more important business."

"This is important. You want to know what happened to me? Do you remember Louis? Well, he was a kid of a drug lord. The cops? They just shot me, but they didn't kill me like they thought. I survived. I was in a coma, but when I woke up, I was somewhere else. Witness protection, so no one could find me. I couldn't come to you, Thomas. I wasn't allowed to."

I slam my fist on the table. "Bullshit! Bull-fucking-shit. I would have come to you. You were all I fucking had, Mason." I hit my chest. "I was alone."

"You went to the Kings."

"Good thing, because they became my family."

"That's what I wanted for you. I really thought I was dead, but when I woke up, I wanted to reach out, but I wasn't allowed. When I turned eighteen, I decided to be an agent and—"

"And you decided to leave me alone anyway. The witness protection was an excuse, but after that? It's been twenty years, Mason. Your excuses mean nothing to me now. You've been dead to me since I was fifteen, and you're still dead to me now."

I sit down, trying to calm my racing heart, and Tongue gives me a nod, a silent way to support me. I'm with my brothers. This is my home. My real home. I'm not with people that will abandon me. "And my name isn't Thomas. It's Knives," I correct him. "What do you know about Mary's father?"

"I've seen Mary—"

Before I can blink or inhale, I have a star in each hand, and I throw them.

Bam.

One in each shoulder.

"What the fuck!" he cries out.

Mercy gives me an annoyed, exasperated look and plucks the metal out of Mason's shoulder.

"You knew her? You knew and you let that happen to her?"

"I didn't know. I made sure she was safe and that she never made it to the underground auction house her father had."

179

"And the other women? What the fuck took so long to get the information you needed?"

"His name was never anywhere. We needed evidence. We had suspicions. A ton of suspicions. But he never does anything himself."

"Except when it comes to Mary," I sneer.

"Yeah, it's what led me here. I followed him, and the agency told me of a contact. I met Mercy, and they put Mercy on the case."

"Okay, do you have any useful information?"

"He and Maximo have been working together for a while. Your ally is not your ally, Reaper."

Reaper doesn't seem surprised, but he also doesn't seem like he believes it. He swings back and forth in his chair by keeping his legs on the ground and using the ground as leverage.

"Daphne," Tongue's voice is dark, demeaning, and holds a vow of murder. His knife stabs the table again, and this time he drags it down to the edge. His shoulders rise in rapid beats, and his tongue flicks out over his lip. He is practically vibrating in his chair to go downstairs and kill Maximo.

"Tongue, deep breaths," Reaper says, giving Tool a warning glance to make sure we are prepared to stop Tongue from leaving.

Tongue doesn't have the ability to control himself, not really, and not when it comes to Daphne. He is… obsessed with her. I would argue it's borderline unhealthy. He watches her constantly, but when he isn't near her, I notice she looks for him.

But he is always there in the darkness.

He loves her more than anything. More than this club, that I know for sure.

I understand. I feel that way—a healthy way—about Mary.

"He was going to take Daphne from me," Tongue says. "No one takes Daphne."

"Tongue, Daphne is safe, remember? She's here. She's in your bedroom, reading, probably. She's always reading," Reaper reminds him, trying to get through the haze that has glassed his eyes over.

When he remembers that Daphne is in his bedroom, he relaxes. "Daphne," he repeats, then brings the knife to his nose and smells it, which turns him into a smiling fool.

Why would he smell it?

"Okay, you have Maximo here, right?" Mason asks me.

Me.

I don't answer him, and Reaper gives me a warning glare.

"We have him."

"Fed Happy three of Maximo's fingers. Happy wasn't happy it wasn't a tongue, but he'll take any treats."

"What the fuck is a Happy?" Mason asks.

"My swamp kitty," Tongue says with a 'duh' tone.

Mason's brows pinch when he tries to think about what a swamp kitty is, but he stares at Reaper for more clarification.

At least he isn't staring at me.

"It's an alligator."

"You have an alligator here?" Mason straightens in his chair.

"Yep and if you try to do anything about it, I'll feed you to him," Tongue warns.

"Okay, we need a plan."

"Mary is the plan," Mason says. "She's bait. Use her, get her father, boom. Done."

I don't remember getting up. I don't remember walking to Mason.

All I know is right now, my hand is wrapped around his throat, and I slam the back of his head against the wall, kind of like how Mary hit her head last night. I lift Mason off the ground until his toes are barely touching the floor, and I hear a commotion behind me, but I'm too focused on Mason to give a damn. I tighten my grip, watching his face turn red, and the veins in his eyes pop. "I'm not that fucking kid

181

anymore, Mason. I'm not weak, so let me be clear to you when I say using Mary in any way is not an option. If you try to use her, I will fucking rip your spine from your body. You might be used to running the show, but here, you don't fucking matter."

"Let go, Knives."

I turn around to see Mary at the door, her beautiful dark hair in a big nest on top of her head. She's sleepy. She's wearing sweatpants, a simple white tank top, and a grey zip-up jacket that hugs her curves.

"Mary, I won't risk you," I inform her in case she doesn't know.

"I'm offering."

I let go of Mason's throat, and the fucking silence in the room   deafens   me.

CHAPTER EIGHTEEN

Do I like the plan? No.

Should I have heard the plan? Also, no. No woman is allowed in Church unless they are invited, but I invited myself when I realized the meeting was mostly about me. I have a right to know, and I opened the door at the perfect time because Knives was choking his brother.

"You can't be serious. You're not thinking straight. You hit your head last night," Knives says, trying to make excuses for why I want to go ahead with the plan. I understand he's scared; I am too. My dad is a horrible man, and what if he does get his hands on me? What if the Ruthless Kings can't find me and I'm lost forever?

It's a chance I have to take. This isn't only about me; it's about all the women my father has sold, auctioning them off like they are pieces of antique furniture.

How long did he keep me prisoner, only to keep other women prisoner too? How can a man like my father get up every day pretending to preach faith, yet steal faith from others?

Mason is gasping for air, rubbing his throat, and staring at Knives with sorrow. He isn't angry. He isn't trying to attack; he just looks... sad. He has missed his brother.

"I wasn't allowed to contact anyone from my past, Knives. Ever. You have to understand," he explains through a raspy, strained voice. "I was done with my past."

"And you're still done with it," Knives says to Mason, turning his head to his shoulder, but not looking behind him to stare at the person that used to be his best friend. Knives makes his way over to me, walking behind the men who are sitting in chairs, and Reaper's eyes harden as he stares at me.

Probably because I entered the room when I wasn't allowed.

"You are not going. You will not be bait. Do I make myself clear?" Knives is stern, pointing a finger at me and setting his jaw. "I won't have you putting yourself in harm's way. I won't."

"Don't talk to me like that. Don't patronize me. Don't talk to me like I'm a child. I know what I'm doing."

"The answer is no, Mary."

"It isn't up to you," I say, noticing the shift in our arguing. This isn't bickering. This isn't to poke fun. This is a real make it or break it argument. I shift on my feet, never meeting the freezing temperature of his eyes.

He's pissed.

"The hell it isn't up to me. I don't care what I have to do. I'll throw your ass in jail again," he threatens.

I gasp, uncrossing my arms from my chest as if he slapped me in the face. "You wouldn't dare."

"I would. If it meant keeping you safe, I'd do anything. If it means you hate me and never talk to me again, I'll do it. Your life is more important than anything else. I'll risk you

184

not loving me anymore if it means your heart is still pounding and your lungs are still breathing. Don't mistake it for one fucking minute, Mary. I'm that man you used to think you hated, remember? Hold onto that if you have to, because I will do anything—" He crowds my space, and I take a step back out of the room. He follows me, and the heat of his body warms mine. "—Anything to keep you safe. Don't raise hell with me about this, I'm begging you," he pleads with me

"Knives—"

"—Mary, please," his words break, like a dam holding in a river, the barrier cracks and threatens to spill. He's on the verge of breaking, because Knives is proving he is already fractured. "What do I need to do? I'll do it."

"We need to know what to do," Mason says from behind him.

Knives spins around and throws a star, slamming his foster brother in the arm again. "You can shut the fuck up before I decide to kill you. For good. You can wait. You waited all these years to show your face; you can wait a while longer."

"Twenty," Mason grunts in annoyance, holding his bicep against him as he yanks the silver out. "It's been twenty years."

"Semantics. All the years blend together when someone dies and goes missing from your life."

The moment he says the words, I know they aren't just meant for Mason, but they are meant for me too. He thinks that I'll go and never come back. In my mind and my heart, I hurt for Knives because of the mindset he has.

I intertwine our fingers together and pull him out the door. "We are going to go talk. We will be back later."

"No the hell we—" I slam the door before Knives can say anything else.

"You're so fucking bossy."

"I learn from the best."

"You—"

"Knives!" Maizey bursts from the kitchen in her princess dress, and she waves her wand in the air and bonks him in the leg with the glittery stick. "You will now be happy!"

Aw. She's so damn cute.

"Kid, not right now," he snaps, in a harsh tone he never uses with Maizey.

"Knives!" I scold him, and Maizey pouts her lip, her large brown eyes well with tears. There is no stopping it. She wails, throws her wand at Knives, and runs right toward Sarah, who is cutting up apples to make a pie.

Skirt will be happy.

Maizey wraps her arms around Sarah's thigh and buries her face to cry.

"Are you kidding me?" I say, the words a harsh hiss directed at Knives. "Apologize to her, right now."

Knives thinks about it for a minute and nods, realizing he fucked up in that moment with Maizey. Our issues can wait. Sarah lifts her chin when Knives stands in front of her, a stance only a mother takes to protect her child, and Knives kneels. "Maizey, I'm sorry. You didn't deserve that. I have a lot going on, and I took it out on you; I shouldn't have. I hope you can forgive me, squirt."

Maizey sniffles, rubbing her wet cheeks against Sarah's jeans before turning her chubby cheeks to Knives. "You mean it?"

"I swear it."

"Pinky promise," she says, lifting her tiny finger in the air.

Knives lifts his pinky, which is so much bigger than hers, and locks it around her tiny one. "Pinky promise."

"You gotta kiss it or it don't matter," she sniffles, waiting for Knives to give in to her demands.

He brings his face down and kisses his hand. The toothless smile beams across her face, and she does the same, plopping a wet kiss on their fingers. "I'm going to go dash Daddy's office with happiness. I need my wand." She runs to where her wand is on the ground, picks it up, and heads for the Church door.

"Oh, no. Maizey, sweetie, you can't bother your dad when he is in the office," Sarah calls out, but it's too late.

Maizey is gone, and the roar of laughter coming from Church can be heard from the kitchen, followed by a high-pitched squeal.

"If you make my daughter cry again, Knives, I'll kill you," Sarah says as if she is having a normal conversation while she cuts the apples with calm, controlled slices.

"Yes ma'am," Knives says, gulping.

"Knives! Get your ass back in here, right fucking now," Reaper bellows from Church.

Not if Reaper kills him first.

"We really need to talk," I tell Knives. "I'll go tell Reaper."

"No, I will," he says. "We will talk, but my stance isn't changing," he says defiantly, leaving no room for argument.

If I know anything about us, there is always room for argument.

I bite my tongue until he leaves the room, and I lift my hands to strangle the air, pretending it's his neck as I let out a frustrated growl. "He is so impossible. He won't listen to me. He doesn't understand that this needs to happen."

"He cares about you, Mary. Think about if it wasn't an issue, what would you think if he agreed with Reaper to put you in harm's way?"

"How do you know it has to do with that?"

"Those walls aren't as thick as Reaper likes to think. I can hear everything they talk about. Don't tell him that, or he will soundproof it," she winks.

I pull out a chair, plop down, and sigh. I don't look away from the hallway, so I know when he is coming back. The longer we wait to talk about this, the more I calm down and realize Sarah is right. It could be worse. Knives could just not give a shit at all about me and let me be dangled as bait.

187

I'm lucky, I know, but what else is there to do? If they can't find my dad in Vegas, we draw him out. I'm the best way to do that.

"I just want to help. I know the risk, and I know Knives has been through so much—"

"—Mary, all the guys have been through so much. These men, they are glued together by pure will alone. Everyone has their story. I don't know much about Knives, but I know enough to know, he has lost so much. He finally has you, a new story, don't you think he is afraid to see how it ends? Especially with what Seer said. He must be freaking out."

It makes me think about all the ol' ladies and what they have been through. I wish more of the girls were here right now. Juliette works with Tool, Joanna seems to need sleep all the time since she's pregnant, Dawn just had a baby, Sunnie…well, I don't know where Sunnie is, actually. All I know is that she isn't here.

"I want him to trust me."

Sarah puts the knife down and takes the seat next to me. "You think he doesn't? It isn't you that he doesn't trust, Mary. It's the world. It's everyone else around us. It's men like your father, men like the Groundskeeper, men like Maximo that make him realize he can never leave you alone or unprotected. After everything this club has been through in the last couple years, the only place trust exists is here."

"Damn it!" Knives roars just before slamming the door, and the slam has my hand falling to my chest.

I exhale and rub my temples. "I know. I know, you're right. I better go check on him. That doesn't sound good."

"It never does. Reaper probably called a vote."

Which means if Knives is mad, Reaper voted in favor of what I wanted.

I steal an apple slice off the counter as I get up and bite into the juicy crisp. The flavor bursts across my tongue, but the Granny Smith apples that are usually sour are muted. It doesn't taste the same when I know Knives is mad at me.

188

Granny Smith apples are my favorite too. "I need to go check on him. I hate how upset he is," I say, throwing the other half of the apple in my mouth as I walk away and head toward the man that has my heart.

But he is also a ticking time bomb. His fuse is becoming shorter and shorter until I'm worried the man I've come to know and love will be gone because of the circumstances around him. Knives has hidden how he really feels for far too long now, and now that his past is back, I doubt he will ever be able to hide how he feels again

"He has a lot going on. Everything he thought he knew, he didn't know at all. Keep that in mind, okay? I'm sure he doesn't know how to process it all." Sarah gives me a warm smile. I appreciate it, but it does nothing to make me feel better.

I tuck my hands in my jacket pockets and give her the best smile I can and head toward the door; the light spilling in from outside shines from the crack.

I feel like I'm about to meet my maker walking toward the light. My dad used to preach that the light holds acceptance and peace, but I think he has it all wrong.

The same things that happen in the dark, happen in the light too. The only difference is that you can see what is happening   rather   than   wonder.

CHAPTER NINETEEN

I've never felt like I've hated Reaper before, but right now, it is debatable. I can't believe they took a vote without me because he said I was too close to the issue. Too close? Too fucking close? What a joke. If that happened with Sarah, Reaper would have raised hell, but because he is Prez, he is able to do whatever he wants.

He has the best interest of the club at heart.

I have to keep telling myself that, even though I feel like no one is taking my heart into consideration. It sounds needy. It sounds like I'm a real fucking pussy when it comes to my feelings.

And maybe I am. I've kept them locked up for so long. I numbed myself, and it worked, for a very long time, until Mary happened.

Fucking Mary.

She reached inside me with her warmth and thawed my soul. Pandora's Box has opened, and now my feelings are spilling out, and I can't contain them. It's like poison, completely killing who I used to be and changing me into this... I don't even know what.

I don't recognize who I am.

"Hey. I've been looking for you."

"You found me." I hang my head and stare at the ground. Even though it rained the other day, the desert is still cracked and dry, as if it hasn't seen water in months.

When I left the clubhouse, I walked around toward the back where Skirt's house used to be. I'm sitting on a stack of cinderblocks that are sitting in the middle of the lot. We are going to try and rebuild it soon. The supplies are slowly coming in. It would be easier if we owned a hardware store. The building process would speed up, and Skirt and his family can have their own space. But right now, the clubhouse is safer for them to live, considering we don't really party anymore, and the whores aren't there. If we want to drink, we go to Kings' Club. And if we get too drunk, Tool has extra rooms in the back with cots where we can sleep it off.

I almost prefer it. I don't miss the sluts. I miss Becks though, even though she wasn't a whore. She was a damn good massage therapist. I could use a backrub right now.

Things at the clubhouse won't be like this forever. Cut sluts come and go all the time, but when they return, the drama between them and the ol' ladies will return, and with Mary's attitude, I have no doubt she would kill one of them.

Not that I'd ever give her a reason to. Ruthless Kings can be bastards, but we don't cheat. Once we find our ol' lady, no other pussy will do.

It's a harsh way of putting it, but it's true. It's because no other woman makes us fucking feel or makes us weak like our ol' ladies.

"Knives, I know you don't want this to happen, and I understand why. I love you. If the tables were turned, I wouldn't want you to do this either. You and the guys, you are always running into danger. Don't you think that bothered me before? You might have driven me crazy, but I worried every time you walked out that door to take care of club business."

"Yeah?" I ask, lifting a thick brow at her.

"Are you so surprised?"

"A little bit. You surprise me, that's all." I open my cut pocket and grab a star, but this one is different. It's old, handmade, and a bit rusted.

"I remember when I met Reaper's dad, and he said, 'I have a son about your age.' And Reaper is a few years older than me, but I think his dad was trying to make me feel better after everything that happened." I'm not sure why I'm telling her this, it doesn't make sense, but I feel like I have to. "His Sergeant at Arms, you don't know him, he died a few years later, took the knives I had in my hand when I arrived at the clubhouse and made me this. They are sharp, so be careful."

"These are the knives you defended yourself with the day you thought Mason died?"

"Yeah, these are it. It's ugly, right? Not smooth and pretty like my other ones, but they are jagged, almost more threatening, since they have that knife feel."

"Your name makes sense now," she teases, nudging me in the shoulder.

"I want you to have it," I tell her. I never thought it would be so emotional to give something to someone I love that was built because I missed someone I cared about.

"I can't take this."

"You need something to protect yourself. Please, if you're going to do this, I need to know you're okay."

"You aren't going to fight me?"

"I don't have the energy to fight you, Hellraiser. I can't go against Prez. He *will* kill me. Especially after I made

Maizey cry." I feel fucking terrible about that. I can't believe I snapped at a little girl who was only trying to make me happy. "I don't want this to happen. I don't know what I'd do if I lost you too, Mary. You're everything I didn't know I needed. After my family died, after Mason, I don't have the heart to go through another loss."

"Mason is back. You didn't lose him," she says, laying her hand on my knee. "Why won't you see that?"

"Because I know eventually, I'll lose him anyway. It's easier to keep myself distant from him. You don't know how much I struggled in the foster homes. You don't know how much I wished I would have died in that car accident with my family. Mason made the little bit of love I had for life worth it."

She lays her head on my shoulder, and the breeze takes the moment to sweep by. Her long hair dances, and the smell of her shampoo hits my face. It's that cheap shit, Suave, but it smells so fucking good, like strawberries and cream. She could have the most expensive shampoo, and all she says is, "nothing makes my hair shine like this."

Good, because I'd miss the scent of her.

We sit there not saying a word to one another, just enjoying the peace and the sun against my face and my girl by my side

That's when it hits me.

It's quiet. There isn't a sound. It's just the wind picking up dust and a few vultures overhead.

The silence isn't bothering me, but it's still speaking volumes. It's still fucking loud.

And it's saying what a lucky sonofabitch I am.

I wrap my arm around Mary, my biggest pain in the ass ever, and pick her up to set her on my lap. "Just don't die, okay?"

"You deal with death every day," she says, pressing her lips against my cheek.

193

"Yeah, but I can get over those deaths." I close my eyes and relish in the feel of her red pouts against me, the softness of the plump flesh grazing against me. I know it won't be the last time I feel her, I'll make sure of that, but it feels like it.

With what Seer said, with the threat of her dad, it's hard for me to stay positive.

"You saying you won't be able to get over me, Thomas Underwood?"

I groan when she uses my full name. I haven't been called that since I was fifteen. "Come here." I turn her around so she can face me, the damn breeze taking another opportunity to blow her hair, so I catch it, holding it down so it doesn't get tangled. I want a picture of her like this. It reminds me that we have no pictures together, and if we do, it's with the rest of the club, and we are as far away as we can be from each other.

We always fought to stay away, but now we have to fight to stay together.

And one kiss changed everything.

"I'd never be able to get over you, Mary. You need to know that—"

"Knives..."

"Look at me." I grip her chin in my hand and force her to. "I can get over a lot of things. I have and I always will, but not you. When all this is over, and you're back right here where you're meant to be—" I grab her ass for good measure, making sure she understands me, "—You're going to be Mrs. Underwood."

She gasps and then slaps me across the face. Mary covers her mouth with her hand, and water sparkles in her eyes.

"Ow, Hellraiser." I lift my hand to my cheek and rub it.

Next, like the crazy ass woman she is, she smashes her lips against mine.

She's going to give me whiplash from not being able to make up her damn mind and what she wants to do to me. She rears back and slaps me again, my cheek blazing and my

194

cock hard. I fucking love it when she makes me insane. "It isn't funny. Don't joke like that. Plus, you know it's too soon—"

"I'm not laughing, am I? I'm not kidding, and I don't give a fuck if it is too soon. We live in Vegas. I'll marry your ass on the strip, in front of Elvis and everybody. Tomorrow. I don't give a fuck."

"You're serious?"

"Deadly." It's way too soon according to society and normal people standards, but fuck society. They have never done a damn thing for me anyway. There is one thing I have in a drawer in my room. It's a plastic bag, pushed all the way in the back. It holds my parents' wedding rings. They're the only items I have from them. They're all I have left of them.

Oddly enough, my dad's ring fits me.

And I'm going to wear it.

Mom's engagement ring was simple, a teardrop diamond on a rose gold band, but I can see Mary wearing it. It suits her. I've saved the rings all these years, not having the heart to part with them, and this is why.

"I could slap you again."

"You better not unless you want to get bent over and fucked," I say, my cheek still tingling from her palm.

"I'm sorry, I was shocked, and I had to make sure I wasn't dreaming."

"You usually pinch yourself if you think you're dreaming, Hellraiser."

"Yeah, but what fun would that be?"

There she goes, checking all my damn boxes and driving me mad. I smash my lips against hers, diving my tongue inside her hot mouth, and this time the kiss is sweeter. My beard rubs against her chin, and my palm slides down her throat, getting a semi-hard hold, so she doesn't move.

I bring the kiss to an end and lay my forehead against hers, panting. "You going to marry me or what?"

195

"And if I say no?" She leans back, her lipstick smeared, so I bring my finger up and wipe it off from her chin. I like it when she's all fucked up and messy because I know I did it.

"Too fucking bad. You're going to marry me anyway. I was only asking to be nice."

She tosses her back and falls back in my arms, laughing at my response. I slide my hand up her spine and make her come back to me, chest against chest. Her arms wrap around my neck, and her laugh finally dies down. "I guess I have no choice in the matter, do I?"

"Nope," I state.

"Then marry me tonight." She ups my ante, trying to see if I'm bluffing.

"Tonight it is, Hellraiser."

No one will take my wife from me.

I'll claw tooth and nail, peel flesh from bone if someone dares.

She's my fucking Hellraiser, my Pandora's Box of fucking emotions.

This wedding has to happen now because in the back of my mind, in eleven days, I might not have that opportunity.

CHAPTER TWENTY

Holy Crap. He asked me to marry him.

I think I said yes. I'm not sure. I wouldn't say no. I'm just surprised. We have known each other for a while, but we have only been lovers for a few days. If my parents knew what I was up to—well—I guess that doesn't matter, because they no longer matter.

This matters. Knives matters. The Ruthless Kings matter. My home matters.

"We're getting married!" Knives hollers as we walk through the door of the clubhouse, and everyone, I mean everyone, including the dogs, stare at us with open mouths. It's comical.

And it's making me nervous, because no one looks happy, but no one is mad.

Well, Reaper doesn't look too thrilled.

Crickets.

This is awkward. I know it isn't the best timing, but a little amount of support would go a long way right now. "Knives, maybe—"

"No," he cuts me off and grips my hand tighter. "I'm marrying her, and I know all of you assholes think it's a bad time, but what better time is there than right now? With all this fucking shit going on, all I want to be is happy. She makes me happy, and I want to live my fucking life before we do go after her father—"

"—Knives, we have a lot to plan. Getting married right now is not a good idea. Her father is here."

"Exactly, he is here, and he isn't going anywhere without her. If in eleven days something happens to her, I want to know I did everything I wanted with her."

"Nothing is going to happen to her, Knives. We will make sure of it."

"I promise, Thomas," Mason has the courage to pipe in.

Knives loses his patience, and his anger engulfs him instead. "You don't fucking know that! You. Don't. Know!" Spittle flies from his mouth as he yells. He points at Mason and sneers, "You have no right to promise me fucking anything. You're nothing but a fucking liar. Her dad, he can wait a day. He's waited nearly a year; he can wait one more day, can't he?"

"Fuck yea! Let's get ye fucking married, brother!" Skirt lifts his fist in the air and cheers.

"Let's do it!"

"I'm in. Oh, hey, can I be the best man? You know I'm your favorite," Slingshot says, taking a swig from his water bottle.

"Can Happy come?" Tongue drawls from the corner. "It would be his first wedding. He can be the flower boy." There is so much excitement in his words that I know Knives will say yes. I'm not sure if they allow alligators wherever we are going, but I'm sure they will figure it out.

"Did someone say they're getting married?" Sarah squeals from the kitchen. She rushes into the main room and pushes Reaper out of the way. "You're getting married?" she asks me and stops right in front of me and takes my hands in hers. "Really?"

"I... think so? Yes? As long as it is okay with everyone."

"Fuck everyone. If they don't want to see me get married, they aren't the family I thought they were," Knives says, staring down at his boots.

I squeeze his hand, and he returns it, but I think they are more surprised than they are against us.

"Hey, you're going to get married," Reaper says, and once his affirmation is heard, the energy changes in the room, and the buzz that I wanted when we walked in is there. I can sense the buzz of anticipation. There is a round of applause, and Knives lets out such a big breath and curses. He doesn't care about anyone else's opinion; he just wants his Prez's approval. "Well, that means all of our ugly asses need to go get cleaned up."

"And we need to get you a dress. Oh my god! You're getting married," Sarah screeches again and starts to prance in place.

"Doll, no bouncing," Reaper suggests, kindly.

If I didn't know why he told her that, I would think he was controlling, but I know he's worried.

"Let's go shopping. There is a little boutique by Daphne's bookstore that is so cute," Sarah says, looping her arm through mine as she guides me to the couch.

"Can I go?" Tongue asks as he sits down next to me. In his arms, he is holding Happy, petting the top of his head, and even though Happy is still somewhat small, his teeth are big.

Big, sharp, pointy teeth.

That can tear into my flesh without a second thought.

"You want to?" Sarah asks him, sitting up straighter and hopeful.

199

"I'd like to."

I know their relationship has been a bit rocky since they got into an argument and Tongue accidentally stabbed her, but they are slowly coming back together as best friends.

"I'd like that," Sarah whispers, playing with a piece of her hair. "You have great advice. I remember when you helped with my prom dress. I couldn't have done that without you."

"I couldn't have done a lot of things without you. Like live," he says, stroking Happy down his spine while he wears his 'emotional support animal' vest.

Apparently, Happy is a docile, soothing alligator that Tongue can take into shops; who knew?

"Well, we don't have much time," Sarah sniffles, slapping her thighs as she gets up. "I'm going to go get changed, and we should go shopping. Pick a place to get married and we will meet you there, Knives!" Sarah wipes her cheek as she walks away. Reaper places his hand on her shoulder as they disappear down the hallway to get to the bedroom they are staying in.

"I say we get married in Maximo's hotel. That's the biggest 'fuck you' I can think of," I say with bite, digging my nails into my forearms as I think about him partnering up with my father.

"Damn, you are a Hellraiser," Patrick says, throwing a peanut in the air and catching it in his mouth.

Knives' hand lands on the back of my neck, warm and calloused, sending arousal down my spine. It's how I respond every time he touches me. "Damn straight she is." He holds me tight and brings his lips down on mine.

"I'm going to marry the fuck out of you, Hellraiser."

"Yeah?"

"Yeah, and you're going to fucking like it."

Like it? I'm going to love it.

"Okay, I'm ready," Sarah chirps. She struts in much happier than she was before. Her neck is flushed, and her hair is in a messier bun now, resembling a nest of some sort. The front of her shirt is tucked in while the back isn't, and she has a hickey on her neck. Reaper comes out next, and his shirt is on backward, but no one is going to say anything to him. "Are you ready?" Sarah asks me.

"Are you? You're the one wearing two different shoes." I point down to her feet, one boot, one slipper.

I'm going to go out on a limb here and say she meant to put on the other boot.

"Oh. I'll... let me... just..." She twirls around and heads toward her room again.

At this rate, I won't be getting married until I'm dead.

Knives' phone rings, and when he pulls it out of his pocket, he bangs it against his forehead. "It's Seer."

"No!" Everyone in the room yells at the same time, not wanting him to answer it.

"Yeah, fuck you all. The last time I didn't answer, my bike exploded, and we nearly died in a freak tornado." His finger swipes across the screen, and he brings the smartphone to his ear. "Hey, Seer." He does not sound enthusiastic at all to talk to Seer. "What? Of course, I am happy to hear from you. I'm just a little nervous, is all." He doesn't say anything as he stops to listen. "Sure, yeah. Hold on." Knives brings the phone down and presses a button. "Okay, you're on speaker."

Seer's Cajun accent comes through the phone immediately. "I just wanted to call and say congratulations. You guys are taking me by surprise. You like to keep me on my toes."

"Thank you, Seer," I say. It's hard to be nice to a man that knows I'm going to die, but it isn't his fault he knows. I'm sure if he had it his way, he wouldn't want to know half of the information in his head because of what he sees.

"And go with the dress that makes you think of the future, Mary."

I almost ask why, but he hangs up the phone, leaving us wondering what that call was about.

"Okay, I'm sorry. Now, I'm ready," announces Sarah.

"I want Bullseye to go with you," Reaper says.

"Tongue is coming with us."

"Tongue is going as a friend, not a guard. I want someone there who will be focused on their surroundings, not tulle."

"I want to go. I want to go! Can I get a princess dress?" Maizey says, already wearing a princess dress. She wears it every day. Sarah is lucky to wash it, and when she does, Maizey throws a damn fit.

"You can get anything you fuc—fudging want, Maze," Reaper says, catching himself before he drops a curse word.

"Yay!" Maizey squeals. "I can walk with Happy down the aisle." Showing how fearless she is, she reaches up to pat Happy on the head, and the damn gator closes its eyes.

I swear, he is smiling, showing me all those teeth.

"Okay, let's go if we don't want to hurry. I might get a little something from Trixie's shop," Sarah says off-handedly, and Reaper's growl can be heard from across the room.

"Doll…" he warns.

"Okay, we are leaving, or we are never going to get out of here." Sarah takes my hand and drags me away from the couch.

"Bye," I say to Knives, blowing him a kiss.

"I'll see you down the aisle, Hellraiser."

This is really happening.

I give him my biggest, cheesiest grin I can before Sarah is opening the door. Tongue and Bullseye are right behind us, a low hiss coming from Happy.

"You just ate," Tongue tsks.

Happy snaps his jaws, and his teeth clank together, which has me flinching back and almost falling down the steps. I'm not sure if I'll ever warm up to the idea of a gator as a pet. I'm trying. I really, really am.

"One more," Tongue reaches into his pocket, and I almost throw up when I see a large tongue. "There you go," he says, dropping it from above his head. Happy catches it and gobbles it down until there is nothing left but a piece of flesh between his teeth.

"What was that?" I ask in horror, wondering how Tongue has tongues on such short notice.

"A bull's tongue. It's not all the time I can use human, so I order from the nearby butcher shop."

"Right," I say, almost in a daze.

Happy stops hissing though, so that's a plus.

"I love my new car," Sarah says as she digs into her purse for the keys.

Reaper bought her a brand new Range Rover. It's top of the line and safe. It's black, like all the other SUVs. The license plate on the front says 'DOLL' in gold block letters, and the windows are tinted black. They are bulletproof too, and I'm pretty sure the metal he had the car customized with is fireproof to a certain degree.

After what happened over Christmas, Reaper took no chances with protecting her when it came to cars.

"Listen, listen," Sarah giggles as she clicks the button that locks.

"Doll, get your ass in the car before I spank it."

"Why would Daddy spank you, Mommy? Are you in trouble?" Maizey says, tugging on her shirt.

Bullseye, Tongue, and I stifle a laugh. Sarah was all too excited to show us the Range Rover.

"I'm always in trouble, sweetie. Always," Sarah says, opening the back door. She holds Maizey's hand and helps her climb into her booster seat.

"I'm gonna have to talk to Daddy about that. That isn't nice."

"Oh my god, kids are the fucking best," Bullseye chuckles from the backseat.

"You said a bad word! Give me five bucks." Maizey holds out her hand and waits, kicking her short legs over the seat.

Bullseye looks astonished by her words, placing his hand on his chest in a dainty position. "Excuse me, what?"

"Daddy said to ask for five bucks from everyone who curses around me. I have fifty dollars. Fifty-five now, cause you cursed."

"Orders from Prez? That's some shit," Bullseye reaches into his pocket, then pauses when he realized what he did. "Damn it!"

"You owe me fifteen. Keep it coming, buddy," Maizey chirps and wiggles her pink painted fingers. Bullseye narrows his eyes at her, pulling out a twenty-dollar bill.

He slaps it in her hand as Sarah gets in the driver's seat. "You have change?"

"Let's call it good. We know you'll slip," Maizey states, and everyone in the car is laughing until they can't breathe.

"Kid, you know your business," Bullseye says.

"Everyone buckled up?" Sarah asks as she adjusts the rear view mirror.

"Yep," I say, turning around in the passenger seat to check on Bullseye and Maizey, then look toward the back to see Tongue buckled up too.

Happy has his own car seat.

How is this my life?

Sarah drops her sunglasses on her face from the top of her head and puts the car in drive. When we get to the gate, Braveheart is there and presses the button to open it. When the accident happened over Christmas and Reaper and the men tried to get out of the compound, the Groundskeeper snipped the wires on the electricity box, and the gate wouldn't move, so Reaper installed backup electrical boxes so that wouldn't happen again.

We wave and get on our way, driving down Route 50. When we pass the tree Sarah and Patrick crashed into, Sarah speeds up, and Bullseye reaches up to pat her shoulder. The tree is broken, the bark is missing, and the body of the trunk is burnt.

It's like it happened yesterday, but it's been weeks.

"I can't wait to see Daphne," Tongue says out of nowhere. "She's meeting with the painters today to paint the bookstore. She doesn't have a name for the store yet."

Tongue was never much of a talker before, but he could go on and on about Daphne. He's happy, which is why I'm assuming he named his gator—wait—his swamp kitty, Happy.

"We will have to help her think of a name," Sarah says.

"She's there with the painters? By herself?" Bullseye asks, and Sarah and I groan because we know what that will do to Tongue.

"She's okay. I installed cameras in every corner. I can see her." He lifts up his phone and shows us. "She's reading a book right now, but...I'm not liking how that guy keeps looking at her. Sarah, hurry up."

"I'm going the speed limit." Sarah scoffs and gives Bullseye the stink eye in her rear view mirror.

The rest of the ride is silent. I'm stuck looking out the window, wondering how I went from being a Preacher's daughter to a biker's wife.

The only thing I'd change is that I wish it'd happened sooner.

CHAPTER TWENTY-ONE

Mary

We pull up to the town next to Vegas, where Daphne works. It isn't a long drive, only about fifteen minutes. The town is one of those that you stop at to use the restroom before coming to Vegas. It's quaint, and there is a candy store named Paula's. It's painted different shades of pink, like bubblegum and hot pink. There is a cotton candy machine in the window, and my mouth waters. It's been forever since I've had cotton candy.

Next to the candy shop is a hardware store; there is a cranky man standing outside, mumbling nonsense to himself as he smokes a cigarette. He has on a tan apron, and when he sees me staring, he sneers at me before heading inside.

Nice guy.

There is one road cutting through the town, and on either side are brick buildings. The place is almost historical. Like it came out of the Wild West a hundred years ago. It's hard to find buildings that look like this anymore in Vegas. Everything is modern and sleek; there is no charm.

Maizey holds Sarah's hand, and Tongue holds Happy in his sling strapped to his chest. Happy's tail sways from side to side, and the people that walk by us give us a wide berth when they see an alligator.

Bullseye leans against a parking meter and sways. I reach out to steady him. His skin is clammy, and his face has lost all color. "Bullseye? Are you okay?"

"I think my sugar is low."

"Have you been checking it?" Sarah asks. "You know you have to check it."

"If it's low, this happens; if not, I feel great. Why bother checking it?"

"So this doesn't happen, or something worse, Bullseye," I say.

"I'll go run across the street and see if the candy shop has a coke or something. I'll be right back," Sarah tells me.

It's on the tip of my tongue to ask for cotton candy, but right now isn't a good time, considering Bullseye looks like he is about to pass out. He's sweating, and he loses his strength, his knees buckling as he falls to the ground. "I'm not feeling that well," he says. "I'm really dizzy."

"I know, I know," I start to panic. What if Sarah doesn't get back in time? What if he goes into shock? "She'll be back soon, Bullseye."

"Uncle Bullseye? You okay?" Maizey asks, waving her wand in the air. "You're going to be all better."

"You bet I am," he says, trying to sound happy and believable, but he doesn't.

A ding sounds in the distance, and I lift my head to see Sarah crossing the street, a bottle of orange juice in her hand along with cotton candy

I bet it's for Bullseye.

Lucky dog.

"Here." Sarah opens the bottle and hands it to Bullseye, who chugs it down; orange juice flows down either side of his mouth. Sarah grabs a chunk of cotton candy and shoves it between his lips. "There, maybe you'll see how important it is to take care of yourself."

Bullseye mumbles around the cotton candy. It's gone in a few seconds after it melts, and he takes another swig of orange juice. We sit there for a few minutes, Bullseye laying down on his back with his eyes shut as he waits for the sugar to kick in. "I'm sorry. I'll try to do better," he says, finishing off the orange juice.

"We just want you to be safe," Sarah says, pushing his dark brown hair back and off his forehead.

He nods, but I can tell he feels weak. Not physically, but mentally. He lifts his hand, and Tongue helps him to his feet. "Let's get you a wedding dress. Gosh, I can't believe Knives, that crazy fu—fudger is getting married."

"Good job, Uncle Bullseye," Maizey compliments him.

Tongue walks inside the bookstore first. The door is open, and the aroma of paint smacks me in the face.

"Hey, I'm going to go inside the boutique. You guys go and talk to Daphne. I want a minute to look alone. Say hi to her for me," I say.

"Yeah, we'll be there soon," Sarah replies.

I step over a piece of gum on the sidewalk, thankful I saw it just in time, so I didn't ruin my shoe. I stop outside the boutique, loving how cute it is. There are two mannequins in the display window. One is wearing a leather skirt with a red crop top, but the one next to it has my attention. It looks like a vintage dress, a soft peach color. The sleeves hang off the shoulders, wrapping around the biceps, and there is a silk slip underneath the beautiful lace detailing. It seems tight at the bust, but fans out on the hips.

I glance up at the name of the boutique, wanting nothing more than to try this dress on.

Ruby's Rarities.

That's adorable.

I skip one of the steps, since there are only three, and when I get to the top, I open the door. The bell jingles, and there is still a mistletoe hanging over the door from Christmas. With one look around the shop, I just know that this is the place where I'm going to get my dress.

"Hi, welcome to Ruby's! I'll be with you in just one minute." A short woman with a pixie cut says from a wobbly ladder as she changes a lightbulb.

"Are you safe up there?" I ask.

"Oh, yeah. I do this all—woah—" the ladder teeters, "—the time."

"Just let me know."

"Everything in the store is fifty-percent off. Have at it."

I want to ask her why everything is on sale, but I figure it isn't my business. "Actually, I'd love to try on the dress in the window, if that's okay. I'm getting married tonight, so I would love to see if that's the one."

"Congratulations!" she says, the metal of the ladder creaking. She isn't tall enough to reach the light with the ladder. She's on her tiptoes, stretching her arms, and is sticking out her tongue as the pads of her fingers graze the bulb. "Just one second," she grunts.

The door opens, and Bullseye walks in, followed by Tongue, Sarah, and everyone else. Bullseye stares at the disaster in the middle of the floor. He runs to the ladder just as it tilts to the side, and Ruby screams.

And witnessing Bullseye saving her is like something out of a movie. He catches her in the nick of time, cradling her in his arms.

"Oh, gosh. Thank you," she says in choppy breaths.

"You're welcome." Bullseye continues to stare at her, and Sarah bumps my hip with hers when we get the same idea.

Bullseye sets Ruby down, well, I think it's Ruby. She never said what her name was, but she has a big ruby ring on her finger, so it has to be her. Bullseye grins when he sees how short she is. Her forehead comes to his stomach, and she's skinny. "You're tiny," he says.

"My attitude is six-foot-six, so you better watch it with the short jokes." She waves a fist in the air. The scowl on her face falls when she turns away from Bullseye and stares at me. "The dress in the window, right? It's been there awhile. I've been waiting for the perfect person to ask for it. I think it's going to look great on you."

"The peach one?" Tongue asks. "That will look gorgeous with your hair up and your complexion. Good choice."

"Oh my god, what the fuck is that?" Ruby screeches when she sees the gator.

"You owe me five bucks," Maizey says. "Pay up."

"She doesn't count, sweetie," Sarah whispers, kissing her daughter on top of the head.

"This is Happy. He is allowed in here. He is my emotional support animal."

She points her finger to all of us and laughs. "You lot are a bit crazy, aren't you?" She side-steps away from Happy and climbs on the stage, then unzips the dress from the mannequin. "I've seen it all now. Damn, gators as emotional support animals. I need me a glass of wine after seeing that; I tell you what."

"Is she talking to us?" Maizey whispers loud enough for her to hear.

"Sorry, I do that." Ruby jumps off the stage and stumble, running right into Bullseye again.

"We keep meeting like this. I'm going to need your name," he says, flashing his cocky smile.

"It's on the shop." She saunters by him and heads toward the dressing room. She slides the red curtain to the side and hangs the dress. "I'll grab some heels. Not stripper ones. Not that I have anything against strippers, but something classy," she tells me.

"Mommy, what's a stripper?"

"A woman who likes to dance and she makes money," Sarah explains with a questionable tone.

"I want to be a stripper!" Maizey cheers.

"Never sweetie, never. Daddy won't allow that ever."

I snicker as I head toward the fitting room. The floors are all shag carpet, but everything is clean. Nothing has been updated, which makes me like this store even more. I play with the material between my fingers, feeling the aged lace. I try to imagine the story this dress holds, but I know anything I think of won't do it justice. "Hey, Ruby? How old is this dress?" I ask.

"From the '50s. It's an original, a real classic." Her voice comes closer, and she places a closed toe, three-inch heel on the ground. The shoes are a nude color with a thin ankle strap and, she's right, the heel isn't a stripper heel.

"Okay, try it on. Let's see it," Tongue says, tickling the chin of his swamp kitty.

I close the curtain and get undressed, starting with my shoes. My toes dig into the harsh material of the carpet, and as I slide off my pants, the mirror exposes the bruises on my thighs from Knives. My heart thumps when I think of him, and it has me getting undressed faster. I can't wait to meet him down the aisle.

Stepping into the dress, I'm careful as I zip, since it's so old. I bend down, slipping my feet into the heels. Before I show my friends, I take a look in the mirror on the wall and gasp. I hardly recognize myself. It fits me just right. The dress stops just below my knee, hugging my curves and showing the delicate ridge of my collarbone since the sleeves hug my arms. I twist my hair up like Tongue suggests, tying it like I usually do without a hair tie. My eyes water.

There is a glow to me I can't explain as I look at myself. Maybe it's the slight sweetheart neckline of the dress or how the events of tonight happened so fast that I can't believe I'm here.

211

All I know is whatever led me here; I need to be the woman Knives deserves. I've been lost this past year, trying to find a way to live again. I've been doing odd jobs for Reaper, nothing special, which has to stop, and I need to try harder to find something I'm good at. For me. For Knives.

He'll help me find my way.

He has so far, and I know with him, I can do anything.

I open the curtain and look down, stepping out for all to see. I'm nervous. What if they hate it?

Everyone gasps in awe.

"That's it."

"I love it."

"So pretty!"

"Give us a twirl, Mary," Bullseye says.

"Oh, I knew it would find the perfect home," Ruby grins, dabbing the tears under her eyes. "Sorry, I'm a sucker for weddings. Don't mind me."

"Let's have the night of our lives before we can't," I say. "I'm going to keep it on, if you don't mind."

"Absolutely not," Ruby says, her ring glittering in the light. "It's all yours."

I want this to be the best night, since my life is on a timer, but my father is going to be in for a rude awakening.

I'm going to fight *for* the rest of my life

They say like father like daughter, but I don't think that's true. I'm nothing like him, unless you consider how much I want Knives, then I guess our greed is the same. We only apply it differently.

"Can you believe you're getting married?" Sarah asks with wobbly lips, her hormones getting the best of her. "You've been through so much."

I   didn't   before,   but   *I*   *do*   now.

CHAPTER TWENTY-TWO

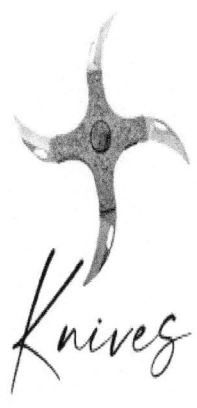

Knives

Holy shit.

I'm nervous.

I've trimmed my beard, shaved the sides of my head, and I'm wearing a suit.

I never wear a fucking suit. The last time any of us dressed up was for Sarah's prom. I look in the mirror, rub my beard with one hand, and make an impressed expression.

Damn, I clean up fucking good. I really do.

I dip my hand into the black silk lining of my inner pocket and pull out the plastic bag holding the rings. I know, it's supposed to be in a pretty box, but I don't have one.

"You okay? Are you getting cold feet?"

I don't have to look to see who it is. I'd know that voice anywhere. "What the hell are you doing in my room, Mason?" I straighten my tie and grab my cologne. I don't wear it often, just for special occasions, and I consider this the most important occasion of my fucking life.

"I'm checking in on you," he says, leaning against my bedroom door.

"Well don't. That isn't your job anymore, remember?" I place the cologne on the dresser and pick up four stars and slide them into my pants pocket.

"It will always be my job. You don't think I kept track of you? That... what? I forgot about you? You're my brother."

"I was your brother. Was." I grip the edge of the dresser before pushing off and facing him. "You left me behind just like everyone else."

"Thomas—"

"My name isn't fucking Thomas, okay? You don't get to call me by my name. There is one person in this world who can call me that, and I'm about to marry her. Stay out of my way tonight, Mason. Just stop," I beg of him. "Just. Stop. Don't ruin this day for me. Act like you don't exist. You seem to be good at it." I shove by him, slamming my shoulder into his as I walk out of the room, leaving my past and who I used to be behind me.

When I walk to the main room, I feel like there is a part of me missing, and it isn't because Mary isn't here. It's the fact that Mason has popped back into my life out of nowhere, and no matter how much I fight him to stay away from me, deep down, I'm fucking glad he is here. I'm happy he is alive, but I can't get over so many years of him being alive and me feeling like I'm drowning.

"Well, look at you. You aren't so ugly after all," Tank says, wearing a powder blue suit that is not easy on the eyes, but it matches him.

I don't know how or why, but he pulls off the look.

"Whatever, I look better than you do. I look better than all of you," I point out. Everyone is in their suit they wore to Sarah's prom.

It's probably the only one they own.

Except for Reaper.

He is wearing black on black, looking more like he is about to go fuck shit up than go to a wedding.

"Is everything set? Where are Moretti and Maximo?"

"Moretti is coming with. Me and Mercy are staying here to keep an eye on Maximo. I'm thinking he can give us more information than he has been saying," Mason says from behind me. "Go get married. We will be here to hold down the fort."

I nod, not having the energy or the heart to bite his head off again. Moretti comes from the basement, a crisp expensive suit on, something he used to wear all the time, and he is pulling at the collar. "I cannot believe I used to wear these all the time. Are you sure?" Moretti directs his question to Reaper.

"Just as sure as you saying you wanted Tool to suck your cock," Reaper laughs, rocking on his toes as he shoves his hands in his pockets.

"Did I really?" Moretti swings his gaze to Tool, who looks very uncomfortable. "I can see why. You are a marvelous looking man. You still don't suck cock?"

Juliette giggles, hiding her face in Tool's shoulder as he stares at the floor, white as a sheet. "Nope. No, cock. Sorry, Moretti. Juliette is my ol' lady."

"Well, we can all suck each other, I don't mind," Moretti says just as Tool takes a sip of water, which he promptly spews out in a massive spray.

And now Patrick is soaked. "Oh, fuck, Patrick. I'm sorry."

Patrick takes out a handkerchief and wipes his face clean. Sunnie helps him too, grabbing a napkin from the shutdown bar in the corner of the main room.

I really miss that fucking bar, but I'd miss Patrick more if he weren't here, and if we had booze lined up everywhere, I don't think he'd have a chance in hell at making it out alive.

215

"It's fine. Just answer the man, okay?" Patrick gives Tool a sly smile, teasing him.

Tool spins on his chair as Moretti waits patiently, unbuttoning the top of his collar. "Sorry, Moretti. Juliette and I only suck each other. I'm flattered, though."

"It's okay, I don't remember liking men too, yet here we are." He fusses with the collar of his shirt again and curses something in Italian. "Are you sure I wore these? This makes no sense. They are fucking uncomfortable. Who would wear something like this?"

"A rich mafia man," I say, hoping he understands that the clothes he has on are the clothes that encompassed the reputation he earned.

"Well, that's not the case anymore, is it?" he says, sadly. "Okay, let's go get Knives married." He cocks his head as he studies me.

"No, sorry, Moretti. I don't either. I'm marrying Mary, remember?"

"None of you are any fun. You're so boring when it comes to your sex lives," he huffs. "Can we go? Being in this clubhouse is making me cranky." Moretti heads out the door, and for some reason, we all follow suit as if he is in charge of getting the show on the road.

When we all walk outside and shut the door, it hits me how serious the moment is. I never thought I'd be here or that I'd get married. I take the first step down the stairs, the first step to start the rest of my life, when my phone rings.

"Don't answer it," Slingshot says, launching a skittle at me. "It's time to marry Mary. See what I did there? Did you?" He laughs at his own joke. "I'm fucking funny."

"You're a fucking idiot, is what you are," Poodle says.

I do what they say. I ignore the call because there is nothing in this world that is going to stop me from enjoying my night unless it is Mary calling to say she doesn't want to get married. Or what if she doesn't show, and I'm standing there at the end of the aisle looking like a real bastard?

Shit. This is how people feel when they are in love? I hope the anxiety ends, because my stomach is in knots.

A bunch of the guys hop on their bikes, and my heart twists, reminding me I have to drive a fucking car. I hate driving a car. I'm not the best at it, but I do it if I have to. My phone rings again as I walk to the Bronco, and when I stop at the driver's side door, my gut turns, and the hair on the back of my neck stands up. Something isn't right. I glance around to see what the issue is, but the guys are laughing and having a good time. It's been too long since we have all gotten together and have had fun. Too much shit has happened. Tonight is the night we deserve for ourselves.

But something is wrong; I feel it. It's like when you wake up one day, and you have that ache in your gut, the one that tells you not to get out of bed because you know something bad will happen. Then, you chalk it up to it being nothing, just stupid negative thoughts, but you walk out the door, drive to work, and get in a car accident, or you spill hot coffee all over you, or you see something you weren't supposed to see, and you tell yourself, 'I should have stayed in bed.'

I feel like we should have never left the clubhouse.

I'm doing my best to chalk it up to nerves and ignore it, but every time someone does that here, bad shit happens.

The sun is setting, the lower temperatures have kicked in, and while the horizon is beautiful on the edge of the desert, the beauty camouflages the ugliness that's being hidden right now.

I just have no idea what it is.

My phone rings again, vibrating more intensely than the last time, or maybe that's just how it feels, and I decide to answer it. My limbs are sluggish; my mind is fuzzy. A cold sweat drenches over me. I lean against the truck, staring at the name on my screen.

I know she's gone when I see Bullseye's name.

I can't say how I know, but I feel it, and that's how I know.

I try my best to answer, I do, but I'm frozen.

"You going to answer that, Knives? It keeps ringing over and over. Is it Seer?" Reaper places a cigarette between his lips and lights it, watching me out of the corner of his eye. When I don't answer him, he blows out the smoke, and the phone rings once more.

Then someone else's phone blares.

And someone else's.

Then Reaper's.

My new phone flashes Bullseye's name again, and with a deep, broken intake of air, I slide my finger across the screen and put it on speaker. "She's gone, isn't she?" I feel dead inside, like Reaper carved a hole in my chest and fucking ripped my heart out.

"Knives, fucking finally!" Bullseye panics as he speaks. He must be running because there is static in the background as if he is moving. "We don't know what happened. She walked out of the store. Dress on. We were walking to the car right behind her and climbed inside, and that's when we realized she wasn't with us. We checked inside the store again. I've run all over, Knives. She isn't here. She just disappeared. It's like she vanished. One minute, she's there, laughing and talking, happy. All she did was talk about the dress, and you know how much she loves you, and then it stopped. Mary isn't here. She isn't anywhere. Mary!" he yells out her name and hearing it without her answering kills something inside me.

Reaper rips the phone out of my hand. "No one fucking vanishes, Bullseye! I want everyone to look, except for Sarah. I'll be there to pick them up. I don't want you leaving that area until you have talked to everyone. Searched everywhere, even the dumpsters. Fucking look!" Reaper hangs up the phone and lets out a ferocious roar, tossing my new phone across the damn desert.

218

It can keep it.

"Knives, look at me," Reaper grabs my shoulders, but I'm limp all over. I can't seem to think, breathe, or move. "Knives? We will find her. We always find them. Always. She's going to be okay. Knives," he snaps his fingers in front of me.

I expect rage. I expect fury to take over, and I go on a warpath, but all I feel is this numbness again. My past is playing on repeat all over again. This is why I didn't want to get close.

Everyone always leaves.

And I'm always left hurting for everyone.

Reaper slaps me across the face, and all eyes are on me. "Fucking listen to me; you don't get to call it quits. Not now. Not when she needs you most." He slaps me again, but his words don't penetrate.

"Aye, Reaper. That isn't what he needs," Skirt says. The brass knuckles glimmer against the sun as he slips them on.

"I didn't want to bruise him on his wedding day."

"He ain't getting married, Reaper," Skirt says, launching his fist through the air and punching me right in the jaw. The pain shoots to my head, my heart, and wakes me up. I'm bloodthirsty.

I fall to the ground and cry out.

"That's it. Let it out, Knives. Let it out."

My ears ring from the hit, and blood pools in my mouth. The taste of it, the pain, it brings me back to the present.

Mary is missing.

I lift my head just as the blood drips down my chin.

"There he is," Skirt says, taking off his brass knuckles.

The sand grinds against my fingertips as I stand, a silent fury filling me as I stare at the clubhouse and head back inside. The scuffing of boots against the ground tells me my brothers are behind me.

There is one man that might know where she is.

And this time, I'm going to listen to my gut.

219

I'm not leaving this clubhouse, not until I have answers, and not until I've raised fucking hell.

CHAPTER TWENTY-THREE

Oh no, I'm going to be late for my own wedding.

No, late isn't the right word

I'm not going to make it.

My head swims with dizziness, and nausea rips away inside my stomach like a storm swirling in the middle of the sea.

Don't throw up on the vintage dress, Mary. Whatever happens, whatever you do, keep the dress safe.

When I get out of here—at least, I hope I'll get out of here—I'm going to marry Knives as we planned. Reaper was right; we should have never left the clubhouse. Now was not the time to be selfish, but I wanted to be. The club never gets to be selfish, and I wanted more for myself, and so did Knives.

This is what we risked. We knew something bad would happen, but I thought we could have one night to ourselves.

What a joke. No one can ever get one night without something bad happening.

"Mary, it's good to see you again. Do you need anything, Sweetheart?"

The sound of my father's voice has me turning over in the silk sheets on the luxurious bed. There's a chandelier in the middle of the room and a chaise lounge in the corner that has gold trim and white cushions.

Turning to my left, I notice the view of Vegas. The flashing array of different lights has me mesmerized for a second. There is a large Ferris wheel in the distance. Reds, whites, greens, blues, neons, the hotels around us putting on a show to attract all the tourists.

My father's fingers graze down my neck as I look out the window, and it has my skin crawling like a thousand cockroaches. "I've missed you so much."

"Don't fucking touch me." I scoot away from him until my back hits the headboard.

"Mary," he tsks. "You know what happens when that pretty mouth leaves a curse in this world." He starts to unbuckle his pants. "I searched everywhere for you. And when Mr. Moretti said you were with a biker group; I knew I had to save you."

The belt cracks in the air as he walks around the corner, looking more threatening than ever. His white hair is combed back, and his beard is a few shades darker, a grey on its way to turning to snow. He has a gold chain around his neck with a gold cross hanging from it, settling in the middle of his chest.

And if I remember correctly, it has his favorite bible verse etched in the metal.

Colossians 3:20.

Children, obey your parents in everything, for this pleases the Lord.

A crock of big fucking shit if you ask me.

222

I've never seen a more despicable man in my entire life. He doesn't serve God; he serves himself.

Instead of wrapping the belt around my wrist like he used to do, he wraps it around my neck, pulling the belt tight. My hands fly to my neck, and I gasp. I kick, and my back bends as I struggle to breathe. My fingers curl around the black belt to pull it away from my airway, but it's too tight.

The blood rushes to my face, and I choke, gasp, and cough.

"You thought you could get away from me? You thought you could run away from me? You can never get away from me. I fucking own you, Mary. You're mine. Wherever you think you can go, I'll follow. You will not disobey me again. You will serve me, you will get on your knees, and fucking worship me. It's what you are meant to do." He tugs tighter to drive home his words, and I'm worried that he isn't going to let up.

I'm going to die.

I know what he means when he says I need to get on my knees. It's something I've never done before with him.

Fear soaks into the marrow of my bones when I dissect his words.

The only man I've ever been on my knees for is Knives, and I don't care if my dad kills me; Knives is the only man I'll ever worship. My father can go to hell.

He rubs his erection against my arm, and tears prickle my eyes. From the pain of the belt against my neck, the terror of feeling him along my arm, my freedom is slowly slipping away. I'm back in his clutches, and I know this time, he will make sure he will never let me go.

He wraps the belt around the post of the headboard, which has me lifting to get the pressure off, but it doesn't work. I can't get a full breath of air. My windpipe is constricted, and it has me barely choking. My heart is racing, and my lungs are already burning. He fumbles with his zipper. The sound of it lowering has me kicking harder, struggling more to get away. I pull on the belt, tightening the constriction further.

Now I can't breathe at all.

"You're a gift from God, Mary. My gift. Your mother hated how much I wanted you. How much I loved you. Still love you. I think you were always supposed to be mine." He pulls out his cock, one I've seen one too many times, and I close my eyes.

His hand rubs up my leg, his fingers digging into the same spots Knives did, pressing against the bruises.

Bruises that were left from love and desire. Knives wanted me so much, he couldn't contain himself, and my father is ruining the passion Knives left for me to remember.

My father groans, fucking his fist as he lifts my dress further. "What's this?" he asks breathlessly, tracing the fingerprints Knives left behind. He knee-walks on the bed and settles between my legs. He tries to jerk them apart, his cock hard and leaking precome, angry that I dared to be with someone else.

"Were you a whore, Mary? Did you spread your legs for someone else?" His hands hook around my thighs to pull them apart, but I keep them shut, the edges of my vision turning black from the lack of air.

The more I struggle, the more I can't breathe.

If I don't struggle, he gets what he wants.

Me.

I refuse to let another man have me.

"Was it that fucking guy with you at the boutique? Was it him?" he roars, yanking my legs apart so hard that the muscles tighten and cramp. I cry out, the pain unbearable in my upper leg. I feel like it's pulled or strained, and in the moment of weakness to try and compose myself, my father bends his head down and inspects the bruises. "I'll forgive you," he says, kissing one of the marks.

A tear trickles down from the corner of my eye from his kiss. "I don't want your forgiveness," I croak, lifting my leg, damn the pain, and kick out again. My foot smacks against his face, but it isn't enough for him to get away from me.

He pins my legs down and crawls up my body, keeping his hands tight on my hips to keep me down. His bare cock rubs against my leg, and I sob, not wanting him anywhere near me. "Please, stop. Stop! I don't want you. I hate you. Get off me. Get off!" My voice is hoarse as I struggle to yell as loud as I can, but the strap around my neck makes it impossible.

He backhands me, drawing blood by splitting my bottom lip open. When he notices, he smashes his lips against mine and licks the droplet off.

I do the only thing I know to do. I bite down on his lip as hard as I can until I can feel the give of his flesh as my teeth sink in. His blood flows into my mouth, and he screams, pulling away from me. His cock is flaccid now, and he is holding his hands over his mouth. I spit, spewing his blood that's gathered on my tongue. A red haze covers his face, and when he drops his hands, the way he looks at me promises nothing but torture.

His brown eyes dance like devils as he looks up me and down. "You found fire while you were away."

I think about Knives' nickname for me: Hellraiser. I suppose I am.

I'm not about to let this monster put my flames out.

"That only makes it more fun for me." He reaches up to the post on the headboard and unwraps the belt, then loosens the clasp, and I gasp, welcoming the oxygen. It's all he gives me, though, before choking me again and wrapping the belt around the post. "I love you so much," he says, rubbing his nose against my cheek.

I stop struggling for a moment, needing to get as much air as I can. The more energy I have, the better chance I have of getting away.

"It's why it's going to hurt so much when someone else will own you."

225

I'm not perfect. I try to school my features, but the shock shakes me.

"Oh, yeah. Your beauty is money, sweetheart." He traces my jaw with his lips, inhaling as he licks the tears off my face. "Our time will come to an end. I think you're going to make someone very happy. There's an auction in ten days. So many other women, so many men wanting to buy."

"You'd sell me?" I choke.

"I love you. I don't want to, but there's an offer on the table for you that is too good to pass up." He checks his watch and sighs, placing a kiss on my cheek. "I have a sermon to give. I do virtual church now, and it's brought in so many new believers, Mary. You could be a part of it; you could be at my side instead, do you want that?"

He is giving me an option?

I tug on the belt around my neck, sneering at him. "You're giving me an option? I thought the money was too good to be true?"

"If you wanted to be with me, start a family, be at my side as my wife, I will not put you in that auction. I want to know if you'll be mine or if you want to be someone else's. Your faithfulness is priceless to me."

The bile creeps up my throat, helping the belt choke me further. A family? He wants his own daughter to have more children with him?

I can't hold back. Bile works its way out of my mouth, down the belt, and my chin. What would his followers think? He can't marry his own daughter. He is delusional.

"Our bloodline will remain pure and holy," he says, finally taking the belt off my neck. I bend over and throw up over the bed, stomach bile searing my throat. "I know it will take some getting used to, but I think you'll be happy. I can tell the buyer I'm no longer interested. It's up to you."

So my options are, get raped by my father for the rest of my life, or get raped by someone else. With my dad, at least, Knives would know how to look for me. What if I'm at the auction, and the man who buys me lives in Europe? Knives will never be able to find me then, but the thought of being with my father, for years, forced to have his children... I don't know if I can do that either.

"Where is Mom?" I ask, spitting out the remainder of spit in my mouth. "Is she okay with this?"

"I sold your mom a year ago, sweetheart. I have no idea where that bitch is. She wasn't a true believer." He tucks himself into his pants and zips up.

"No! You fucking bastard. How could you do that to her?" I launch myself across the bed to... I don't know, kill him? But with one backhand to the face, my head snaps to the side, and I fly to the floor, landing with a hard thud on my shoulder.

"If you don't choose correctly, maybe you'll see her." On that note, he walks away, shutting the hotel door behind him.

I'm slipping in my own puke, crying, and I know whatever choice I make, it will kill me. I used to want that, but now that I have something to live for, the last thing I want to do is die.

Putting my elbow on the mattress, I use it to lift myself up. I have to try my best to make sure not to look at the puke against my arm or leg. I need to call Knives, but as I look around the room, I notice there isn't a phone.

But there is a notepad.

Walking over to it, my heart broken because of my mom and what's she is going through, I pick up the thick pad of paper. My eyes widen when I see the name.

Maximo has to be behind this auction.

The notepad says, "Circus Circus." It's an old notepad, because the hotel and casino no longer have a name while he renovates.

I'm in a web full of lies and deceit.

And the more I struggle, the further I sink.

CHAPTER TWENTY-FOUR

Knives

It's been ten days since I've last seen Mary. Ten, long, depressing days. I've lost myself. All I do is search the city. Day in and day out. At night I torture Maximo, but the bastard has stayed quiet. His wounds are infected, and he fucking smells like shit. If he doesn't speak soon, I'm going to have his tongue cut out, and right in front of Maximo, I'll feed it to Happy.

Then I'll start taking from other body parts.

I haven't slept. I've drunk myself into a stupor.

And I wake up at night, crying out her name, fear gripping my heart when my dreams turn into nightmares. I'm always clutching the sheet, drenching the blankets with sweat and reaching out for her.

Only to find her side of the bed cold.

I miss her.

We were supposed to get married, and my job, my one job, was to protect her.

I'm running out of time.

Today is the day Seer said Mary was going to die. I have to make sure that does not happen. The last ten days have made me realize just how precious life is with Mary. I didn't understand it before, but now that I think about it, all the fighting we did before I kissed her, I wouldn't have been able to be without it.

"Knives, you need to go get some rest," Reaper says, standing by the sink. He leans against the counter, crosses his legs at the ankle, and sips his coffee. I'm not the only one tired. Everyone is.

We have searched every single hotel in Vegas. From top to fucking bottom. She's vanished, and it's time for me to start thinking that maybe she isn't here anymore. I'll need to search the globe for her.

Every damn city, town, and abandoned building this damn world has to offer, I'll tear it down. I'll find her.

And if I find her in her grave, I'll join her.

I need my Hellraiser.

The bickering, the frustration, the madness she makes me feel, I need it. I've always needed it.

"Rest?" I laugh bitterly, rubbing my eyes with the palms of my hands to bring life back into them. "You wouldn't rest if this was Sarah, just like any of you wouldn't. You want me to rest? You want me to laugh too? Tell a joke? Dance? What the fuck do you want!" I slam my fist on the table, and everyone looks away from me. "She's gone."

"Our answers are downstairs, I know it," Mercy says. "Maximo knows a lot more than he is saying. I can feel it."

"Me too," Mason says, running a hand through his hair.

He's changed so much and hasn't changed at all. His hair is longer, and the scruff on his face isn't to grow a beard, but because he keeps forgetting to shave.

229

"I say we get a little more creative," Tongue adds, staring down at Happy, who is at his feet.

"You want us to threaten him with a baby gator? What's that going to do?"

"Torture. Happy is growing, but his bite is strong," Tongue says proudly, puffing out his chest as if his kid is the best there is.

I can only imagine Tongue as an actual dad. He would be so protective, so intense, and his kids would probably be just as fucked in the head.

I drop my head in my hands, and my stomach growls, but I ignore it. I can't even think about eating right now. I haven't been able to stomach anything. Not with the vivid images playing in my mind every second of every day.

What if she's been calling out for me? What if she's been crying every day? What if she's been fighting and it hasn't mattered? What if he has been using her? I can't get her eyes out of my head. They are pleading for me to save her, and I can't.

I'm fucking done with this. I'll kill Maximo for what he has done. I don't give a fuck if he is Moretti's brother or not.

No one deserves to live after what he has done, but as long as Natalia's life is in his hands, I can't go too crazy. We have to save Natalia too. Innocent lives cannot be sacrificed. I have to try and think smart.

We find Mary. We find Natalia.

We kill Maximo.

I will kill her father.

This bullshit is done, and Moretti can take over as the mafia boss again. At least with him, we didn't have to worry about shit like this.

I check to make sure I have my ninja stars and get up from the chair. My girl's life has a fucking time bomb on it. I'm not about to let it go off.

I swing the basement door open and hurry down the steps. I don't tell anyone what I'm doing. I'm not asking

Reaper for permission for what I can and cannot do to Maximo.

I'm just going to fucking do it.

Opening the playroom door, the metal hits against the wall as I stomp in. Maximo's head is bent, his breathing is labored and choppy, and his suit is nothing but soggy scraps from the blood, cuts, and piss saturating him.

His days are fucking numbered.

I grab him by the thick of his hair and yank his head back, then slap him across the face. "Wake the hell up!" He doesn't move; he just groans. "I said, wake up!"

When he doesn't, I let go and move around him. Along the wall is a counter with various tools, but it's the gasoline I'm after.

I'll set him on fire and send his rotten soul back to hell.

Taking a page from Boomer's book, I grab the red jug of gasoline and head toward Maximo, circling him like a lion, a beast waiting to fucking kill.

It's amazing how I went from feeling nothing to feeling everything in just a few days of being with Mary.

I sit the jug down on the floor, the floor vibrating a high-pitched frequency from the weight, and slip a few ninja stars from my pocket.

Maybe this will wake him up.

Gripping the silver between my fingers, I admire the pointed hooks on the tips of the star, then fling it through the air. A whoosh of a blade spinning sounds before thudding against Maximo's eye. His left eye opens, and he begins to scream. Blood flows down his right cheek in thick streams, and my nostrils flare when I hear his pain.

I was taking it too easy on him before.

I fling another, landing right in his crotch, and another painful wail begs for me to stop.

Never.

231

"You took my fucking eye! You took my eye!" Maximo pulls on the restraints doing his best to get out of the trap he is in. "And my dick! My dick is bleeding."

"And you'll lose it if you don't start talking." I hold my star up to the light and let it shine. Maximo's reflection mirrors off the metal. His mouth is open, begging for mercy, begging for me to let him go because he can't handle the pain anymore.

Footsteps sound at the door, and I see Reaper, Tool, Bullseye, Tongue, and Happy. And that crazy fucker is off his leash, opening his mouth in a deadly hiss when he smells blood.

"What the hell is that? What is that!" Maximo rocks back and forth to get the chair loose, but it's pointless. It's welded to the floor, and it isn't going anywhere.

"That is the reptile that is going to eat you for dinner if you don't start talking, and you better tell me everything, Maximo. Or I'm going to skin the flesh from your cock with the very tip of my ninja star. I'll take my time. I'll make sure every second is you in complete agony." I yank the star from his dick, which was more in his groin, but the threat was close enough. "Do you take me seriously, yet? Do you understand? Moretti has already told us to do whatever we wanted to you, because even he doesn't trust you. The man that can't remember anything remembers how he feels about you. What's that say?"

I yank his head back again so I can get a better look at his face in the light. His good eye is watering, and the star is stuck deep in his other eye. To drill in how serious I am, I pull it out, and his eyeball comes with it.

He screams until he pukes. I barely have enough time to get out of the way, so it doesn't get on my boots. The eye is nearly sliced in two, the nerves red and dripping from the back, and the hole in his eye socket is about to become a home for gasoline. With two fingers, I pinch the eye and pluck it off my weapon. It's squishier than I thought it would be.

"Have at it, Happy," I say, tossing the gator the eye. He catches it quickly, snapping his jaws before he swallows it down.

"Good boy," Tongue says, praising him as he pats him on the head.

"I promise I'll feed you bit by bit to Happy, and then I'll burn your goddamn bones, but not before I make you watch Happy eat your dick. Then, my Prez will rip your heart from your chest, and you'll see it stop pumping. Happy will eat that too. I'm done fucking around, Maximo. Where is she!"

Silence.

This is so fucking frustrating. I hate silence.

I pick up the jug and start to pour gasoline over his body. I know it burns the open wounds, but I don't care. I don't care about anything right now. I shove the nozzle between his lips, and he coughs from the fumes he inhales from the gasoline. "I'll make you drink this. What is your role in this? What is her father's plan? Why the hell were you at the barn? Where is she? What's so special about today?"

He nods eagerly, wide brown eye dripping with tears while the abyss on the other side cries blood. I rip the nozzle from his lips and toss it to the side, then take the same star that blinded him and put it against his neck. "Talk," I say.

"He's a business partner. At first, it was just drugs. I didn't want to get into anything else. When you're in my line of work, it isn't hard to figure out who is who. Everyone knows about the Preacher who doesn't follow the bible, if you know what I mean. I heard he was looking for his daughter. I got a picture, and any information would have my network tripling. The fights would grow, money would grow, power. It's all about the power," he says, blood spraying from his lips when he speaks.

"I didn't know she was an ol' lady at first. When he came to the hotel, he saw Natalia, and he said until he got Mary, he

233

would keep her. I met him at the barn, which is where all transactions, drug, human, and whatever else related goes down. He said there was going to be an auction. The last one of the year. Natalia would be in it if I didn't comply, but then I started thinking, what's the harm? Moretti doesn't remember her anyway, and she'll be alright. She's a smart girl. She can get out of this—"

I stop him from talking by grabbing his shoulders and shaking them "—Where is the auction? What time does it start?" I remember Mason warning us that her father was going to do something like this.

"It's at my hotel. Elevator, east side, takes you to a level no one has ever seen before."

"What about the attack on the club a few months ago?" Reaper asks. "I knew it was fucking fishy that that college kid happened to shoot us up after working your club. That was you, wasn't it?"

"Yes," Maximo says. "I wanted to be on top. I wanted to be the one that controlled Vegas. I told you the truth, please, let me go. Please. I'm sorry."

Reaper gets in Maximo's face. "When we get back, I'm going to soak in your fucking soul, Maximo. You better count down the hours of your life as a free man."

"Please. I'll work for you. I'll put all my men at your disposal. I'll give you money. Anything. Please, just let me go. I'm sorry. I'm so sorry."

"Save it," Reaper snaps. "I don't want your money. I don't want your apology. I don't want shit from you but your goddamn heart beating in my hands as I crush the life out of you."

"Please, just let me go. I'll do anything. I never meant for our alliance to end up like this."

"You should have thought about that before you decided to fuck with the Ruthless Kings."

We storm out of the playroom and lock the door.

Leaving him alive is hard, but there is no more time to waste.

I have to get to Mary before someone buys her.

They don't even know that what they bid would never be enough.

She's   fucking   priceless.

CHAPTER TWENTY-FIVE

My energy is gone.

I've been starved, slapped, jerked-off on, but at least my dad hasn't had sex with me.

That's the one silver lining in all of this.

I told him I didn't want to marry him, because maybe when someone buys me, they won't be as cruel as he is. Maybe I'll get lucky.

He's kept me drugged with a tranquilizer to keep me in line over the last ten days. Not enough to knock me out, but enough to keep me loopy. I've taken a thousand pictures in lingerie. I'm sure they are posted on every website imaginable. My father even made a brochure, so when the buyers come in, they have something to reference while they hide behind tinted windows.

Right now, all of the women are in a room, shoulder to shoulder, shivering from the cold and shock of the situation.

There are no windows, no fan; it's a basic, plain room with four walls and a door we can't go out of.

"Mary?" a familiar voice says from behind me.

I turn around and gasp when I see Natalia, Moretti's daughter. She's a little younger than me, and I can see the innocence in her red eyes and wet cheeks. "Natalia, what are you doing here?" This is the first time I've seen all the women. I didn't know if I was going to be the only one or what, but of course, I'm not.

Men always think they can do whatever they want to us.

"My Uncle, Maximo. He gave me up," Natalia cries.

I'm not surprised. Maximo has always rubbed me the wrong way.

"Everything is going to be okay." I wrap my arms around her and bring her in for a tight hug. "They are going to find us, okay? They will." I have to believe that, or I will be lost the moment I step out onto that stage. I'm wearing a sheer bra that crisscrosses in the front, black lace panties, and stockings. My hair is down, but I've been ordered to play with it and give the buyers a show.

Natalia is wearing a light blue teddy, a short sexy nightgown that showcases her small chest and flat stomach.

"Do I hear three million?" my father announces over the speaker that's attached in the right corner of the room. "Sold!"

I almost expect to hear a slam of a gavel, but it's quiet.

"Next up, we have a special guest," he says, quickening the pace of my heart.

The door opens, and a man I've never seen before surveys the room. He's tall and buff, reminding me of a bodybuilder, and his eyes fall on me. He doesn't ask; he doesn't gesture for me to come to him; instead, he reaches out and snags me by my hair.

"No!" Natalia screams, trying to hold my hands to keep me from being dragged out the door. "No, Mary! Please, don't do this," she begs while the other women cry along the back wall, away from the door.

The guy still doesn't say anything. The way he has my hair has my scalp burning. I reach up to grab his hands to take the pressure off, but he trips me with his big boot and proceeds to pull me across the floor.

The hallway turns into a long tunnel the further away I get from the room that holds a dozen women. The walls are grey, the floor is black, and it's like I'm sliding along pools of ink. I'm waiting to sink into the ground. The tile is so spotless, so shiny, that as the light shines against it, I know it's going to suck me under into the unknown.

My captor's boots pound against the floor, loud drums that strike fear into my soul. When he comes to a stop, a door opens, and he throws me into the room. I roll to the middle, and the carpet leaves burns across my skin. I'm too afraid to get up.

But I do.

I push myself up onto my hands, then again to get to my feet. I'm surrounded by black glass. I can't see what's on the other side, but I have no doubt it is sleazy men in expensive suits debating if they want me.

Lifting my chin, I do my best to show I'm not scared of what will happen to me. My heart is ripped out, and I know my fate. Anything these men do to me will be nothing to the pain I already feel.

"Gentlemen." My father's voice is heard over the speaker again. "This lovely lady is named Mary St. James. She's beautiful, feisty, and has hair you can grip for days while you pound into her from behind. She's only ever been with one man, and that's me. You're going to want to get your hands on this one."

I fling my hair over my shoulder and give every window the middle finger.

My father laughs over the intercom, and a red light flashes above one of the windows.

"Oh, we have a bet coming in already," he whistles. "The betting is starting at 5 million. We can do better than that. You'll never have a pussy like it. It's tight, hot, and wet."

The way my father talks about me makes me sick. I can barely stay on my own two feet, and he is lying to them.

He is not the only man I've ever been with, and I hate that I have twelve years of memories to prove he wasn't a dream, but—shudder—experience.

Another red light goes off, then another from the left, one more to the right. It's a light show, and they won't stop flickering.

"Twelve million," my dad's voice lowers in a sexual hue. "Can I get fifteen?" But as soon as he asks the question, the glass to my right shatters from a gunshot. I scream in surprise, and through the glass I can hear shocked gasps and murmurs.

I glance up to see Knives there, holding the neck of a stranger, a star to his throat.

My heart leaps into my throat.

"Sold," Knives says, slicing the blade across the man's neck until he is bleeding out.

I flinch when another glass wall breaks from another bullet, and Slingshot is standing there. I've never seen him use his weapon besides to launch skittles, but when he does use it, it's a sharpened rock that's thrown. It hits the guy against the temple, and when he falls backward unconscious, Slingshot snaps his neck.

Another window breaks.

And another.

Then another.

All the Kings are there, their boots crunching against glass as they kill every single threat. Bullseye's dart hits a man between the eyes, Tool shoves his screwdriver into a man's throat, Tongue cuts out another villain's tongue, then walks to every room to do the same to the others, and Reaper appears.

With my father in his clutches.

"Mary!" Knives drops down from the window, landing on his feet, and slowly standing like some sort of superhero. "You're okay? Did he hurt you? Christ, he did. Look at your neck, Hellraiser—" He swings me into his arms and kisses me all over my face until our lips meet. "I was so goddamn worried about you."

I suddenly realize I'm weeping. Big, heaving sobs rack my body. But he is here. He rescued me. He is keeping me safe. Knives' strong, muscular arms hold me tight, and I am able to calm down and lose myself in his grip again.

I finally gather the strength to open my eyes and look at him. He looks horrible. His hair has grown out, his beard is longer and scraggly, which is not like him, and he has dark circles under his eyes.

"My dad liked to use his belt on my neck every day and masturbate until he got off."

"Did he…"

I glance away, ashamed, but shake my head. "He only jacked off on me after watching me struggle against his belt," I say, lifting my fingers to my black and blue neck.

"Only?" Knives growls. "Only?"

"What do you want to do?" Reaper says. "A quick death is too easy."

My father is shaking. "No, no, wait! Wait! I have money. I have a lot of money. Mary, you won't let them do this to me, right? You love me. You love me!"

"I hate you!" I don't know what comes over me, but I steal Knives' star, which is the one he gave me, his original one. The one he made when he was just fifteen. He must have found my jacket in the chaos of all this. Before I move another inch, Knives throws his jacket over me, and I make my way to Reaper.

But I can't get up there.

Reaper grins, then pushes my father down. He hits the ground, lands on his back, and groans. Knives steps on his arms and Reaper jumps down, landing on his legs. One breaks from the force, and my father exhales a wail of pain.

"I hate you so much, it physically aches my bones," I tell him as I straddle his stomach. "You want to kiss me?" I pinch his lips together with tears burning my eyes and, with the star, start slicing his lips off. I toss them to the side until all I see are teeth and gums.

Tongue laughs, giddy and excited to add to his collection.

"You stole my innocence. You raped me." I slide back, unzip his pants, and squeeze his pathetic cock until I know it hurts.

"Please," he cries. "Don't." The words are hard to hear, since he has no lips to speak with.

"You never listened to me! You never stopped! Twelve years!" Hot, fat tears drip down my cheeks. I yank his pants down and use the serrated edge of the star to cut his dick off. My father screams in agony, and it is the most cathartic sound I have ever heard in my life. I throw the inches to Tongue, but he ignores it.

"I want Happy to eat it! I want nothing left of my father, you hear me? Nothing!" I scream, then with bloody hands, I stab him right in the heart, a tear falling from my chin to his exposed mouth. "You wanted me to love you. You sick, twisted bastard."

"I'll take it from here," Reaper tells me gently, and Knives grabs my shoulders to steer me away.

"I want him so far gone, Reaper. I want him erased from the planet." My entire body is shaking uncontrollably, and when I glance down at my hands, all I see is blood.

"You got it, Mary," Reaper says, using the star embedded in the Preacher's chest as he cuts to rip his heart out. "May the Devil chew you up and spit you out, and may God have no mercy on your soul."

Knives turns me away, and my father's screams sound eerily familiar to mine over the years. We walk out the door that I came in from, and the bodyguard that brought me to the

241

stage is there, aiming a gun right in the middle of Knives' chest.

I guess this is it. This is where I die to save Knives. It was worth it.

I do the only thing that enters my mind. I jump in front of him to take the bullet as the barrel rings release, but nothing ever comes.

I finally open my eyes to see Mason jumping in front of us, taking the shot in the chest. A gun in his own hand, he aims it at the guard and fires.

The guard falls to the floor in a useless giant heap when the bullet catches between his eyes.

"Mason! Mason, no. No!" Knives drops to the ground next to his brother, and I do the same, taking Mason's hand in mine. "I just got you back. I was supposed to work out my feelings. You can't... no," Knives is full of denial as he presses his hand against the bloody wound on Mason's chest. "We were supposed to be brothers again. What were you thinking taking a bullet for me, again?" Knives lifts Mason's head onto his lap. "You're going to be fine. You'll be okay."

"I wanted you to have the life you always deserved. It was me or Mary," he wheezes, a hint of blood foaming his mouth. "It had to be me. You were right—" he coughs roughly, struggling to gain his breath, "—I shouldn't have left you alone. I should have found you. Consider this—" he coughs again, "—taking responsibility."

"You saved her for me," Knives cries. "Thank you."

"I never stopped having your six, Knives."

"Thomas. Call me Thomas."

Mason grins, his face white as death and sweat dripping down his temples. "Thomas. My brother."

"Your brother," Knives says. "It's okay. It's okay, Mason. You can go. I'll be okay. Thanks to you, I'll always be okay."

Mason locks eyes with me, another weak grin on his lips, and his hand falls on top of Knives' that is pressing against his chest. And then his chest deflates as he exhales his very last breath.

"No," Knives clutches his brother against him, hugging his dead body. "I'm sorry, I'm sorry, I'm sorry, I'm sorry," he whispers.

The guys from the other room pile in. Reaper is soaked in blood, but he kneels down next to Knives and uncurls his fingers from Mason's shirt. "It's time to let go, Knives. We have to get out of here. We will bring him with us and have a proper burial."

"Let go?" Knives asks with red eyes.

"Let go," Reaper affirms.

"I'm not good at that," Knives replies, holding out his arm for me. "I'm not good at letting go at all."

I take his hands immediately, and Knives pulls me into a tight hug. "I'll never be able to repay him. He always saved me, and now he gave me you."

Mason made sure Seer's prediction didn't come true.

"There are more girls in a room down the hall, on the left," I tell Reaper.

Reaper takes charge and grabs the keys off the dead guards' body before handing them to Skirt and telling him, "Go get the girls."

"Thank you for coming for me, and I'm so sorry about Mason." I begin to cry. The adrenaline is starting to wear off. I'm overwhelmed and exhausted.

"I'll always come for you, just like my brother always came for me. You'll never have to worry about that." Knives lays a kiss on my forehead.

A minute later, Natalia comes out of the other room with the girls.

Reaper bends over and picks up Mason's body. "Come on everyone; we are going home."

We follow Reaper out, the women covered by jackets from the guys as we all huddle in the trucks.

When we get home, we can tell something is wrong.

It's quiet.

"Moretti and Maximo are gone!" Sarah screams out the front door as Reaper jumps out of the driver's side of the Ford Raptor.

And nothing good ever happens in silence.

EPILOGUE

Knives

One month later

"You may now kiss the bride," Reaper officiates, finally telling me to kiss my bride. And I'm not going to half-ass this either. I dip her down over my leg, hold the back of her head, and kiss her until I know her knees are weak, and her pussy is wet.

Whistles and catcalls sound, and when I bring the kiss to an end, she nips my lip. "You put on a show on purpose."

"As if you don't like being the center of attention," I wink, lifting her up until she's standing straight again. I clasp her hand in mine and lift it in the air as another round of cheers sound.

I only wish my brother could have been here to see it.

I spent too much time being mad at him, too much time holding on to the past and the anger I felt, that I could have

245

built new memories over his last few days on earth. We could have had a beer as men, talked as men, laughed as men, and not some silly little boys.

But I'm stubborn, and I know how to hold a fucking grudge, but I'll never do it again.

We left a seat open for him, and Mercy is sitting next to it, my brother's badge lying flat on the chair.

I'll never be able to thank him enough for saving Mary's life.

We decided to get married at the clubhouse. With friends and family around us. Yeti, Tyrant, and Chaos are on the ground.

Lady is in Poodle's arms. She's lasted so long, but we don't know why she's holding on. I'm glad she's here, though. I'm happy everyone I love is here to see me move on with my life.

Mary leans over and whispers, "I'm pregnant, and if it's a boy, I want to name him Mason."

My head whips to the side so damn hard and fast, I nearly lose my balance. I can't find the words. My mind is jumbled. I grab her hand, the one with my mom's ring on it, and hold on tight. "Are you serious? Don't play with me, Hellraiser. That's a cruel joke."

"No joking. I found out this morning," she says, laying her hand against my cheek. "Are you happy?" she asks, her long lashes shadowing her cheeks as she blinks.

The gold band that belonged to my father now sits on my hand, and as I stare at the wedding rings, the emotion bubbling up in my chest almost stops my heart.

There was a time when I thought happiness was something earned, but it isn't.

Happiness is something someone waits for.

And I couldn't be happier.

"Sonofabitch! She's pregnant!" I cheer, smiling from ear to ear, then swing her up in my arms.

"You owe me five bucks!" Maizey says, the little hustler wearing a purple princess dress.

I grin and lay another kiss on my wife. When her lips touch mine, everything fades away. It's her. It's me. It's our baby.

And as my world rights itself, I realize it's quiet. The background noise is muted by love and happiness.

This. This is the silence I can live in, because I'm no longer alone.

I have a family.

And my ninja stars, of course.

THE END.

KNIVES PLAYLIST

HELLRAISER BY: MOTORHEAD

MAGIC BY: THE BLUE STONES

I WANT A LOVE LIKE JOHNNY AND JUNE BY: HEIDI NEWFIELD

MUTHAFUCKA BY: BEWARE OF DARKNESS

WALKING DISASTER BY: SAYWECANFLY

TOGETHER, WE'RE ALONE BY: SAYWECANFLY

CHASING HIGHS BY: TOO CLOSE TOO TOUCH

SCUMBAG BY: GOODY GRACE

AS ABOVE, SO BELOW BY: IN THIS MOMENT

HEADSPACE BY: FAME ON FIRE

ACKNOWLEDGMENTS

To our Ruthless Readers thanks for sticking with us another year!

Give Me Books here's to another great year.

To all the bloggers and reviewed and shared Knives thanks y'all are the best.

To Wander and Andrey here's to another PHENOMENIAL YEAR.

Donna we love you! #BOOMERISDONNAS

Stacey at Champagne Book Design thanks for all your amazing work.

To my Instigator you're the best decision I've made.

Lynn as always thanks for being my rock all these years

Silla here's to another great year!

Carolina your enthusiasm is infectious

Harloe you are amazing

Mom love you

Jeff 5 LITTLE WORDS

Austin as always y'all are such a blessing

David Cowboys are gonna still suck this year!!

ALSO BY
K.L. SAVAGE

PREQUEL - REAPER'S RISE
BOOK ONE - REAPER
BOOK TWO - BOOMER
BOOK THREE - TOOL
BOOK FOUR - POODLE
BOOK FIVE - SKIRT
BOOK SIX - PIRATE
BOOK SEVEN - DOC
BOOK EIGHT - TONGUE
BOOK NINE – A RUTHLESS CHRISTMAS
BOOK TEN – KNIVES

OTHER BOOKS IN THE RUTHLESS KINGS SERIES
A RUTHLESS HALLOWEEN

RUTHLESS KINGS MC IS NOW ON AUDIBLE.
ALREADY AN AUDIBLE SUBSCRIBER? CLICK HERE
TO LISTEN NOW. NON AUDIBLE SUBSCRIBERS,
CLICK HERE TO ENJOY A MONTH NOW.

CLICK HERE TO JOIN RUTHLESS READERS AND GET
THE LATEST UPDATES BEFORE ANYONE ELSE. OR
SIMPLY SCAN THE QR CODE TO

VISIT AUTHORKLSAVAGE.COM OR STALK THEM AT THE LINKS BELOW.

FACEBOOK | INSTAGRAM | RUTHLESS READERS TWITTER | BOOKBUB | GOODREADS | PINTEREST | WEBSITE

Printed in Great Britain
by Amazon

33333145R00145